SOLITUDE
OF ILLUSIONS

Adib Khan was born in Dhaka, Bangladesh where he lived until 1973. That year he came to Australia where he completed a Masters degree in English literature. Khan currently lives and works as a teacher in Ballarat. Among his interests are reading, philately, cooking, listening to Western and Indian classical music, chess and cricket.

Seasonal Adjustments was Khan's first novel which won the Christina Stead Prize for fiction and the Book of the Year in the 1994 NSW Premier's Prize, was shortlisted for the 1994 *Age* Book of the Year Award, and won the 1995 Commonwealth Writer's Prize for First Book.

SOLITUDE OF ILLUSIONS
ADIB KHAN

ALLEN & UNWIN

Copyright © Adib Khan 1996

All rights reserved. No part of this book may be reproduced or transmitted in any form or by any means, electronic or mechanical, including photocopying, recording or by any information storage and retrieval system, without prior permission in writing from the publisher.

Publication of this title was assisted by the Australia Council, the Federal Government's arts funding and advisory body.

First published in 1996 by
Allen & Unwin Pty Ltd
9 Atchison Street, St Leonards, NSW 2065 Australia
Phone: (61 2) 9901 4088
Fax: (61 2) 9906 2218
E-mail: 100252.103@compuserve.com

National Library of Australia
Cataloguing-in-Publication entry:

Khan, Adib.
   Solitude of illusions.

   ISBN 1 86448 147 1.

   I. Title.

A823.3

Set in 10/13 pt Palatino by DOCUPRO, Sydney
Printed by Australian Print Group, Maryborough, Victoria

10 9 8 7 6 5 4 3 2 1

For Papa—wherever the place

Memory often failed me or furnished but imperfect recollections, and I filled up space by details supplied by imagination to supplement those recollections . . . I sometimes lent strange charms to truth.

Jean-Jacques Rousseau, Confessions

ONE

It was a night when the world nearly died.
Earlier that afternoon the clouds began to roam the southern sky like a pack of marauding dogs growling in the distance, waiting . . . waiting to overthrow April's frenzied madness that had parched the land and cracked it open like the pods of dry seeds.

The *djinns* were stirring after a long slumber. It was impossible to predict what mischief these creatures of smokeless fire would bring with them.

Anxious farmers scanned the horizon where billowy clouds, in shades of deepening grey, foamed and puffed out like the sales of a giant *nauka* favoured with a mighty wind.

'The dry spell is nearly over,' they said to each other uneasily. '*Boishak* is about to arrive.'

But the djinns . . . what were they coming to celebrate?

The sky paled and the temperature dropped.

A flurry of activity aroused the enervated village from its prolonged stupor.

The meagrely stocked grocer's shop was suddenly besieged by impatient housewives clamouring for quick service.

Accompanied by chaotic shouting, goats, cows and hens were chased, rounded up and shepherded inside the bamboo sheds. Outside their shacks, women lit *chulas*, using twigs, leaves and dry cow-dung. In earthen pots they cooked rice, *dhal* and modest quantities of spinach for an early dinner.

The local schoolmaster convinced himself that a slightly premature celebration, to welcome the first of the monsoonal rains, warranted a shorter school day. Children screamed with pleasure as they streamed out of the solitary classroom without their slates and pencils.

> *Allah meg dey panni dey*
> *Chayah dey reh*
> *Allah meg dey . . .*

They sang and danced their way home, only to be yelled at by distraught mothers who feared the worst for their flimsy dwellings of clay and straw which rarely withstood the ferocity of the wet season. The ebullient children were not to be bullied into domestic chores. Watched by their helpless mothers, who could only shout abuses and brandish sticks in futile threats of corporal punishment, they ran to the fields to await the drenching. Their spirits were high among the clouds, and their dreams were with the croaking toads and jumping fishes in the half-empty ponds.

The angry women sank into a mood of utter despair. They fumed and cursed their husbands who were not to be seen. There was a prevalent feeling of abandonment.

'Men!' The older wives sighed. 'It is Allah's Will that we should carry the burden of their irresponsibilities.'

The males had slipped away quietly to the *cha dhokan* for their mandatory cups of tea and to speculate on the timing of the next rice harvest. The conversation was subdued. There was a growing apprehension about the wildness of the approaching storm. The clouds were dense and ominously dark. After their long hibernation, the *djinns* were bound to be brimming with wickedness.

The talk shifted to Bau Ma and Boro Saheb's sister. The *begums* were unfamiliar with the turbulence of rural nights.

The villagers feared for the delicate constitution of the Calcuttan ladies, although their physical safety could not be jeopardised in the *pucca* house built by Zahid Sharif.

Other than the weather, everything augured well. Servants, acting as spies, kept the locals informed about the Sharifs. There were signs that both women might give birth on the same day. Such a shame that Boro Saheb's sister had lost her husband so soon after the wedding!

Despite their cunning efforts, the villagers were unable to elicit details about the man who had been honoured and accepted into the family as a *jamai*. They knew nothing about his background or the reason for his death. The only news circulated in the village was about the family's grief and Hasina Begum's hysteria over the loss of her husband.

Had they known the facts, the village folk would have recoiled with horror. Boro Saheb's sister was not a widow. She had never been married. The tyranny of *purdah*, rigidly imposed by her brother, had driven Hasina to an unspeakable deed of darkness with a trusted, elderly neighbour employed to teach her Bangla and Urdu.

On an empty terrace, under the bewitching light of a summer's moon, the tutor had his virility miraculously restored, and fleetingly experienced the ecstasy of *Behaesht*.

As for Hasina . . . She was lumbered with an unwanted burden.

Shahid Sharif's rage was frightening. His frustrated anger was fuelled with the discovery that the nefarious offender, the cursed son of Iblis and a vile seducer of women, had packed up and left the city.

For Hasina, the punishment for violating the family's honour was severe—permanent banishment from Calcutta and a quiet life in the country with the illegitimate child.

Hasina wept and begged her brother's forgiveness.

Shahid Sharif remained unmoved. 'You have soiled our name and committed a heinous crime against the family! Our *izzat* has been compromised! It is not in my power to forgive you.'

The invasion from Calcutta had begun several weeks before the babies were due. Shahid Sharif was the last to arrive with his brothers and the reputable *hajjam*, Adalat Shah, who had been handsomely paid to accompany them in the hope that favourable circumstances would necessitate a circumcision . . . or two. Cousins, aunts, uncles and servants arrived at odd hours of the day in ox-drawn carts, from the railway station in Haripal, and headed for the house without stopping to acknowledge and talk to the locals.

Despite being a Hindu, the midwife, Suchitra, was allowed to live with the family and was given a room next to Shahid Sharif's wife.

Everything was in readiness. All that Providence had to deliver was a male heir to the house of Sharifs.

On their own initiative, there were a number of peasants who sneaked off to consult Bimal, the Hindu fortune-teller in Haripal. They carried gifts of *shondesh* and *mishti doi* in anticipation that the hermit would respond to their generosity with a propitious prediction. They were peeved with Bimal's lack of graciousness about what he had to say, especially about the boy who was to be born to Hasina Begum.

Bristling with indignation, the villagers returned to Modhunagar and headed for the mosque to pray fervently to Allah.

Let Allah bless the house of Sharifs with a saintly son who will bring prosperity and happiness to Modhunagar. Aameen!

May Boro Saheb's sister have a child who will be a credit to the village. Aameen!

It was the commonly held view that the village desperately needed a strong leader; someone like Boro Saheb's father who had spent most of his time in Modhunagar and had ruled firmly, settling disputes and handing out punishments for misdemeanours with a supremely confident mien of authority.

SOLITUDE OF ILLUSIONS

Things worked well in Modhunagar in the old days. There was no ambiguity in the established order of the ruler and those who obeyed him. Ambitions were unknown, and the slightest hint of dissent was deemed to indicate the influence of the Devil. The children were brought up to believe that their destinies were predetermined, and irrevocably linked with the services they could offer to the Sharifs. After all, the youngsters owed much to the generosity of the ruling family.

In a moment of whimsical fancy, Zahid Sharif had established a one-room school, appointed the only semi-literate man in Modhunagar as the master and derived immense satisfaction from what he considered to be his magnanimous contribution to the modernisation of rural India so monstrously neglected by the *Angrez*. Children received gifts of slates and pencils. They were taught how to write their names, sing songs and learn the family history of the Sharifs. The school hours were flexible and largely dependent on the mood of the master in the morning. When they were needed, the children went to work in the fields.

Life continued peacefully without noticeable manifestations of discontentment. Zahid Sharif had managed to create a credible illusion of progress without threatening his own hierarchical privileges and the security of the entrenched ways of the villagers.

Even now there were those who revered the memory of Zahid Sharif. He was an exceptional being, blessed with the wisdom of a demi-god.

As for the present Boro Saheb . . . well, he did not possess his father's calmness and foresight. Without expressing their concerns, the people lived uneasily with the way he neglected his ancestral home, allowing things to drift without asserting his authority. Shahid Sharif was known to be more interested in the family's textile business in Calcutta and far too busy to involve himself in the affairs of Modhunagar. As a compensation for his blatant negligence, Shahid Sharif made a great fuss about appointing a village head. After some deliberation he decided to honour Polash Mia, the *imam* of the mosque and reputedly a pious man. The *imam* was a kind and good-natured person, but too weak and indecisive to be an effective leader.

'The perfect choice!' Shahid Sharif declared enthusiastically at a village *majlis*.

That was not, however, the prevalent view in Modhunagar. There were murmurings of dissatisfaction, but nothing of any alarming significance reached Shahid Sharif. The older peasants accepted Polash Mia grudgingly, and the younger men indicated their displeasure in puerile acts of defiance. The guava trees in the Sharifs' orchard were raided and stripped of all the fruits. Several goats disappeared mysteriously. Sacks of rice went missing from the godown. Nothing terribly serious . . . merely the sorts of happenings that could be credibly blamed on invisible creatures of the night.

No, it wasn't quite the same as when Zahid Sharif was alive and spent most of his days in Modhunagar.

The people desperately needed another Sharif to restore the harmony of the past and put an end to the unsettling changes that were creeping into the rural community.

And so they waited as the evening approached like a sick patient, racked with pain, moaning and spluttering.

They watched the fireworks in the sky.

The great *djinns* were at a celebratory dinner.

It threatened to be one of those nights when spirits were set free to wander in search of malicious amusement.

The mind became a dark pit of frenzied creativity. Fear leapt up from its depth to be shaped into grotesque and spiteful creatures. Stories were born and the words stored in sharp memories.

Men accompanied each other to their flimsy huts, since it was prudent not to walk alone in the gathering darkness with *bhoots* lurking behind trees and bushes, waiting to spring on lonely mortals. Such was the fear of the supernatural that the village was asleep by early evening, after the oldest male in each family had walked thrice around his hut, reciting *suras* and blowing the words on the outside walls to protect the inmates from bodily harm.

Later that night the rain arrived. Some demonic force unleashed the storm clouds. They swept across the sky like a vengeful army venting its anger on a helpless world. The rain hammered down all night and breathed life into the dying earth. Even those who normally slept soundly heard the ghoulish cries as spirits snapped branches, uprooted trees and blew away roofs. The thunderous laughter of the *djinns* reverberated across the troubled sky. People were hurt and made homeless.

A terrible night. The village elders agreed. The worst they had seen. Terrible . . .

But somehow Modhunagar survived.

A wounded but freshly washed village arose to a calm and clear morning. The peasants rallied to help those who had been adversely affected. The radiant day prompted smiles and congratulations. The earth had revived.

There was further reason for rejoicing. A servant walked the length of the muddy track that ran through the centre of the village and announced the auspicious news in a voice that reminded everyone of the previous night's thunder.

It was Boro Saheb's privilege to inform the village that, by Allah's Grace, he was a fortunate man. Bau Ma was well. Assisted by the midwife, she had given birth to a robust baby boy.

'A boy!' The villagers rejoiced, their misfortunes forgotten. '*Mashallah! Allahar Rohmoth!* A boy to bring luck to the village!'

There was further good news. Boro Saheb's sister had also made the family proud by having a boy. In deference to Shahid Sharif's wishes, Hasina Begum had decided to settle in the village with her son.

The women prayed at home and the men thronged to the mosque where Polash Mia beamed his welcome and spouted flattering words in praise of their courage against the adversities the night had flung at them. Allah was profusely thanked for His Mercy and Generosity. Polash Mia was delighted. Such a large gathering was a rarity in the mosque. He relished waving away the latecomers to congregate in the muddy yard outside. Polash Mia felt justifiably pompous. He had been asked to tell the gathering that Boro Saheb had invited the entire village for lunch the following Friday.

Shahid Sharif, after consulting his three brothers, Rashid, Anwar and Firdaus, had determined that it would be appropriate if the babies were circumcised before sunrise on the very day of the feast. Adalat Shah was informed, and the male servants were instructed to be prepared with hot water and fresh towels.

Adalat Shah rose before dawn on Friday. He checked his sharpened razors and the jars of herbal ointments and soothing creams. The bandages, imported from Great Britain, were unsealed and made ready for use. Adalat Shah felt cheerfully confident. There was a milestone to be reached with the second circumcision. The figure sounded impressive. Forty-nine thousand, nine hundred and ninety-eight so far. Each one had been performed with the proficiency of a divinely inspired surgeon. Never had he struck a significant problem during or after the operations.

Fifty thousand. He liked the wholeness of the large number. Its weight was worthy of his reputation in Calcutta. Adalat Shah prayed in his room, asking Allah for success.

The sleeping babies were undressed and washed. Shahid Sharif paced the floor and waited for the *hajjam*. His brothers talked among themselves near a window.

'My son first!' Shahid Sharif commanded, as soon as Adalat Shah entered the room.

Candles and lanterns provided adequate light for the *hajjam*'s sharp eyes and skilled hands. As usual, it was a smooth and flawless performance. The baby barely whimpered as the foreskin was cleanly severed. In an instant a liberal amount of herbal ointment was applied to the affected area and the penis bandaged.

The baby's cry of pain was no more than was to be expected. Adalat Shah was exultant. One more and . . . He was certain that it would be a record among the *hajjams* of Calcutta.

Shahid Sharif and his brothers muttered their thanks to the Almighty.

'Now the other one. I have to say my morning prayer,' Shahid Sharif said curtly and left.

In the privacy of his room, Shahid Sharif washed himself and changed. As he spread the prayer mat on the floor, there was a tentative tap on the door. A servant had been sent to request Shahid Sharif's presence in the room where the babies lay in separate cots.

Shahid Sharif's lingering euphoria overcame his irritability at the unexpected disturbance. He followed the servant.

A panic-stricken *hajjam* met him at the door.

'Sharif Saheb, the *sunnat* . . . It cannot be performed,' Adalat Shah whispered, his eyes widening with fear and embarrassment. 'I have never witnessed anything like it.'

'Cannot be performed?' Shahid Sharif snorted scornfully. 'And why not?' He marched into the room to confront his brothers.

They were bent over one of the cots as if a matter of unusual interest had captivated their attention.

'What nonsense is this?'

Shahid Sharif's infuriated voice made them turn around guiltily. No one spoke.

'Well?'

Adalat Shah crept closer to the brothers. Rashid whispered in his ear. The *hajjam* nodded vigorously.

'*Bhai Jan* . . .' Rashid began and then looked at Anwar whose attention was closely focused on a rash on his hand. '*Bhai Jan* . . . the circumcision cannot . . .'

'So I have been told!' Shahid Sharif interrupted impatiently. 'Can someone tell me why?'

'Anwar!' Rashid snapped at his brother who cleared his throat and looked up.

'*Bhai Jan* . . . it appears . . .' Anwar glanced apprehensively at Firdaus, ' . . . it seems . . . well, it cannot be done because every time the baby is touched . . . Firdaus, you can tell *Bhai Jan*.'

Firdaus, the youngest of the brothers and the one least intimidated by Shahid Sharif, had already formulated the words to explain the difficulty.

'*Bhai Jan*, this is unbelievable! But whenever the baby is touched between his legs, he has an erection and the foreskin disappears.'

Rashid and Anwar giggled. Adalat Shah moved toward the door.

'What?' Shahid Sharif's voice was a bewildered whisper.

'It's true, Shahid Sharif!' Adalat Shah confirmed boldly. 'In all my thirty years as a reputable *hajjam*, I have never seen anything like it! The . . . the . . . er . . . organ springs to life as soon as it is touched. And the size!' He grinned slyly. '*Mashallah!*'

'*Chup!*' Shahid Sharif screamed. 'If this is a joke . . .'

'It is no joke, *Bhai Jan*,' Rashid assured his hysterical brother. 'Come and see!'

The baby was asleep. The *hajjam* reached out gently and parted the legs. With an index finger Adalat Shah barely touched the penis. Immediately the organ swelled and shot up into the air. It stood like a hypnotised snake before collapsing sideways to rest against the inside of the left thigh.

Adalat Shah made another attempt. The effect was the same.

'This is a Devil's child!' Shahid Sharif gasped with shock. There was a compulsion to keep his eyes on the abomination. 'What has Allah given us?'

The baby's face was unsurpassably ugly. His head was unusually large, and a huge, bumpy nose protruded, like a lump of clay, from a flat face. The flappy ears were better suited to an elephant's head.

'He . . . he is not human!' Shahid Sharif pronounced with fearful amazement. 'What is this thing? I want my son separated from this creature of a trickster's foul imagination.'

A *milad* was celebrated prior to lunch. The deeds of the Prophet were explicated in minute details. The congregation was sprinkled with rose water, and sweetmeats, wrapped in red paper, were distributed. Afterwards the villagers gathered under *shamiyanas* to feast on mutton *biryani* and listen to Shahid Sharif's long-winded speech about Allah's Blessings on those who accepted their destiny in life, and the virtues of hardwork. Suchitra was called up to a raised platform, where Boro Saheb lunched with the male members of his family, and lavished with gifts of money, jewellery and sweetmeats.

Then the anticipated moment reached its fruition. An *ayah* appeared with a baby in her arms.

A roar of approval greeted her. Five of the oldest villagers had been chosen by Polash Mia to bless the child. They filed up the steps of the platform and recited verses from the Holy Koran before whispering in the baby's ears.

'May Allah grant you a long life!'
'Be blessed with the gift of patience!'
'May you grow up to be a wise man!'
'Let your dreams always guide you!'
'May you know more than there is to know!'

There was music. Dancing and story-telling. Magical shows. A perfect day.

In the excitement of the festivities, no one remembered to question the absence of the other baby . . .

The celebration lasted until the clouds rumbled again.

* * *

Khalid Sharif awoke, as he frequently did, with the words of the village elders echoing faintly in the darkness. During his childhood he had strung together the fragmented accounts of the first few days of his life from his mother and Firdaus *chacha*.

A strange tale, he reflected. Full of elusiveness and wonderment. He thought of the old men he had never seen.

May you never know the curse of loneliness.
Let your life be inspired by the grace of love.

They had withheld the most precious blessings of all.

Khalid Sharif fought to shake off the drowsiness. It had been a night of twisted dreams charred by the ferocity of a vengeful fire.

Familiar voices. Young faces untarnished by time and preserved by memory. And then the flames . . . They leapt suddenly from the darkness. Women ran down the stairs, spilling outside, as the fire licked the corners of the house, consuming it with the wrath of a jealous lover.

Allah's judgement! the thin-faced *mullah* claimed triumphantly.

And above the noise, a sad, clear voice. *I do not know how to love.* The rose bush crackled in protest. He had never believed it to be true . . .

Images merged into a gyration of vivid colours and then faded suddenly.

A hospital room.

The death bed where . . .

That was one of the cumbersome problems of old age. The

past rarely appeared as a coherent sequence. It came out of memory like a handful of confetti which drifted beyond Khalid Sharif before he could catch one and linger with its significance.

The mind settled on the final moments with his wife. He had felt like a cheat, a moral destitute, at the way she confronted him with the last words she had spoken.

And do you still remember and love her? she gasped, clutching the front of his damp shirt with an unexpected strength. *I know, Khalid Sharif. I know . . .*

He tensed with surprise. Never before, in all their years of married life, had Jahan Ara ever called her husband by his name. It was always *Aey jeh* or *Sunyeh jeh. Sharif Saheb* to outsiders. *Your uncle* or *your nephew . . .* to members of the family.

Tell me, Khalid Sharif! I must know! Briefly her eyes glowed fiercely, demanding a reply. *I am not afraid! Khalid . . .*

He felt a slap of breath on his cheek as he lifted her gently by the shoulders and cradled her in his arms. He could not bear to look at her emaciated face twisted with pain. Involuntarily his hold tightened as if his embrace would preserve life inside the frail body.

Their final moments together were bound by a silence that denoted the impenetrable barrier between life and death, ignorance and the knowledge which might exist beyond mortal experience. There was so much he wanted to say, but the forbidding silence, which strangled the room, held back his words. It was a force too formidable to defy. There was something sacred in the quietness. He imagined a distant, blue flame, against the background of a starless sky, waiting for her. It burned steadily without a flicker, demanding a speechless surrender.

Khalid Sharif forced himself to look beyond the whitewashed walls of the room decorated with cheaply framed prints depicting the stories of creation in Hindu mythology.

His eyes wandered to the top of the solitary palm tree visible through the parted curtains. The window was left open at her request.

It will be easier that way, she had whispered deliriously.

He lacked the courage to ask what she meant.

Khalid Sharif was vaguely aware of the muffled sound of the outside world. Out there life was untouched by what was happening to him. It continued to hum in a monotone of busy indifference. Loneliness taunted him. Memories thrashed in the shadows of the past. Self-pity exaggerated fear. A silhouette of darkness was to be his only companion in the inevitable changes to be thrust on his life. There would be no one else, he realised. He couldn't repeat a life tainted by unstated lies for the sake of companionship. He remembered Pascal's despairing words. *We shall die alone.*

There was a slight movement of her head. The grip loosened.

We shall die alone.

The words smashed into his life, releasing the guilt he had accumulated silently over the years.

The others waited outside the door at his request. They would also feel the pain and mourn the loss. But not like this, not with the intensity of so many regrets. It was a moment when he felt the entire burden of his lies of silence. She knew, she had said. How much and for how long?

The others could wait. This had to be his loss; his anguish more than theirs. There was an absence of guilt in his selfishness. He preferred suffering to be an exclusive and solitary experience. That was the way of a great tragedy. Communal grieving diluted the purity of sorrow. He had no desire to endure the additional presence of people around the hospital bed, sniffling and bawling in a vulgar display of transient sadness.

Her breathing slackened. He resisted the urge to press the

buzzer. It would be a futile gesture. The doctor had been gently candid, his face professionally impassive.

We can only pray now, Mr Sharif.

Then, with a slight shudder of her shoulders, as if she was shrugging off all the responsibilities she had carried for forty years, Jahan Ara slipped away.

Khalid Sharif continued to hold her, his mind floating in a blankness of incomprehension. His eyes did not waver. They remained fixed on the yawning expanse above the tree-top, as if he expected to catch a glimpse of her soul deserting him.

The others . . . they were amazed at his composure. He did not cry at the funeral to reveal the measure of his grief. They waited patiently and watched him closely. He performed the rituals with an unwavering precision which indicated no personal commitment. Not a twitch of emotion crinkled his face. The eyes were clear and steady.

Khalid Sharif heard the whispered rumours.

He couldn't tell them someone else had reached deep inside him and stolen everything. That was *her* revenge, a retaliation for the rash promise he had been unable to fulfil. It was a secret far too personal to disclose.

Khalid Sharif's inability to articulate a reply had become the nagging regret of his life. He was unable to console Jahan Ara by saying that whatever she had heard was untrue. He wasn't able to tell her that it would not be long before he followed her, that his grief would make him unfit for a world that would soon forget, a world that had become timid about loving and incapable of understanding the life they had shared.

He had failed to lie when it was a moral necessity.

That was twelve years ago.

Even a life lived in memories and dreams can be hurtful, he thought wearily.

Habit, rather than conviction, dragged Khalid Sharif out of bed.

Pensively he stood near the window. With a rueful resignation he began to rub the numbness out of his right arm. It was customary for Khalid Sharif to awaken each day with an uncomfortable stiffness in his body. His lower limbs felt leaden, and the fingers of his right hand were perceptibly swollen and refused to flex. He responded gradually to the massage and exercises he tolerated as a daily chore. Just as he began to relax, a ripple of pain knifed across his upper abdomen, sending him lurching toward the handbag on the bedside table.

Khalid Sharif groped in the darkness. The alarm clock slid across the table and crashed to the floor. His fingers managed to find the switch of the table lamp. Impatiently he unzipped the bag and turned it over on the doona.

The spillage summed up his life. Memorabilia from another world. Flakes, of what had once been rose petals, sealed in a plastic bag. Dark and crumbling, like bits of ancient parchment. A discoloured ivory comb with several missing teeth. *Her* comb. Medicine . . . more medicine. A notebook with a schedule for capsules and tablets. Khalid Sharif scanned several pages and then pawed through the bottles and packets until he found the appropriate medicine. He checked his scrawly handwriting again. *Red and blue capsules for severe pain. Two.*

He washed them down with several gulps of water. The pain gradually subsided into a tightness in his abdominal muscles.

But that other ache . . . It was relentless as the torpid days crept toward the finality of an ending that could not be too far away.

Darkness pressed against the window. Tentatively he reached out with his left hand and wiped the dampness from the middle of the pane. He leaned forward and pressed his face against the cold glass. It was like peering into what was left of the future—a cavernous void untouched by faint streaks of grey and pink.

Involuntarily Khalid Sharif stepped back, daunted by the sudden fear of a blood-stained hand reaching through the window to grab his neck and hurl him down to a waiting crowd devoid of compassion, intent on revenge . . .

He forced his mind to focus on the reality of the presence outside. Hidden in the darkness was one of the very few interests left in his life. With a rare enthusiasm, Khalid Sharif had taken it upon himself to spend a significant proportion of his time rejuvenating the badly neglected garden. His preoccupation with gardening stemmed from a feeling of power over the degenerative process of ageing. There was vitality and hope in nature's cyclic rhythm of life. Decay and regeneration. Nothing really ever died in a garden.

Watering, raking, weeding and pruning occupied his morning hours. In the shade of the late afternoon he potted, planted and replanted with a caring attention which amused his grandchildren and pleased Javed and Shanaz. Within a few weeks Khalid Sharif had managed to create a symmetrical harmony in the yard. A sense of order was important to him. To an extent it negated the terrifying chaos and the uncontrollable uncertainty he perceived to be the culmination of old age. Here he could manipulate nature, losing himself in an illusion of creative energy which distracted him from a life that had bled itself of meaningful purpose.

He paid special attention to the rose bushes and planted petunias on either side of the paved pathway which was now free from weeds. Where the path ended, there was an artificially raised area partly shaded by the branches of a lemon tree. The tree was flanked with boxed-in vegetable patches covered with leaves and crawling with snails. Within days of his arrival, Khalid Sharif had cleaned the space, turned over the soil, staked, fed and watered the wilting tomato plants. Enthused by his father's dedication, Javed spent a Sunday afternoon with Khalid Sharif, planting spinach, silver beet, cucumbers and hot capsicums.

Along the length of the treated pine fence at the back, there was a narrow strip of enriched soil where Khalid Sharif planted mint and coriander on either side of a Japanese plum tree which was surprisingly fecund and laden with fruits.

To Khalid Sharif's immense satisfaction, the backyard was beginning to exhale a mixture of odours which challenged even the least discerning of nostrils. The pungency of the open mound of steamy compost clashed with the fresh smell of ripe lemon and the cloying fragrance of the red and yellow roses. It was not a garden with an idyllic aesthetic appeal; rather, it seemed to bring together the contrary life forces of decay and growth without being unduly offensive.

The back fence did not please the old man. Its entire length was straddled with the additional barrier of latticed trellises, threaded and knotted with passion fruit vines which he did not find particularly attractive. There was a small break between two trellises, an unexpected opening created more by accident than design. And beyond the fence was another country, ruled by the elusive and forbidding Mrs Barrett who, Khalid Sharif was warned, did not care for people of Indian descent despite the fact that she herself was born in the subcontinent. Shanaz was reluctant to talk about Mrs Barrett beyond cautioning her father-in-law not to allow his curiosity to wander across the fence.

It was too early for the morning prayer. The *wazuh* could be delayed for another half an hour, Khalid Sharif convinced himself. He dreaded the ritual of the dawn ablution in this strange city of perpetually cold mornings.

He felt a sudden longing for the sticky, oppressive heat of Calcutta and its broken footpaths crowded with the agony of a destitute humanity. He missed its amplified heartbeat and its blackened, monumental soul.

He had to be quiet, Khalid Sharif reminded himself. Twice

Shanaz had spoken very gently to him about the noise he made as he limped his way to the bathroom. He was angered and humiliated. Khalid Sharif was conscious of his own clumsiness, and it was a source of immense irritation to him. It compromised his fiercely independent spirit and sharpened his awareness of the increasing loss of control over his bodily functions. He was constantly knocking against walls and banging into doors, despite the corridor being illuminated by a ceiling light that was not switched off at night for his convenience.

It embarrassed Khalid Sharif to overhear the boys muttering restrained complaints to their mother about the drops of water on the tiled bathroom floor. This happened regularly despite his conscious effort not to leave behind any traces of the *wazuh*.

Khalid Sharif sensed that his grandsons, Asif and Safdar, were mystified by what appeared to be the idiosyncrasies of an old man tottering on the brink of insanity. The day he arrived, Khalid Sharif had insisted on rearranging the furniture in the spare room so that the foot of the bed did not point to the west.

Asif, the older of the two boys, had the temerity to question his grandfather's decision.

'So that my feet are not pointing toward Mecca when I lie down,' Khalid Sharif explained patiently, slightly taken aback by his grandson's ignorance. 'Muslims pray facing the holy city to the west.' A note of disapproval crept into his voice. 'You should know that.'

Asif remained silent.

Sceptically Safdar tugged the peak of his baseball cap. 'Where is Mecca?' he whispered to his mother who had dutifully complied and helped to move the bed.

'Saudi Arabia,' she replied tersely, touched by a fleeting guilt about her son's lack of knowledge.

The boys looked at each other and grinned. That was where men wore those funny dresses and rode around on camels.

'What's in Mecca?'

Khalid Sharif straightened up and turned toward them. He forgot about unpacking his suitcase. 'The *Kahbah*!' he said indignantly, darting an accusatory look at Shanaz.

She avoided his eyes and continued to slip the doona into its freshly laundered cover.

The boys exchanged glances again, only this time there was genuine bewilderment on their faces.

Safdar opened his mouth and silently formed the word *Kahbah*.

Asif shook his head in a rare admission of ignorance.

The boys remained unconvinced. Whatever *Kahbah* was, it could not possibly have any relevance to the movement of the bed.

Asif spun a cricket ball in his hands, his mind mulling over the irrationality of his grandfather's uncompromising demand. Discreetly he nudged his brother with the left elbow.

'What?' Safdar snapped irritably, punching Asif on the arm.

Asif leaned over and whispered in Safdar's ear.

'We are in the southern hemisphere,' Safdar said slowly. He paused and swallowed hard. It was too late. He had to continue. His grandfather was listening attentively. He could feel his mother's eyes loitering on him. 'If you pray facing the west, the prayers will reach Brazil.'

'Argentina, you idiot!' Asif corrected him sharply, losing control of the ball which bounced off his hands and thudded against the door.

'That's enough!' Shanaz's ominous tone prevented a bout of adolescent jostling. 'Let's not carry on! I've had enough problems with your sister today.'

'It's true!' Asif persisted in a rare defence of his brother who nimbly picked up the ball and pocketed it.

The boys shuffled forward reluctantly in response to Shanaz's instruction to help her with the bed-making.

The old man grunted non-commitally and squatted on his haunches to tackle the suitcase again. He was alert enough to recognise the heartless accuracy of what had been said, though unwilling to ponder its implications. He remained silent, determined not to demonstrate any sign of confusion or admission.

Khalid Sharif frowned at the memory of his first day in his son's house. He had been unsettled by the frantic pace of life he encountered. He was like a pedestrian stranded in the middle of a busy highway. There was an absence of calm which he associated with a settled family life. He sensed a perceptible lack of cohesion, a discernible fragmentation in their relationships as they hurried in and out at various hours—beginning with the morning's departure which was invariably preceded by trivial arguments at the front door. Their lives were fraught with activities and noise. At home they grabbed sandwiches, played loud music, fought over the right to use the phone and watch television, with the children occasionally using language which offended him. They always appeared to be on the move. He was unable to recall a single meal when they had gathered together to eat and talk without being whipped along by their acute consciousness of time and its tyrannical demands on their lives. He was often left on his own at the kitchen table and compelled, by the activity near the kitchen sink and the dishwasher, to wolf down the remainder of the normally bland food from his plate.

Khalid Sharif looked at the clock again. He could indulge in the luxury of another twenty minutes in bed. He decided to lie down and lose himself in the comforting familiarity of a world which deferentially tuned itself to his leisurely routines, and where time was not as rigidly segmented. He switched off the lamp, straightened the pillow and lay flat on his back. The warmth of the electric blanket made him drowsy.

His mother appeared almost immediately, smiling gently with that look of tolerant patience which blunted male anger and overcame the patriarchal obstacles in the family.

He felt himself drifting. It was a giddy sensation. There were faint voices around him. A gust of cold air rushed past his face. Suddenly an invisible force lifted him above the misty darkness to an immutable land where life was not armed with the serrated edges of pain and unfulfilment.

Khalid Sharif was never quite certain when and how he managed to arrive . . .

There was his mother waiting with his favourite stories. He was fascinated by the spell Shahrazad cast on King Shahriya. Khalid Sharif often fancied himself as the omnipotent king on the verge of taking yet another wife's life, only to be made powerless by the story-telling skills of the Vizier's daughter. Even at a young age Khalid Sharif instinctively felt that there was something rather noble in the act of surrendering himself to the imagination. His mother had brought him up to believe that it was no disgrace to be under the influence of females. The fact that it was a woman who ultimately humanised King Shahriya struck a romantic note in his illusory world populated with royalty, warriors and unhappy women destined to be rescued from brutal endings.

Mumtaz Sharif knew all the stories from *The Thousand and One Nights*, but she chose to tell him only the ones she judged to be suitable for a boy of his age. He listened to them repeatedly. He discovered the magic of transformation. He became Bakbook, Al-Haddar, Al-Ashar and King Yunan. Sindbad and Aladdin were his closest companions. He sought them in the remote, uninhabited corners of the huge family house in Tengra where he enacted heroic deeds with bravado and melodramatic words.

He was about to embark on a voyage in search of the land of eternal life. Sindbad beckoned him for a dawn sailing . . .

A door slammed.

He lay quietly.

Cars pulled out of the driveway.

Even before he opened his eyes, Khalid Sharif knew that he had missed the morning prayer.

TWO

To her utter dismay Angela Barrett discovered that she had run out of tea-leaves.

She bristled with frustrated indignation. How could she? She admonished herself repeatedly. How could she forget? Such an oversight was without precedence. The possibility of advancing age debilitating her memory was not even worthy of a momentary consideration, lest it became an inadvertent admission of fallibility. Mortality was her arch foe, an enemy with whom an honourable compromise was unthinkable. She was obsessed with preventing its cold, gaunt shadows from terrorising her into a state of passive submission. Yet she was not foolishly stubborn enough to reject the certainty of ultimate defeat. What eventually defined the worthiness of life was the dignity of its surrender. Angela Barrett had determined that it would be a heroic act of proud defiance and, finally, a fortitudinous acceptance of the inevitable. No tears. Noiseless. No regrets or fuss. A quiet slipping away.

The kettle began a shrill whistle.

With a desperate hope, Angela searched the pantry's bottom shelf where she stored the empty cardboard packets of *Brooke Bond* tea. Her eagerness had the nervous edge of a drug addict. With unsteady hands she shook each container before allowing her fingers to explore the emptiness inside.

In a barren moment of rage, she flattened several packets and then tore them into small pieces. The rest were shovelled back inside the pantry, their purpose unknown beyond fulfilling an instinctive desire for hoarding.

Reluctantly she reached for the nearly full jar of coffee. At half-past eleven even instant coffee was preferable to those ghastly tea-bags, bought nearly a year ago and stored in an air-tight container, intended for the unexpected visitor.

Mindlessly she made herself a cup of heavily sugared white coffee and reached into the biscuit tin for her daily indulgence. Wearily she slumped into a chair. Her elbows rested on the kitchen table and she clasped her head with both hands to regain her composure. The sudden flash of irrationality had embarrassed her into a resolution of stricter self-control.

Angela hated these occasionally disruptive mornings which thrust her into unpleasant confrontations with people who lacked the good sense and civility to resolve their problems without an ugly display of temper.

Normally her day unfurled leisurely with the morning papers, toast with home-made marmalade and a pot of strong tea. In the confined space of the kitchen and the tiniest of dining areas, she gradually attuned herself to the emptiness of the morning hours. After a second cup of tea, Angela allowed her thoughts to spread themselves beyond her immediate surroundings to the diversity of three continents where she dwelled among the people she loved. Her imagination recreated the past with an uncharacteristic fervour. It was her way of escaping the enfeebling chill of loneliness that permeated every room in the house.

She was young and pretty again, the men gentle and refined in their manners. They spoke without the coarse directness with which women were pursued these days. Angela retreated to a world of ballroom dancing and long, flowing dresses, teasing laughter and whispered conversations under a jasmine-scented tropical sky, glistening with unspoken promises. She pictured the young men in their spotless uniforms. There was Robert with the bluest of eyes. Cedric, with his charming lisp. Robin and Albert. They discussed everything with a serious earnestness. Trade and commerce. *Shikars*. Polo. Summer holidays in Simla and Kashmir. Turbaned Sikhs slid among them with silver trays laden with hors-d'oeuvres and canapes. The champagne was expensive and the flutes never empty . . .

The sacred domain of her morning's reminiscings had been rudely disturbed by Simon's angry phone call. Initially he was restrained enough, but her refusal to divulge any information about Judy's whereabouts had provoked a mouthful of abuses before he slammed down the receiver in an explosion of impotent fury.

Then there was Adam's tantrum. Her eight-year-old grandson had decided that the promised trip to the milk bar was to be undertaken immediately after breakfast instead of late in the afternoon as Angela had planned.

The failure to make an impression on his grandmother mobilised Adam into retaliatory acts of domestic anarchy. He launched an impromptu attack on her composure by pushing his bowl of cereal and milk off the table.

Angela's immediate impulse was to treat the incident as an accident. She went down on her knees with a sponge and a bucket of hot water. The mess reminded her of fresh puke, without the accompanying smell. Angela grimaced and returned to the laundry for a pair of gloves. Fortunately the bowl had not broken. It was chipped on one side but it need not be thrown away. When she emerged from under the table, Adam had disappeared.

Angela found him in the bathroom, slathering the mirror over the sink with toothpaste. The concentric, white circles in the centre were being edged with outlines of what she perceived to be domestic animals. Adam was using a toothbrush with a dexterity which suggested considerable familiarity with the process.

'That is very naughty!'

Angela hadn't intended to bend down so close to his face and shake a stern index finger at him. She stepped back apologetically as she saw him cringe. His left arm was raised protectively across his face as if he expected a blow on his cheek. His lips trembled and she detected a glaze of fear in his eyes.

'You mustn't do that,' she said kindly and immediately realised her tactical blunder.

Sensing a victory in her retreat, Adam stuck out his tongue at his grandmother and ran out of the bathroom.

Angela heard the front door slam. It slammed again, with more force. And again.

With determined steps she caught up with him in the small front yard where Adam was angrily pulling off the petals from her favourite white roses. He stopped as she approached him. Then, in a display of deliberate defiance, he reached behind him to yank a flower from its stem. The bush shook and showered the ground with petals. His strength surprised Angela. The violence with which he had snapped the flower upset her.

Angela relented with mixed feelings of confusion and inadequacy. She had very few definitive ideas about coping with his unpredictable behaviour. Adam had destroyed her angelic image of gentle, happy grandchildren craving for obsolete bedtime stories. Adam's fixation with unsuitable cartoons on television made her uneasy.

'Kids are different these days, Mum,' Judy had casually shrugged off her mother's concern.

Relationships with grandchildren were infinitely more complicated than with one's children, Angela concluded. Years ago such outrageous behaviour from her own children would have encountered a swift, punitive response—smacked bottoms, confinement to their rooms and no dessert for tea. Mumbled apologies would have been effortlessly extracted under the threat of prolonging the punishment. She could always draw on the reservoir of Tom's silent support if the children became unmanageable. If he had to speak, the children calmed down and listened. Her husband never raised his voice or displayed any anger. It was simply the overpowering strength of his presence which commanded obedience.

The way Angela brought up her two children was strongly influenced by her sense of cultural identity. She did not think of herself as being anything but English. Angela remembered her Hindu mother, without nostalgia, as a shadowy, silent figure lurking behind Robert Morton's domineering presence, someone who had fulfilled her life's function in giving birth to his offspring and was, afterwards, destined to be redundant until her death. There were no regrets or guilt associated with the absence of close emotional ties with Indra. Angela had been raised to ignore the Indian connections in her life, so that the term *Anglo-Indian* was never a cause for a conflict of identities and had no bearing in determining the cultural boundaries of her life. She adopted propriety, correctness and decorum as the essential features of her imperial heritage. Robert Morton had been a strict disciplinarian who consistently extolled the virtues of moderation and restraint, although he was extremely lenient with himself in venturing well beyond the rigid framework of morality he established for his daughters. Angela had grown up with the belief that the imposition of a string of disciplinary measures for children were integral to parental responsibilities.

Age had not only mellowed and softened Angela, but made her belatedly aware of the futility of corporal punishment. Adam had become a guilty reminder of her own lack of perspicacity, and a starched maternal love which did not tolerate any behavioural excesses vital for the development of formative personalities. Angela sometimes wondered whether Judy's impulsiveness had been triggered by a rejection of the dull predictability of her childhood life. Perhaps Tim, as well, had been adversely affected. She often speculated about his remoteness and lack of warmth. He had chosen to live in the United States. He wrote sparingly to his mother, mostly about his work, and phoned Angela every Christmas with polite inquiries about her health, warding off questions about himself. His replies were brief. No, there was no immediate prospect of marriage. There was no space in his life for girlfriends. He was in good health. He had a few close friends . . .

Six years. It was a long time without a visit. He was too busy to contemplate an Australian holiday, she was told. Maybe in a couple of years. Always *maybe*. Reticent and elusive. There were times when Angela felt that she existed only as a familiar voice on the phone for her son. That was all he seemed to need from his past.

Even as Angela told her grandson that she had changed her mind, that they would be walking to the milk bar as soon as she slipped on her runners, Adam remained rigidly unmoved, his hands clenched into fists of unyielding anger. There was something terribly vulnerable about the small, defiant figure, silently daring her to enter his perplexed world scarred by a few moments of brutality.

The walk to the milk bar exasperated her. Adam insisted on walking several steps behind his grandmother. As if to emphasise his intention, he sank his hands deep inside the pockets of his tracksuit pants and refused to look at her. Angela wanted to stop and wrap him in a reassuring hug. But true to habit, her world of yearning remained closeted inside her, unable to find a spontaneous expression of emotion.

The mild morning curled itself around the edge of Angela's consciousness, but failed to arouse her into a sensory appreciation of Melbourne's short-lived summer. Her troubled mind mulled over the familial problems, and her own reluctant involvement in a crisis without any promise of a satisfactory resolution.

'Only a few days, Mum! He won't be any trouble,' Judy had pleaded. 'I only need a bit of space to sort out my life. Please?'

The days had stretched to a week, and still Judy hadn't called. Instead, it was Simon who rang.

'Sticky-beaked bitch!' he yelled as Angela insisted that she hadn't heard from Judy. Simon's assumption that Adam would be with his mother did not necessitate any lies. 'Why don't you keep your fucking nose out of my affairs?'

The vehemence of his words frightened Angela. She gripped the receiver and fought to calm herself as he continued to scream and bully her with a barrage of insults which made her feel as though she was a parasite, feeding on the misery of others to give purpose to her life.

I didn't ask for this! she wanted to shout back at him. *I don't know where your wife is! Your son is here! With me! Come and take him.* Immediately she regretted even thinking of such a betrayal. It was mean and selfish. However reluctant she was to be drawn into such an ugly conflict, and regardless of the encroachment on her privacy, Adam had to be protected.

Slowly a fierce stubbornness asserted itself and pushed aside her fear. There was a moral reason for standing up to Simon. Without speaking, she absorbed the vile words and the hurtful accusations until his accumulated anger burnt itself out in a prolonged moment of awkward silence. She clung to the receiver even after he hung up.

Long afterwards she felt cold. Her forehead was damp and a nagging headache made her wretched. *This would have never happened if Tom was alive*, she brooded miserably. The entire house was like a morgue, lifeless and frigid. She submitted to the surge of self-pity which swept over her, and retreated into the safety of the memory where Tom waited.

There he was in his crumpled shirt and creased trousers, his big, grimy hands like feathers on her shoulders. She missed his mild-mannered ways which belied his awesome strength. With relish, Angela remembered the day his patience had been exhausted by an over-enthusiastic Mormon who insisted on coming back the next afternoon to tell them more about Joseph Smith's way to salvation. Without speaking, Tom picked up the zealot by the collar of his navy-blue jacket and deposited him gently on the nature strip outside the gate. That was the last they saw of the suited young man.

Tom would have slipped in quietly and handled Simon without being intimidated. Later he would have embraced and comforted her in a bear-like hold, whispering clumsy phrases of endearment.

There was a time when Angela faced life with confidence, though it did not stem from her own strength of personality but from her husband's bolstering presence. He hovered in the background, a kind-hearted man devoted to his hardware store, emerging from the unexciting landscape of their marriage to be with her whenever she needed support. Total independence was the hardest adjustment she had to make as a widow. She was still learning.

Except for the girl behind the counter, the milk bar was empty. It was a working day. The early morning rush for milk, bread and newspapers had subsided. It was still too early for the pensioners in the neighbourhood.

'Good morning, Tina!' Angela greeted the girl with a forced cheerfulness. 'You know Adam, don't you?'

'Hi, Mrs Barrett,' Tina responded without enthusiasm. She eyed Adam as though he was an unwelcome nuisance, a stray from the afternoon's mob, clamouring for ten cents worth of jelly beans, packets of wizz fizz, twenty of strawberries and cream . . . shoving and elbowing . . . It was enough to make her think that life on the dole wasn't bad after all. She was accustomed to a quiet hour at this time of the day. 'No school, Adam?'

'Ah . . . Adam is staying with me for a few days while his mother recovers from a bad attack of flu,' Angela explained limply.

'I wanna have these!' A fistful of small chocolate bars clattered on the counter between Angela and the girl. 'And chocolate frogs! And . . .'

'Not so many! Adam!' Before she could turn, Angela heard the crash.

'Oh no!' Tina's hand flew to her mouth. She was unable to keep the rage out of her voice.

Adam had pulled the small chocolate stand over him.

Angela's immediate concern was for his safety.

It was easy enough for Tina to put the cardboard rack back to its upright position.

'Are you all right?' Angela cried, going down on her knees to see if her grandson was hurt.

Adam was sitting on the floor, his legs outstretched in front of him, a wide grin slicing his face. The floor around him was littered with foil-wrapped sweets.

'And these!' He held up several bars of chocolate in each hand as if they were treasures he had managed to salvage from an unexpected disaster.

From the kitchen table, Angela had a view of the Sharifs' backyard. In her opinion it was a decided advantage to own a property on an elevated block of land, even if the slope caused the topsoil to be washed away during the winter rain. To Angela, the raised position was compatible with the moral superiority she enjoyed over her materialistic and status-conscious neighbours.

It was a quiet, upper middle-class neighbourhood buoyed by hefty bank loans and purring with the sounds of new Falcons and the odd Volvo. The rows of brick-veneer houses were inhabited mostly by dual-income couples with the resources to maintain the extra car, employ cleaning ladies and once-a-week gardeners, and educate their children in private schools. It was the kind of suburb where people went to absurd lengths to maintain the facade of domestic equilibrium. Couples argued in low voices and, in the case of more serious rows, made certain that doors and windows were tightly shut. An outward show of restraint was a mark of civilised behaviour in this predominantly Christian community.

Among the quiet affluence lived a few scattered and tenacious pensioners who had seen their neighbourhood transform over the years. Now they were the outsiders, politely ignored by the new residents. It was an unexciting suburb which had settled itself into an insular lifestyle of comfortable habits without being affected, or concerned about Melbourne's growing problems of underprivileged people and the deprivations they endured. The parameters of contented living included an obligatory annual holiday in Queensland, memberships of football clubs, summer tennis on Saturday afternoons, golf on Sundays and clannish barbecues, when the weather permitted the ritual of camaraderie, where the myth of living in the world's best country was reinforced with stories of overseas travels—mishaps in southeast Asia, the impossible cost of living in Europe and the rising violence in America.

It pleased Angela that the Sharifs had finally tidied up their backyard. It was essential for the neighbourhood to maintain its orderly appearance. That was the problem of having non-European foreigners living in one's midst. They did not place enough value on the aesthetic dimension of living.

A well-kept garden is a reflection of a civilised soul, her father used to say. *In that respect, most Indians are inadequate.*

Approvingly, her eyes swept over the pruned trees and shrubs, over the neat rows of vegetables.

She blinked and dabbed her eyes with a tissue.

He didn't go away.

There he was, sitting on the grass near the tomato plants. It was that man again! She resisted the initial impulse to open the sliding door and stand on the timber deck for a better view. Instead, she made her way to the window over the kitchen sink.

She couldn't see him too well. Angela admitted to herself that, even with spectacles, her eyesight was not as sharp as it used to be.

He was wearing a broad-rimmed hat, and his face was buried in a book that commanded his unwavering attention. She was overwhelmed by an intense curiosity to see his face. An elderly relative, Angela concluded. An Indian of her vintage.

A current of anger surged through her. Her face felt hot. Aware of the irrationality of her reaction, Angela forced her imagination to place him among those in the rampant mob that had hurt her father on that fateful afternoon.

An idea occurred. She knew they were stored among Tom's camping gear. After her husband's death, Angela had sorted out his things and moved them to the third bedroom which she used for storage.

Adam's voice stopped her. The door to his room was slightly ajar. He was engaged in an imaginary dialogue. Angela crept closer.

'Will you be a good daddy to me? Say *Yes*, or you'll be punished! You won't ever see me or Mum again. Say *Yes!*'

Quietly Angela moved on.

The room felt claustrophobic. Impulsively Angela resolved to get rid of some of the boxes piled high against the walls. She would only keep those items which Tom had used regularly. The rest . . . she would give away. But not yet, she told herself. The sorting out was bound to be a slow, tedious process. Later . . . in the winter months, she decided. When she could find more time.

Angela parted the curtains and pushed aside the memories, telling herself sternly that this was no time for nostalgia. She found them in a large cardboard box among coils of rope, tent pegs and a pair of walking boots. She hesitated, feeling like a robber plundering an ancient burial chamber.

Those are Tom's, a voice inside cautioned her. *You know how fussy he is about his camping gear.*

Tentatively, Angela opened the dust covered case. The binoculars were heavy.

'I will bring them back!' she said emphatically.

Angela tiptoed back to the kitchen window and, with trembling hands, attempted to focus the binoculars on the man in the neighbouring yard. She adjusted the vision and saw, with startling clarity, a rosella feeding on a cluster of ripe plums on the tree across the fence. With a methodical slowness, she scanned the yard until she spotted him. She attempted to sharpen the focus. The vision blurred and then cleared again.

Indian. Very definitely Indian, though not as dark as the southerners. Aquiline nose. Angular face. He might have been handsome once, she conceded. The skin under the chin hung loosely like the folds of a sari drying on a wash-line. His eyes . . . it was impossible to tell from this distance . . . would be dark and full of the mysteries of a life she had never quite understood. She leaned further over the sink as though a few centimetres would make a difference. Angela wished that he would remove his hat. The head was important in determining age. His face appeared to be thoughtful and sad.

He was no longer engrossed in the book but staring at the fence.

Angela coaxed her imagination to sketch a host of animated faces from the rampaging crowd that had disappeared when she reached her father. She saw the old Indian's face as it might have been all those years ago—young and twisted with fanaticism, his charcoal eyes burning with a bigot's hatred of the English.

She rested the binoculars on the edge of the sink and closed her eyes. The humid heat and dust of that fierce afternoon consumed her. Patriotic slogans echoed all around. She imagined the *lathis*, knives and crudely made spears. Broken bricks in eager, vengeful hands.

The crowd had moved on, its passion spent in an unforgivable act of senseless violence.

A tearful servant brought the news. Her mother fainted without uttering a sound, and her sisters ran sobbing to their rooms and locked the doors.

Despite warnings and pleas from the servants, Angela stepped outside the house. She burned with a slow anger against a world that had torn off its mask to reveal its hideous blemishes and vindictiveness. She felt no sympathy for her mother or sisters. Their responses were unmistakable signs of cowardice, an inability to face a crisis. She instructed the panic-stricken servants to look after the distraught females and left the house.

A gust of hot air slapped her face. In the open, Angela felt vulnerable and estranged from the land of her birth. India was not her country, she determined. For the first time in her life she allowed herself a generous measure of self-pity. Her birthday party would have to be cancelled. There would be no need to decorate the drawing room. No party games or dancing. The candled cake, sandwiches, savouries, champagne and lemonade were mashed into a huge lump in her stomach. She sensed that a way of life was being torn away from her, leaving the Mortons marooned in a darkness of uncertainty.

Only a few days from her twentieth birthday, Angela was dragged into the ugliness of an adult world. She was powerless and untrained to cope with the unstoppable currents of hatred and prejudice.

The street was empty. Abandoned pushcarts were scattered along the sides of the raised footpaths. A scrawny dog whimpered and limped into an alley. The eerie cries of whorling eagles prompted Angela to break into a run.

A shrill voice yelled, *'Tesua kuthee!'*

She pulled up and whipped around to seek the offending voice.

Nothing. Beads of perspiration tickled the corners of her eyes.

So what if she was an Anglo-Indian? She wanted to call out. It didn't make her any worse than the rest of them. She didn't know why *tesua* was such a derogatory word, uttered with unbridled scorn by adults and children.

Anglo-Indian bitch.

Tilting her face upwards, she let out a yell of uncontrollable rage.

The street remained conspiratorially silent.

The desire to vent her protest against the cruelty of a lopsided Fate made her grab a fistful of small stones lying on the side of the street. Mustering all her strength, she hurled each one at a lamp-post, and missed.

Years later she recalled the incident, with the bemused cynicism of accumulated experience, which had taught her that adversities in life often had to be accepted without any form of compensatory justice.

She remembered the lamp-post, defaced with scrawled political messages and anti-British posters. It stood there like a manifestation of Fate she had attempted to hurt but failed miserably as the stones flew by on either side.

Angela found her father on the footpath, lying face down in a coagulated pool of blood. She went down on her knees and touched his face. He did not move. She thought she heard a faint moan. Her bravery deserted her. Angela was on the verge of running back to the house when she heard the comforting voice of Ghulam Mohammad, their old servant, calling her. Behind him were the *mali* and the cook casting furtive looks on either side of the street, evidently uneasy about the prospect of being seen to help an *Angrez*, a detested foreigner known for his snobbery and unflattering opinion of the Indians.

The Indians really killed Robert Morton that afternoon, Angela concluded much later in her life. The administrative power of an imperial civil servant had deceived him into an assumption that he was invincible. Suddenly his arrogance was crushed. He was humiliated for the first time in his life. Confined permanently to a wheelchair, Robert Morton left India for the gentler climate of his native Dorset where he settled into a life of bilious retirement.

Robert Morton was a changed person, someone who functioned mechanically without displaying a flicker of emotion. He rarely spoke to his daughters and treated his wife with an icy indifference, as though she was to blame for the unthinkable daring and impertinent savagery of her countrymen. The shadow of disbelief veiled his lustreless eyes.

Indra withered away. Doctors could not diagnose her ailment. She became thin and pale, pining for India and often crying quietly in her room. She willed herself to death. Pneumonia, a local doctor pronounced, after a neighbour found her wandering the streets on a cold winter's morning. She barely survived a day in the hospital.

After his wife's death, Robert Morton faced the tattered remains of his life in a state of perpetual inebriation. He spent most of his time sitting near the bay window, staring at the unchanging dreariness of the narrow lane beyond the low hedge. Angela came back whenever she could, from her nursing job in London, to lavish attention on him with anecdotal incidents about their happier days in India.

It was during one crystalline autumn afternoon that Robert Morton suddenly turned to Angela.

'Can you hear that?' He cried, gripping the arm of his wheelchair. 'Can you hear it?' He cocked his head on one side and began to hum.

'Hear what?' She asked cautiously.

'Strauss waltzes, girl!' He snorted. *'Blue Danube!'*

Angela smiled at the sharpness of his voice.

Robert Morton closed his eyes. The pallor of his normally expressionless face was replaced by a refulgent glow, radiating the happiness of an era they had shared in an orderly world of rank and privileges. She stood behind his wheelchair and gently massaged his shoulders, as if to tell him that she too understood and missed those days of irrepressible gaiety.

It wasn't as if Angela had been a scatty socialite in her younger days or that she was irresponsible and lacked a conscience. Far from it. Her Anglican upbringing had taught her that a dutiful sense of charity and a generosity of spirit were the definitive qualities of a Christian. But Angela's moral world was not expansive enough to embrace those precepts without identifying them as being strongly British, as if the Holy Trinity originated in the islands themselves. If there were perceptible moral anomalies in the Raj, then they were regrettable exceptions which merely emphasised her carefully nurtured notion that the British were only human. Such flaws were inevitable in the complexity of the great scheme for the continuing benefit of Britain and, indeed, India herself.

'Do you remember your first Christmas ball? At Fort William?' His voice was clear and demanding.

'I remember.'

That was another planet under a tropical sky spread like a silver spangled awning under which the chosen had gathered for a night of revelry. Tentatively Angela sipped champagne until she felt giddy and bold. There was no shortage of impeccably bred young men to dance with her and whisper words of flirtatious endearment, which both flattered and embarrassed the naive, young woman.

The young hopefuls were ignorant of Angela's maternal background. In the modulated dimness of the evening's light, her slightly darker and more robust complexion did not create suspicious speculations, but made her even more desirable as a rarity among the pallid-faced men with their darting eyes, rehearsed smiles and strong, wandering hands. And when it was time for lingering and reluctant farewells in the early light of the drowsy dawn, Angela gave away her gloves with a magnanimous indifference and exchanged addresses with coy assurances to write, without the slightest intention of furthering the unspoken promises communicated throughout the evening.

'I remember,' she repeated, and saw her father smile with a misty sheen in his eyes that saw far beyond their front garden.

Robert Morton never spoke again. The next day when Angela took an early morning cup of tea to his room, she found him dead in bed, clutching one of the trophies he had won in a polo tournament.

It was 15 August 1947.

Angela's hysterical sorrow did not permit even a fleeting thought of India's independence. Not that she cared. The country had damned itself to wallow in a cesspool of poverty and ignorance. The celebrations would be short-lived. It wasn't her problem. She was British.

The memory of her father in his retirement scraped the scars that were permanent reminders of the torment she had endured. The injustice of it all was a searing pain that had not been dulled by the analgesia of time.

Over the past two decades Angela had allowed her mother to invade her memory. It was as if the belated regret and guilt which accompanied her remembrances of Indra were a punishment, deliberately invoked, for the heinous crime of filial negligence that had shattered Robert Morton's wife. Guilt grew more robust with old age and did not hide behind clumsy excuses. It was a regular visitor, prone to lengthy sojourns in Angela's memory.

She picked up the binoculars again. He had disappeared. Angela searched frantically as if she was a *shikari* who had sighted a prized prey, only to lose it again. She did not realise that she had viewed the old stranger as an emblem of all that had reduced her to a state of ordinariness.

The backyard of the Sharifs looked disconsolately empty. That was the horrible nature of reality itself, she reminded herself. Since Tom's death, Angela had struggled to adjust her entire being to the yawning emptiness of solitude. She had to admit that it had created for her the time and freedom to repair all those intricate strands which were essential for her to communicate with her former life. Her memory had gradually rediscovered a suburb of many familiar streets. She found it comforting to dwell among its crowded details in the company of remembrances whose balance between happiness and fretful moments she could monitor and alter whenever it was necessary to align them with her moods. It was a source of immense relief that she could manipulate the past in a way that no other dimension of time would allow her. The present was superfluous and mechanical in the rigidity of its unvarying routine. At best it provided the necessary provocation for her to slip back where she really belonged. As for the *future* . . . the word really belonged to a foreign language.

Instinctively she had used the old Indian to propel her back into the glaring brightness of that long afternoon which had irrevocably altered her life. She began to creep toward it again when the doorbell rang and aborted her journey. The Police Commissioner and the ambulance, with the men in white, were instantly vaporised, leaving Angela stranded in front of the sink, feeling the weariness of her seventy-two years.

She heard the scurrying of Adam's feet and his whoop of delight. Angela filled the kettle and reached for the cups and saucers, ignoring the convenience of the mugs in the dish rack.

She composed herself and turned to greet her daughter. The tranquillity of her life, for the day, was over. Now she would have to involve herself with complicated realities.

'Hello darling!' Angela welcomed Judy with her best smile and a peck on the cheek. Her mind was still hovering on the elusive man in her neighbour's backyard.

THREE

It is a delicate matter which has to be handled with tact and sensitivity, Nasreen warned toward the end of her long-winded letter.

His feelings must not be hurt, and yet he has to understand that he is creating too many unnecessary problems. Papa is really quite impossible these days. How can a person change so much in old age? He is secretive and seldom lets us know what he is up to. The village has suddenly become a focus of great interest for whatever reason. We have made discreet inquiries. Fortunately there isn't . . . At his age it is unthinkable! But there is always that possibility. He likes spending time there, he told me. Just before getting his visa for Australia, he said something about reaching a point in life where a person has to live for himself. How selfish! Now his only responsibility, he claims, is to his memories. What does that mean? But wait . . . you won't believe this . . . he insists that he owes a great deal to Pagla Chacha! Sometimes he makes no sense. I don't understand what he means by 'I am trying to look at life the way Munir does.' Fancy using a psychologically unstable man as a model for anything in life!

I know we can rely on you to do the right thing. We are all very grateful to you. It is very sad that Papa has become so touchy and difficult with age! Please be gentle. I could cry when I think of the easy-going, quiet and accommodating person we once knew . . .

Javed paused to determine the tone of the letter. He was familiar with his sister's felicity for flattering, or maudlin, words when they suited her purpose. He read the letter again before crumpling it into a ball and tossing it in the wastepaper basket. His irritation stemmed from a feeling of helplessness. A disagreeable encounter with his father appeared to be inevitable. He did not question the fairness of his sisters' collective agreement to thrust the important familial responsibilities on him. He was the oldest and the only male among the four children, and they recognised his right to deal with the more weighty decisions. But Javed could not escape a nagging suspicion that he was being used, that his sisters were more than relieved to let him exercise the incumbent prerogatives of the older brother in the family.

The awareness of the manipulative cunning of his sisters increased his trepidation about approaching his father. It was impossible to guess how Khalid Sharif might react. Communication with his father was stilted and constipated, as if they were strangers reluctantly brought together for the sole purpose of discovering their differences. Javed was unable to determine, with any authority, the extent to which his father had changed in the decade since their previous meeting.

A fair bit, his sisters had complained in their correspondence without elaborating at length on the nature of the perceived transformation. Amina had mentioned a certain *self-centred irresponsibility* that had crept into his character, and Sharifa had drawn Javed's attention to their father's *increasingly frequent outbursts of temper* whenever he was cautioned against his growing idiosyncrasies.

Javed had spent considerable time thinking about the content of the letters he had received within a fortnight. He divested them of their excessive emotions with an indifference which characterised his attitude toward his sisters. In his judgement of the females in his family, irrationality was their more debilitating drawback, often creating serious complications from trivial concerns.

Javed was cautious by nature. He was reluctant to engage his father in a conversation which might make him appear greedy for an inheritance. His migrant's obsession with self-preservation made him reluctant to venture into areas which threatened his sense of well-being. Behind his finely developed instinct for a comfortable survival lay a tenaciously held belief that a permanent foreigner in a foreign land could not depend on others in times of financial crisis. What he perceived to be a mild form of muted hostility to his presence, in a vicinity dominated by Anglo-Saxon descendants, was, to a large extent, a lack of understanding about the way most suburban lives operated in Melbourne. Reluctantly Javed had adjusted himself to its cautious formality toward anyone or anything markedly different from what was tacitly accepted to be the Australian norm.

The desire to flout the landmarks of his monetary success had played a pivotal part in the choice of an affluent suburb whose residents were not particularly curious about ways of life other than their own. They had acquired and achieved most of what they hankered after within the parameters of their own insularity. There wasn't much point in seeking the unknown beyond their established experiences.

Even as Javed's personality changed, and he adapted himself to the conformity of suburbia and the restrained and often emotionless behaviour expected from chartered accountants at work, the vestiges of family responsibility, in that other life he had left behind, were not entirely uprooted. They stirred faintly and unsettled him into a conscientious endeavour to fulfil a filial obligation, despite a mild voice of caution. The overwhelming concern, which made him wary, was inheritance. He knew exactly how Islamic laws on inheritance were weighed in his favour. All he had to do was wait patiently without upsetting his father.

Javed had chosen the time with the utmost deliberation. Saturday afternoon. The boys were playing cricket. Shanaz had taken Zareen to the South Melbourne market with the assurance that they would not return for several hours.

'Whatever you do, don't be pushy and unpleasant!' Shanaz had advised her husband before leaving. 'He is probably very confused at this stage in his life.'

Javed himself was scheduled to play squash later that afternoon.

It had been a hectic morning with the plumber arriving late and then handing Javed an outrageous quote for installing a spa in the en suite.

'I have to go out for a few minutes. My wife will talk to you,' Javed muttered, leaving Shanaz to discuss the price and the details of colour, type and size.

There was a dark-haired girl, with false eyelashes and wearing heavy make-up, speaking animatedly on the phone when Javed reached the booth near the milk bar.

'All you fucking men are the same! Oh don't give me that shit! What? You bastard!'

She caught Javed staring at her and disdainfully turned her back to him.

He stepped back a few paces and lit a cigarette.

It was one of those Friday evening's *Come and have a drink* at a client's house. A professional presence was necessary. Javed grabbed a beer and stood in a corner, wishing that an hour would pass quickly so that he could excuse himself and head home. He felt himself being grabbed by the arm. Steven insisted on introducing him to all the men.

Smile in place. They were potential clients.

Handshakes . . . Nods . . . Hellos . . .

'And I am Theresa . . .' The voice came from behind him. He turned quickly and stuck out his right hand.

'Pleased to meet you!'

A sudden spurt of energy revitalised him. He would stay on. After all, there would be little more than the sound of the washing machine to greet him. The kids would be in front of the TV. The best he could expect was a laconic *Hi Dad*.

And Shanaz, of course. *God what a day I've had . . . Can you make it a bit easier for me by sorting out your coloured clothes from the whites?*

He shuddered. It was the same every fucking Friday. There was little conversation. Shanaz expected him to listen . . .

'What do you do?'

'I'm a nurse.'

He glanced at her left hand.

Trite conversation. Cautious probings. She sounded as bored as he was.

'Would you like to go out for something to eat?' He didn't mean to sound so abrupt.

'Not tonight.'

He began to think about a slow drive home.

'But you can call me next week if you like.' She scribbled a phone number on a scrap of paper.

He lit another cigarette. The craving for something different, he decided. It makes one blind to everything else.

The girl flounced off.

Javed entered the booth in a state of apprehension. He hadn't quite figured out how to tell Theresa. The excuses he had considered sounded limp and implausible. To tell her the truth would be hurtful, even cruel.

He dialled the wrong number. Javed cursed himself and dug into his jeans' pocket. There were enough coins for another call.

Theresa's reaction was not unexpected. She sounded forbidding and distant. Javed immediately apologised for not seeing her the previous week and promised a visit the following Wednesday, the night he played pennant. Mentally he dropped her into a time slot. A couple of hours. He would give the sauna and drinks a miss.

Javed felt helpless as Theresa's pretence collapsed and she burst into one of her tearful diatribes about being neglected and her dissatisfaction with part-time love. He listened patiently. Love? How could she have taken him so literally? That was the difficulty one faced with females. They wanted to ennoble sex and bestow on it a profundity of meaning. As his passion for Theresa ebbed, Javed sought moral reasons to justify the termination of their fortnightly arrangement.

A puckered-faced woman tapped on the glass door. Irritably she tapped her watch. Javed glared at her and mumbled into the receiver. 'I must go now. There are people waiting to use the phone.'

As he sat under the shade of a wattle tree, waiting for his father, Javed permitted himself the unaccustomed luxury of meditating on the complications which enmeshed him. He was troubled by his inability to tackle the disquiet he felt about everything in his life. He was reluctantly convinced that it was a state of crisis far more complex and persistent than those fractious periods of moodiness he weathered with a patient knowledge that they would eventually pass. He dreaded the term *mid-life crisis*. It was banal and defined an inescapable condition of mediocrity. All it suggested was the symptom of being trapped within one's limitations. Javed had no wish to be stereotyped as a lost soul, destined to redeem himself with an introspective journey on a therapist's couch.

He felt estranged from life itself. He apprehended an invisible force in the process of removing him from the mainstream of existence. A barrier existed between himself and those he knew. Javed experienced a haunting sensation of emptiness at the oddest of times. At work he sometimes imagined himself on a long and deserted road, walking toward an unspecified destination, shedding his clothes as he went, his weary footfalls echoing the ultimate futility of the travel.

What Javed craved was the intimacy of knowing someone without the encumbrance of responsibilities and the pressures of set commitments. Freedom and relationships were incompatible, he realised. Javed wished to float high above himself in the openness of an expansive life, to explore those horizons he knew were within him, but which did not respond to his sensory probings. He yearned to expose himself—his frailties and desires—and allow the aches of his muddled frustrations to be examined and cured by some mystical force which would not mock or accuse him of caving in to unmanly weaknesses in his character.

There was an *ashram* in Rocklyn, someone at work had said. Perfect for a weekend's retreat. Away from clients, money matters, and business lunches parenthesised by puerile jokes and talk of football. He had laughed with the other sceptics but secretly decided to find out where Rocklyn was. If only time permitted . . .

Shanaz was beyond any hope of intimacy. Their relationship was now one of utilitarian convenience. Suffering from emotional fatigue, the marriage had meandered into the wilderness of consumer living. There it derived some satisfaction from acquisitions and monetary hoarding under the comforting pretext that the family's security was being ensured. The vaguely perceived loss of a close relationship was overshadowed by their mutual anxiety to establish the children in a life without struggle—education in reputable schools, designer clothes, an array of expensive cultural activities and a variety of holidays, all packaged in the implicit belief that the primary duty in life was to cushion one's children from any form of deprivation. They had to be imbued with a sense of worthiness that would negate the disadvantages of being the children of coloured migrants.

For themselves, Javed and Shanaz continued to maintain an empty shell without any serious consideration of its demolition. Tacitly they moved into opposite corners of an arena whose centre was dominated by their children. Separately their professional lives became the pivotal points of satisfaction and filled the vacuum which might have otherwise led to a despairing and irretrievable breakdown in their marriage. They managed to do enough together with their children to support the illusion of a reasonably contented family life.

As Khalid Sharif slowly made his way toward the chairs, with a book in his hand, Javed decided to confront Theresa directly with his resolution. No excuses. No lies. There were enough reasons to justify his decision. He was plagued with a growing conviction that he was bored with the predictable and unvarying sequence of domestic make-believe whenever he visited her in the small unit.

Javed enjoyed Filipino cuisine. She pampered him with food before unleashing the torrential woes of her professional life. Usually it was a one-sided conversation punctuated with Javed's perfunctory remarks. Rarely did Theresa cease talking, even when Javed began to fumble and prod without any spontaneous ardour. As he moaned, grunted and undulated, Theresa's verbosity merely changed directions and her passion was poured into a lengthy complaint against his thoughtlessness and lack of romantic involvement.

There were never any flowers, chocolates or restaurant dinners. He didn't visit her often enough. Did he love her? Really love her? Did he ever consider a more permanent relationship? She was so lonely on other evenings. Couldn't he perhaps . . .

Javed warded off a rush of panic as her limbs wrapped around him like a pitcher plant closing on an unsuspecting insect. He was overcome with a claustrophobic feeling as he imagined being squeezed into the confines of her life without retaining even a semblance of independence. Later, under the shower, Javed pondered on the advantages of a celibate's life spent in solitude, far removed from the ridiculous temptations of the flesh. Some day, he promised himself. Some day . . .

Javed stood up in deference to his father. He moved the spare chair closer to him. It took an agonisingly long moment for Khalid Sharif to seat himself.

Javed was determined not to skirt around the issue. He poured a drink for his father and then reached out to touch his hand.

'Papa, there is something we have to discuss . . .' Javed hesitated, looking at him.

Eyes closed, Khalid Sharif was leaning back in his chair.

'Papa?'

The old man held up his left hand in an assurance that he was listening.

'Papa, we are all very keen for you to be comfortably settled in one place . . .' Javed paused, making a snap decision against mentioning anything about the limitations of old age.

Khalid Sharif's face looked peaceful as if he had reached a state of tranquillity which made his son's concerns entirely irrelevant.

Javed scratched the back of his neck, uncertain if he should continue.

'I am settled and very comfortable in my mind. That is where I now live. I am sorry I cannot give you an address. The streets are unnamed. Narrow and twisted.' Khalid Sharif opened his eyes and stared at his son. 'The houses are without numbers.'

Javed's bewilderment was obvious. His chubby face reflected the consternation of a man whose meticulously laid plans were being cruelly thwarted. He shifted uncomfortably in his chair, desperate for the consolation of a cigarette.

A good beginning, Khalid Sharif commended himself, taking a sip of the lemon cordial. *A very good beginning*. He had managed to confuse Javed. The cordial wasn't sweet enough. He asked for more sugar.

Javed hurried back inside, irked by his father's evasiveness.

His mind worked quickly as he attempted to reformulate his strategies.

Khalid Sharif permitted himself a faint smile of triumph. If he had a worry, it was thousands of kilometres away. His thoughts revolved around his cousin, Munir. By this time Ashraf had surely sorted out the paperwork with some hefty bribes, and the house in Park Circus and the flat in Camac Street would have passed on to their new owners. Before leaving Calcutta, Khalid Sharif had instructed his solicitor-friend about the money from the sale of the properties. The house in Modhunagar was to be extensively renovated, and Munir was to be given a fixed sum of cash every fortnight. Khalid Sharif was anxious to complete the transactions without unnecessary delays. His intention was to thwart the Islamic laws of inheritance and ensure that his cousin and life-long friend would not have to struggle financially, should Khalid Sharif terminate his business with the world without sounding a warning of his imminent departure to relatives and friends.

Khalid Sharif thought about Munir with a gentle affection, recalling their farewell at Calcutta airport. Munir was in a state of sorrowful panic, tears rolling down his cheeks, unashamedly demonstrative at the departure of the one person who had consistently protected him from a world that derived pleasure from ridiculing the illegitimate Sharif.

'I wish Munir *Chacha* wouldn't embarrass us like this!' Nasreen had hissed to her sisters.

'What's new?' Amina responded.

'Who asked him to come here?' Sharifa demanded, ensuring that her father heard the query.

'I did.' Khalid Sharif turned to his daughters. 'I wanted Munir to come. Don't concern yourselves! He is not staying in Calcutta. He is taking the late train back to Haripal.'

Before walking into customs and immigration, Khalid

Sharif hugged his cousin and consoled him with promises of exciting changes in their lives.

'Kha . . . Khalid.' Munir stuttered. 'What . . . what will happen to me?'

'You will be looked after,' Khalid Sharif assured him, stroking the back of Munir's head. 'Be brave! You will be all right. Someone from Ashraf's office will visit you regularly. Remember to behave yourself. And!' He waved an admonishing finger. 'Don't go near the girls!'

'Kha . . . Khalid!' Munir's plaintive cry echoed beyond the door guarded by a security man.

Khalid Sharif boarded the aircraft with some reluctance, fearful of his cousin's vulnerability in the commonplace situations of everyday life. There was little he could do to prevent the teasing. The villagers called him *Pagla*, and the tag of a madman had given Munir the licence to behave in odd ways which amused the villagers and landed him in frequent trouble.

Khalid Sharif's daughters had vented their anger and embarrassment when their father paid a large sum of money to one of Calcutta's top lawyers to defend Munir against charges of accosting young girls, and offering money to married women to accompany him into the forest for *heavenly entertainment*.

'What else can I do?' Khalid Sharif implored, knowing that his excuses for Munir's behaviour would not be accepted. 'I cannot abandon him.'

'He is wicked and irresponsible!'

'He has to understand the consequences of such behaviour! And at his age! Papa, how can you defend him?'

'He is not as stupid as he pretends to be!'

'I cannot abandon him,' Khalid Sharif stoutly defended his decision. 'You won't understand. I don't expect you to.' His memory flitted back to a warm day in the village, years ago. 'I owe him more than a lifetime's debt.'

Khalid Sharif's daughters remained indignantly silent, doubting their father's judgement that so generously pardoned Munir's scandalous offences.

'Papa,' Javed began more assertively. 'We must talk about what is to be done for you.'

Khalid Sharif's eyelids snapped open. His eyes were cold and steady like a vulture's stare.

'Papa, you must try to understand how concerned we are about you. You are our responsibility!' Javed whined, cursing himself for sounding so weak and ineffectual. His father's clenched jaws and the stubborn, upward tilt of the head did not augur well.

'What exactly is the problem that I am being lavished with so much attention?' Khalid Sharif spoke slowly, his eyes narrowing as he continued to stare at his son.

Javed avoided meeting his father's eyes. He was furious at his inability to marshal his thoughts in some sort of a sequential order. In his state of nervous anxiety, Javed had forgotten to articulate his rehearsed gambit, specifying their preference for Khalid Sharif's future.

'Papa,' Javed's voice trembled with uncertainty. 'It is my considered opinion . . . er . . . ah . . . it is *our* view that you should sell the house in Park Circus and the Camac Street flat and live with one of your children. You are more than welcome to stay with . . . well, with any one of us, I suppose,' Javed's willingness to include himself in the offer was the result of some shrewd thinking about the improbability of such an eventuality. Australian Immigration was unlikely to be receptive to an applicant who already had three children living in his native country.

'And why should I do that?' Khalid Sharif demanded, sitting upright in his chair, outraged by Javed's suggestion. 'Have you considered what I want? What my wishes are? Or am I too old to think and have an opinion?'

'It is only for your benefit that we are making the suggestion!' Javed lapsed into a form of idiomatic Urdu, derogatorily referred to as *gulabi* Urdu among the purists of the language in Lucknow and New Delhi, and peculiar to the Muslims of Calcutta. 'We have to face the time when . . .' He hesitated, groping for words without a patronising connotation. 'We feel it would be much easier to look after you if . . .'

Khalid Sharif banged his hands on the armrests of the chair.

Javed braced himself for the verbal mauling he had been warned to expect on such matters. To his amazement, Khalid Sharif appeared to lose all interest in the conversation.

The old man began to flip through the pages of the book he had brought out with him. He hunted for a specific passage, found it and began to read silently.

Javed waited in a state of tense bewilderment, convinced that he needed no further proof of the senility that had engulfed his father. It was distressing to see his father like this—forgetful and confused, lacking the power to concentrate on anything at length. Yet, in his condition, there was the distinct possibility that the old man's stubborn pride might be worn down into conforming with their plans.

Javed's sisters had expressed their disquiet about the family assets. Their father, they complained resentfully, controlled everything in a shroud of secrecy, unwilling to reveal the extent of his wealth and how he intended to distribute it. They had failed to convince him of the importance of a will.

Javed was far less concerned about his share of the inheritance. Being the oldest and the only male offspring, he was guaranteed, by the tenets of Islamic laws, to gain much more than an equal share of the assets. But he had seen enough of his father's erratic behaviour to rattle his complacency. The old man was now quite capable of acting irrationally for the mere satisfaction of shocking his children.

Khalid Sharif looked up suddenly from the page he was intently reading. 'Can you tell me why a snail has a house?'

There was the barest hint of a mischievous smile lurking on his face.

'Huh?' Javed rubbed his forehead with his right hand. This was becoming quite intolerable.

'Can you tell me why a snail has a house?'

'Papa, we are trying to sort something out for you! Please be serious!' Curiosity compelled Javed to lean toward his father. 'What's that book you are reading?' The title had all but rubbed off the faded and tattered cover.

'You haven't answered the question!'

'At this point snails and their houses are neither relevant nor exactly the most fascinating subjects of discussion!' Javed retorted testily.

'They are to me! I shall tell you what Shakespeare had to say!' Khalid Sharif grimaced and rubbed his stomach.

'Papa, are you . . .'

'I am fine . . . fine. Just to make it more pertinent, I shall insert a few words of my own.' He brought the book closer to his face. *'Why, to put's head in; not to give it away to his daughters . . .'* He coughed to clear his throat. 'And . . . and sons *and leave his horns without a case.* Every man must fiercely protect his horns!' He tapped his forehead with an index finger. 'Great wisdom there!' He snapped the book shut as if the flash of insight he had gained would suffice for the remainder of the day. 'But you may be right in what you say. I need care in my old age.' He brightened visibly, as if he was suddenly inspired with the ideal solution. 'I might come here and live with you. After all, you are my only son. It is only proper for an old man to seek the family comforts his son can provide.'

Javed fidgeted in his chair. The look of panic on his face saddened Khalid Sharif.

I cannot blame him for not wanting me. I am no more than a stranger in their lives. I can only be a disruptive influence in their domestic rhythm. I am unfamiliar with its beat. Why does he . . . why do they have to pretend that they want me? Duty and desire . . . they are not the same. They will have their share of whatever there is. I never wished to have saints in the family. So why should greed not be a flaw in my children?

He felt the familiar tug of loneliness. The same futile questions. *What use? What is the purpose of a lingering twilight?*

His mind tunnelled back to the beach in Puri. Dusk was the most seductive time of the day, inviting explorations of the mystery of darkness that was inside every human. He continued to seek solitude even a fortnight before his marriage, and escaped to the seaside resort in Orissa.

As the evening pulled its way across the sky like a dark cloth to cover the face of a dead day, the sea reached into his mind . . . his heart . . . his soul . . . murmuring a song of enticement.

Khalid Sharif walked into the water. Unafraid.

A passage deep under the waves. All he had to do was go under and follow the voice until he found her. She would be waiting to forgive him, her face dimpled with a patient smile.

He was almost there.

Khalid Sharif did not hear the fishermen until their hands gripped his shoulders . . .

Now life was supposedly meant to be an open grave where he expected to lie with quiet obedience until someone noticed him and shovelled in the dirt.

'I . . . we would love to have you,' Javed rambled on. 'But there are difficulties. Getting a resident status for you will be a major problem . . .' He paused for a reaction.

Khalid Sharif did not respond.

'Besides, *they* will miss you. It is easy for me to go to India to see you whenever it is necessary, but for them . . .' Javed trailed off with a look of helpless plea on his face, as if it was Destiny, rather than human connivance, that would determine where Khalid Sharif lived.

'I see,' Khalid Sharif said slowly. 'And which of your sisters is prepared to have me?'

'All of them!' Javed cried enthusiastically, sensing the beginning of a satisfactory resolution. 'You can live wherever you wish. Papa, we love you very much. We want the best for you.'

Papa, we love you very much.

The same words, spoken dutifully. Without sincerity. They were Khalid Sharif's utterance, devoid of feeling, that summer evening when a trembling servant announced the arrival of Shahid Sharif with his entourage of servants and several cart-loads of furniture from the house in Tengra.

Khalid Sharif rushed down the stairs. He met his father in the foyer. Two servants carried the chair in which the old man sat hunched like a stunned emperor whose territory had been whittled away to the confined space of his seat.

Shahid Sharif commanded the servants to lower the chair to the floor. He glared at his son as though Khalid Sharif was guilty of a monumental and unpardonable filial negligence. 'Do you know I fainted in my room today?' He clutched his walking stick like an imperial sceptre and waved it wildly in front of him. 'It was half an hour before a servant found me!'

Mechanically Khalid Sharif murmured words of commiseration and consoled his father. A message was sent to their family doctor, summoning him immediately. A servant appeared with a hand *punkah*. Other servants brought in a velvet covered *chaise longue* with pillows and bolsters. Shahid Sharif was lifted from the chair by his son and laid gently on his back.

The fuss and attention calmed Shahid Sharif. His anger, directed at no one in particular except, perhaps, the thoughtlessness of a rampant Time, dissipated. This was the way it should be. He had lost none of his power in the family. He reached out to his son with both hands.

'Papa, we are here to look after all your needs,' Khalid Sharif assured him. 'We love you very much.'

'May Allah bless you, *baeta*!' The old man responded. He fumbled in the left pocket of his *kurta*. 'I have decided to move in with you. Here are the keys to the house. Do whatever you think best with the rest of the furniture.'

Silently Khalid Sharif pocketed the keys. Later he would hand them to Jahan Ara. 'Papa, Jahan and I are honoured and very happy to have you.' The words were dry and inert. Sound and no meaning. It was his obligation to suppress the cruel finality of the way Shahid Sharif had altered a young man's life. 'It is our duty and pleasure to care for you. Will you have something to drink?'

'Lemon water,' Shahid Sharif said quietly, pleased with his son's behaviour. 'With ice.' He was already feeling infinitely better.

Khalid Sharif ordered the drink and went upstairs to tell his wife to prepare a room for his father. She was already supervising a clean-up of their bedroom. *Dhobi* washed sheets and pillow cases had been brought in. A servant was on his way out after sweeping the floor with a broom and wiping it with a damp cloth. Rose water was sprinkled in the corners of the room by a maid servant.

'This is where Papa must stay,' Jahan Ara said to her husband. 'It is the biggest bedroom in the house. We shall move to one of the other rooms.' There was no resentment in her voice. Her upbringing had taught her that it was a filial imperative for the head of the family to be treated with tangible tokens of respect.

Khalid Sharif nodded his satisfaction with the faultless arrangements. He made up his mind to order a gold necklace inlaid with pearls and a pair of matching earrings. Jahan Ara had conducted herself faultlessly with composure and commonsense that once again demonstrated her domestic skills and an unerring ability to handle a crisis.

When everything was to her satisfaction, Jahan Ara covered her head with a *duppata* and went downstairs, keeping a discreet pace behind her husband.

'*Aadaab* Papa!' She greeted her father-in-law, curtsying and touching her forehead with the fingers of her right hand. Try as she did, Jahan Ara could not accustom herself to the ritual of touching the feet of her husband's older relatives. It was a custom foreign to her family. Calcuttan Muslims often surprised her with their practices. She inquired about her father-in-law's health and listened patiently to his catalogue of complaints.

Jahan Ara and Shahid Sharif rarely conversed and never, even briefly, looked each other in the face. It was a strained relationship, formal to the point of extreme awkwardness and based on a tacit understanding of a fragile balance of conventions.

Satisfied with his reception, Shahid Sharif moved in without a fleeting thought of the inconvenience he may have caused his son. He had no doubt that it was his prerogative, as a father of a male offspring, to disrupt the privacy of Khalid Sharif's domestic life with impunity. It was an intrusion so demanding that it necessitated an elaborate hoax of pretended obedience to convey the impression that the old man was firmly entrenched as the omnipotent head of the household. Jahan Ara's diplomatic cunning managed to create a host of illusions to feed the desperate vanity of a sick, old man who stubbornly chose to ignore the hovering presence of mortality as it danced all around him.

Shahid Sharif began a short-lived and ineffectual reign of patriarchal tyranny which ended quite suddenly, if not unexpectedly, with a fatal heart attack.

He died during an afternoon nap.

For forty days the *chula* was not lit, and there was no cooking in the house. Relatives, friends and neighbours were overwhelmingly generous in maintaining an abundant supply of food. Khalid Sharif grew a beard for the only time in his life and visited the graveyard every day while the house was in mourning. He suffered a prolonged fit of depression which was really a composite of regrets about a relationship that had been soured by the events of 1943. Guilt and the subsidiaries of a young man's anger tussled for a definitive attitude toward Shahid Sharif. Neither won.

At home Jahan Ara conducted the affairs of a grieving family with a meticulous eye to conventions. Wearing black *shilwar* and *kameez*, with a matching *duppata* covering her head, she received a steady stream of mourners, some of whom had never laid eyes on her father-in-law. She ensured that no visitor left the house without something to eat and drink. Under her instruction, a *maulvi* was engaged to visit the house every evening to read from the Holy Koran. Beggars were fed and gifts of clothing and money were sent to orphanages. Forty days after the death of Shahid Sharif, *milads* were held both in Modhunagar and Calcutta to mark the end of the formal period of mourning.

. . . *we love you very much.* Same words spoken in different times. This was another world, shrunken and miserable with its obsession with the self. A life of self-sacrificing generosity was foreign to Khalid Sharif's children. They were unwilling to give themselves fully to their emotions and experience the giddy extremes of happiness and sorrow. Their preference was the safety of a dull and flat middle-ground from where they cautiously sipped on life without gulping it to eliminate the risk of choking themselves. Self-preservation was the primary rule of individual freedom.

Khalid Sharif pulled away from the tide of memories and turned to what his son was saying.

Javed droned on. His emphasis was entirely on the practicalities which had guided him and his sisters toward a commonality of views about their father's future. Javed talked about comfort, rest and contentment. The joys of being with grandchildren. Security. Fulfilment of needs. Constant attention.

Khalid Sharif listened, unmoved by the tranquil image of old-aged sedateness. How little his son knew!

'Papa?' Javed looked discreetly at his watch.

Khalid Sharif concentrated on remembering the words that had baffled him as a young man. He tried to recall the way Munni Bai had sung Ghalib's *ghazal* as though it meant something special to her.

'Have you ever listened to Gahlib's *ghazals*?'
'Who?'
'Mirza Asadullah Khan Ghalib.'
'No. I am a chartered accountant!'
'Even they have souls, don't they?'
'Papa, we have to . . .'

*'I wish to go away and live
In a lonely and forsaken place,
Where not a soul will talk to me,
Nor I behold a face.'*

'Papa, we must settle . . .'

*'And I will build myself a house
With neither roof nor walls nor doors
And not a neighbour nor a friend
To listen to my woes.*

*Where if bad luck would have me ill
There will be none to care for me;
And when death lays me low, no one
Will ever mourn for me . . .'*

Javed was startled by the fluency of his father's Urdu. 'Where did you learn to speak like that?' he asked suspiciously.

'That was Mirza Ghalib speaking. Sometimes his spirit possesses me.' Khalid Sharif smiled slyly.

Javed's helplessness escaped in a sigh of exasperation. 'I have to go out now,' he said morosely.

Khalid Sharif's eyelids closed again. He waved his son away with an extravagant movement of his right hand. Slowly he mumbled,

'The feverish activities of this transient world
Are no more enduring than the flash of lightning . . .'

The old man opened one eye, barely in time to see his son disappearing through the sliding door into the kitchen.

Khalid Sharif made no effort to fight the drowsiness.

The afternoon sun was kind to his memories.

FOUR

An accidental sighting.
The sliver of red was like a fresh blood stain on an uneven mat of green. It prompted a grunt of satisfaction from Khalid Sharif. He dropped the hose and moved closer. It was no illusion, he convinced himself.

He reached out with the caution of a surgeon's exploratory hands, parting leaves and stems before touching the ripe tomato. With the tips of his fingers he warily stroked the smoothness of its skin as if he was caressing a baby's face. He leaned forward. There was a desperation to get closer to the visible triumph of his backyard labour. It was a vindication of his belief that he was not merely an obsolete entity waiting to be tossed into the bin of oblivion.

His legs began to tremble. The uncertainty of maintaining his balance forced Khalid Sharif to withdraw his hands. He squatted on his haunches, his feet touching the railway sleeper that boxed the front of the vegetable patch.

He reached out again to lift a cluster of leaves for an unfettered view of the first ripe fruit of the season. His excitement was barely containable. It tingled with the same intensity that marks the sudden and unexpected discovery of something instantly recognisable as very precious.

The fruit's perfection was irresistibly sensual. The unblemished, plump roundness of the tomato and the inviting richness of its colour filled him with a giddy sense of fulfilment. He tilted his head and moved sideways to look at the fruit from different angles. The desire to protect it and preserve its fragile beauty became an overwhelming concern. It looked so vulnerable, even lonely, hanging in isolation from its stem, some distance away from a bunch of unripe, green tomatoes huddled together as if they were conspiring enviously against its mature splendour.

Khalid Sharif had no wish to pluck the fruit. The thought of eating it horrified him as an act of wanton destruction. And yet it must perish, he thought sadly. The human inevitability was the fate of all forms of life. It was only in the past few years that Khalid Sharif had apprehensively begun to confront the commonest of universal cliches with a mixture of emotions. In his earlier years scepticism was a feeble force, easily subdued and throttled by the fervour of his religious indoctrination. The conviction of a transcendental state, beyond the grasp of mortality, was a conditioned imperative which killed doubt in its infancy. It prevented the growth of despair which shadowed his later years. This smugness of belief was facilitated by the impression that Death was at a distance too far for serious contemplation. When Khalid Sharif experienced the loss of family members, the tragedies were conceptually dismissed as the medium for the final migration of souls to a timeless dimension where an eternal sanctuary promised all the joys that could be perceived by the senses. Even when Jahan Ara passed away, the blow was partly compensated by a vague belief in a celestial domain where she would continue to dwell without the constraints of time.

In more recent times, Khalid Sharif felt his mind drifting out of control toward a terrifying infinity of inert darkness which simply swallowed all his monumental questions without the faintest echo of a comforting response. His mind became an expanding universe of disquieting thoughts and unanswerable questions which were elusive from the experiential reality of living. What if there was no afterlife? No angels or devils? No meeting of souls? Suppose the deceased in his family could only be reached as a reflection in the ripples of his memory while he was alive? Was life ultimately no more than a despairing creation of an unreliable imagination?

Khalid Sharif understood the futility of his bleak hopelessness. He fought to concentrate on the present and focused his energies on how he ought to conduct his life in the days ahead. His children had made it difficult for him to reject the notion of *retirement*. It had assumed an even more insidious meaning since his abortive talk with Javed. Khalid Sharif bitterly resented the unstated supposition that he was no longer capable of looking after himself and needed to be supervised and helped. He had already been subjected to the restrictions likely to be imposed on him if he agreed to surrender his independence.

Living with Javed and Shanaz induced in him a feeling of rebellion. He had to eat at certain hours, hand in his clothes for washing on Thursdays, leave his room between half-past nine and ten on Tuesday mornings for the cleaning lady, return home from his tram rides and forays into the suburbs of Melbourne no later than half-past six in the evening, head for bed by eleven and not expose himself excessively to the strain of watching television. The mild nagging was persistent under the pretext of filial concern. The unwelcome fuss and intrusion in his life stiffened his resolution not to accept a rationed enjoyment of the cultural ethos of an unfamiliar city.

Khalid Sharif removed his hands and allowed the leaves to fall into their natural configuration. They reminded him of a veil over a woman's face. It prompted curiosity and intensified the hope of a rare beauty lurking behind the barrier.

The sensation was similar to the feeling of awe, which had rendered him speechless, before he was finally allowed to enter the bedroom on his wedding night. His silence had been mistakenly interpreted as a surly impatience to be with his bride, and exposed him to a flood of wisecracks, sexual innuendos and raucous laughter.

'*Bhabi* has to be prepared,' his cousin, Salima, giggled.

'*Aarey yar, jaldi kya hai?* The entire night waits patiently for you,' chortled Aftab, a childhood friend.

Good-naturedly Khalid Sharif fended off the remarks, but he longed to leave the room crowded with babbling relatives, boisterous friends and amused acquaintances. He continued to be teased mercilessly by the females and taunted by the men who knew him well.

When he was finally rescued by his oldest uncle and aunt, who led him up the stairs to the bedroom, a great cheer went up in the drawing-room where he had been sitting in his cream-coloured *achkan* and white *chooridar* pyjama. The older members of the family pretended to ignore the rowdy advice which accompanied Khalid Sharif up the stairs. That such a dignified occasion should be trivialised and verbally vulgarised was irrefutable proof of the alarming lack of *tahzeeb* that characterised the behaviour of the younger generation.

Khalid Sharif was left at the door to his bedroom with the gentlest of smiles from his aunt, and a manly thump on his back from Rashid *Chacha*.

'*Shabash baeta!*' His uncle whispered before turning around to head downstairs. 'Remember what you learned in *Khush Manzil*! Be gentle and patient.'

Khalid Sharif felt his damp forehead. He clenched his clammy hands and felt a reassuring strength in his fingers. He attempted to recall his evenings at Tabassum Begum's house of culture. The learning and experience he had acquired were not meant to fail him now. He made a desperate effort not to think of Nazli . . .

Khalid Sharif raised his right hand and then allowed it to fall to his side. He didn't have to knock. This was *his* room.

The reality of the moment became the source of tormented self-doubt. The fear of clumsiness immobilised him.

'Our pleasure is to teach young men the art of civilised behaviour,' Tabassum Begum had informed Khalid Sharif during their introductory meeting. 'To be gentle and refined in their manners. We do not use books here, Sharif Saheb. People are our words, music and poetry our nourishment, and life our inspiration.'

Fortified by the recollection, Khalid Sharif pushed the door. It opened noiselessly. He stepped inside, his movements slowed by an awkward uncertainty. A heavy fragrance of *attar* permeated the air. The room was dimly lit by several oil lamps in the corners. A huge double bed stood in the centre like a ship marooned in a calm sea. The massive bedposts were garlanded with flowers and twined with tinsel.

The changes in his life were now irreversible. He missed the familiar sight of the unpretentious, single bed which had given him ample space on all sides to move around.

His eyes adjusted quickly to the light, and he confronted the outline of the shrouded, motionless figure sitting in the centre of the bed.

The ache was familiar. If only by some miracle Nazli could . . . That was in the past, he chastised himself. He had been steered in another direction.

Through the perforation of the white mosquito net, Jahan Ara looked like a statue carved in a posture of humble resignation. She sat with her knees raised to her chin, her head bowed and her hands clasped together in front of her ankles. Her face was hidden by a *duppata* draped over her head.

Khalid Sharif walked to the other side of the bed where the flaps of the net had been neatly bunched together and swung back over the top of the sagging canopy. He gathered the marigolds scattered in front of her feet and piled them on the carpet covering the middle of the floor. Timidly he sat on the edge of the bed. His nervousness was a severe impediment to speech. He watched her closely. There was no sign of movement.

Khalid Sharif sat still, mulling over the ways of making an initial contact without giving the impression of being unduly eager. He couldn't think of a question to ask her. He contemplated a light touch on her arm or wrist. Her right hand was uncovered. The fingers and palm were bright red. A better quality of henna, he concluded. The vividness of the colour was a marked contrast to the pale orange which stained the tip of the little finger of his left hand. A dozen gold bangles covered her wrist. On the back of the hand the *rathan chur* sat like a huge, golden spider. The chains, which branched out from the intricately patterned disc and joined the rings on each finger, were like the spindly feet of the insect. The large ruby which crowned the centre of the golden round resembled a glowing ember in the subdued light. The *rathan chur* on her left hand would be adorned with a slightly smaller ruby, a replacement for the original stone that had fallen off during his mother's wedding. The jewellery had originated as gifts to Khalid Sharif's great grandmother and, in the strict family tradition, had passed on to the successive brides of the oldest male offspring in the family.

Khalid Sharif slid his hand along the soft, embroidered linen. He stopped near her feet. If she didn't respond, what was the alternative? Should he say something first? A few words to initiate a conversation? There was nothing he could utter to make him sound more witless than the words he was obliged to mumble at the *nikka*.

He had been given no choice. It was customary for the groom to lift the veil covering the bride's face and beg her to open her eyes.

Earlier that day Khalid Sharif had been instructed by Rashid and told what to say. The flustered groom argued and raged against the humiliation of such self-effacing words.

'It has to be said!' Rashid thundered. '*Aarey bhai*, what harm can it do?'

'I won't say it!' Khalid Sharif protested. 'Imagine saying I am her slave! I won't do it!'

'*Yar*, don't behave like a child,' Firdaus interposed. 'You are merely doing what most clever men generally do with women! Don't you know that the way to keep women contented is by telling them beautiful lies?'

Khalid Sharif held firm until the moment he sat across from Jahan Ara on the raised platform. Watched by over five hundred guests, he surrendered meekly. Guided by his aunts, he lifted the veil and saw Jahan Ara's face. Afreen *Chachi* placed her fingers under the bride's chin and tilted her face upwards for everyone to see.

'He has seen the moon!' A squeaky voice piped behind Khalid Sharif.

Nudged and prodded by several hands, Khalid Sharif muttered, 'Wife, open your eyes and I will be your slave.'

'Louder!' His aunt commanded, enjoying a rare moment of authority over a male in her husband's family.

He repeated the words. A great cheer went up. The guests clapped.

'Again!'

'*Bibi, aanke kholoh mai thumarah ghulam houn.*'

Jahan Ara opened her eyes. Her face was expressionless, as it was meant to be, but in the shiny orbs he thought he saw another face, pained by the knowledge of a terrible betrayal.

People around him were talking animatedly.

Khalid Sharif smiled weakly. Jahan Ara lowered her eyes.

The ceremony dragged on . . .

The ordeal of sitting on a carpet, wearing the tight wedding clothes and keeping his legs crossed through the long hours, had made Khalid Sharif irritable. Through the *sehra* it was nearly impossible to see the patchwork of multitudinous colours and smiling faces. The veil of flowers brushed his face and made him sniffle. His eyes itched and the turban felt uncomfortably tight. He enjoyed a brief respite when he was brought back to sit with Jahan Ara. The stringed flowers were lifted back over his head for him to sign the marriage document and perform the other innumerable rituals which were meant to do more than bore Khalid Sharif. The evening taxed his patience and made him weary.

Sitting on the bed, it occurred to Khalid Sharif that he had forgotten to remove his *pagri*, despite the constriction around his head. He removed the headgear and shoved it under the bed. The relief was immediate.

Khalid Sharif reached over and lifted the *duppata* to reveal Jahan Ara's face. He recoiled at the sight. *Kajal* was smeared under her eyes and her cheeks glistened with tears. Uncertainty and shyness rushed back to confound him. That he was in some way responsible for her crying upset him into a reverie of self-loathing.

He allowed himself to think of Nazli and the way she had smiled when he told her about his plans for their future. There was pain and sorrow . . . a great reservoir of sadness behind the mask she presented to the world. He had not been sensitive enough to recognise the hidden anguish of her unrealisable dreams.

Khalid Sharif felt a renewed yearning for everything left behind. He was back in Nazli's cramped, little room, lying on the bed, unfurling the future as though he was in charge of Destiny.

He would never see *Khush Manzil* and its inmates again. Those were Tabassum Begum's inflexible rules rather than his expressed wishes. On the last day Tabassum Begum had given him a gift of his favourite *ghazals* written in her own beautifully ornate handwriting in a leather-bound book.

'I don't do this for everyone,' she whispered, handing him the present. If she was sorry to see him leave, she did nothing further to demonstrate her regret. She knew life too intimately to allow it to flow away in sentimental words.

Khalid Sharif willed himself to look at his wife. There was an elusive beauty about her, enhanced by an innocence that could be felt rather than seen. She made him feel inadequate—emotionally shallow, unworthy and incapable of loving again with a grand, self-denigrating passion. He was entranced by the glossy darkness of her hair which framed a round face with prominent cheekbones, a straight nose and fleshy lips.

His thumbs brushed her cheeks and wiped away the moisture.

'What would you have me do?' Immediately Khalid Sharif felt foolish. It was a silly question, tactless in its abruptness. He sounded helpless and awkward, but there was enough concern in his voice to elicit a reply from Jahan Ara.

'I would . . . just for tonight . . .' Her voice was diffident and fearful of a brusque rejection.

'Yes?' he said eagerly, encouraging her to speak. 'Anything.'

'Tonight . . . I would like to sleep by myself.'

Khalid Sharif turned his face away, in case she detected some sign of the immense relief which drained the tension from him. But it had not occurred to him that she could, in any way, be afraid of his presence.

'Of course,' he agreed, managing to keep the eagerness out of his voice.

It was impossible for Khalid Sharif to seek another room or find a bed in an inconspicuous part of the house. The place was teeming with overnight guests willing to kindle rumours and malicious gossip. An attempt to sleep separately from his new bride, on their wedding night, would dishonour his family and cast aspersions on himself. Reputations would be wrecked. The Sharifs would never recover. It could not be done.

'I shall sleep on the floor,' Khalid Sharif declared gallantly, although the firmness in his voice suggested that no further compromise was possible.

He covered one side of the thick carpet with a cotton sheet and dragged down a pillow from the bed. He did not change. Without another word he lay down and turned his back to her. Exhaustion rescued him from further perturbation.

When he woke the next morning, Khalid Sharif discovered that he was covered with a blanket. Next to him Jahan Ara was asleep, her forehead resting on his shoulder and her right arm flung across his chest.

The memory of his wedding night made the old man smile. He fondly remembered his wife's supreme courage in effecting a conciliation. He often recalled the details when trapped as a silent bystander in a domestic dispute involving his children.

The previous evening had been particularly unpleasant. He thought of Javed and Shanaz with a paternal trepidation. He wished he could help to repair the damage they were blindly inflicting on themselves. But he was aware that any advice he offered would be spurned as the interference of an old man with no comprehension of the dynamics of relationships in an alien culture.

Javed's vehement opposition to Zareen's request to go to the movies with an Italian boy had sparked off a verbal storm with Shanaz. It swept through their lives and damaged many of the shelters they had built to hide their mutual dissatisfactions.

As soon as he heard the rumblings, Khalid Sharif slipped away discreetly to his room and shut the door. The voices filtered through without distortion. Zareen's tantrum was briefly hysterical. She sobbed her hatred of her father and his obsolete notions of propriety before dashing off to her room and slamming the door.

Shanaz tried to reason with her husband and promptly lost her temper. The argument spiralled out of control into unrelated areas. The ugliness of the confrontation lay in the merciless exposure of their own private lives and the accusations they hurled at each other without any regard for their long-term consequences. There were names that Khalid Sharif did not know, incidents and events which made no sense.

They knew too much about each other, Khalid Sharif concluded. There were corners in one's lives best kept hidden from even the most intimate companion. It needed a reciprocal understanding. There was much skill involved in ignoring these accidental discoveries which only shocked and hurt if they were probed at length. It was one of those supreme paradoxes of existence. A measure of secrecy, even dishonesty, was a necessity for maintaining an equilibrium in a relationship.

There was no thought given to a strategic retreat. Javed and Shanaz reminded Khalid Sharif of two reckless soldiers in a hand-to-hand combat, intent on bludgeoning each other with the most primitive of clubs. Eventually exhaustion would win, forcing them to stagger away with their injuries. The period of recuperation would be a lengthy one, with the pain lingering for days afterwards before hiding itself in one of the bypaths of memory. Assuming that they recovered, the battle scars would remain as ugly and permanent reminders of their inability to negotiate one of the many sharp bends encountered in marriage.

Khalid Sharif was vaguely aware of a trend encouraged by liberal societies for couples to *bring it all out in the open*. A frank, even a vitriolic, exchange supposedly had therapeutic merit. It often triggered a commitment from people to evaluate themselves and reach some form of self-understanding. It was the ability to cope with the reality of the self, once it was unearthed, that Khalid Sharif questioned. Illusions were essential for nourishing the human spirit. A life that could not occasionally fool itself and others into a justification of its deeds, a belief in its own goodness, its potential for creativity, one which could not take flight and soar into the realm of impossible achievements, was destined to droop and languish in a world crowded with pain and imperfection.

The old man heard Shanaz mentioning him several times. He wondered how he had managed to enter the fray. Perhaps he was like an innocent bystander dragged into the melee simply because he happened to be present. Whatever the context of the argument was at that point, it had goaded Javed into expressions of greater fury.

Khalid Sharif immediately retreated beyond hearing. He made his way into the roomy, walk-in wardrobe and slid the door shut behind him. He stood suspended between the desire to know what was being said about him, and the promptings of an inner voice cautioning him to remain hidden in the comforting obscurity of ignorance.

Khalid Sharif emerged only after the yelling had subsided and the evening sounds in the house were restored to their high level. The noise from Zareen's room sounded as if someone was in agonising pain. He could identify a harsh metallic voice, but the words were welded together in an undistinguishable shout, accompanied by a cacophony of instruments which his granddaughter championed as the sound of *unreal music*.

The boys were watching television and conversing sporadically in subdued voices, as though chastened into a consciousness of domestic insecurity they hadn't seriously contemplated before. Their usually boisterous behaviour, manifested in ceaseless and clumsy movements of restless limbs, had given way to a lethargic sprawl. The bag of crisps they shared made Khalid Sharif think of dinner.

He looked at his grandsons with an affectionate pride, although he could not claim to know them. His inability to talk to the boys, beyond superficial conversations, was his most enduring disappointment since arriving in Melbourne.

He had soon discovered that a lack of commonality made it almost impossible to establish even a fundamental line of communication. Their interests were outside his experiences, and the cultural ethos which nourished their personalities was beyond his emotional grasp. They were friendly and considerate enough in a polite and distant kind of way. It had been drummed into them that behaviour toward a grandparent in an Indian family could not be too casual. Familiarity could be misinterpreted as rudeness. Before his father's arrival, Javed had spoken to his sons about those conventions which characterised respect for older relatives. His words merely had the effect of distancing the boys from their grandfather from the moment they greeted him at the airport. Their uncertainty of what *tahzeeb* exactly entailed, and their inability to understand the distinguishing subtleties of good and bad manners, made them reticent and cautious. They were unable to understand their mother's anger after they had teased Khalid Sharif about the direction he faced during prayers. Good-humoured fun, they deduced, was totally unacceptable.

Zareen was more affectionate toward her grandfather. She often hugged him impulsively and thought he was *kinda cute,* a description which did not meet with her father's approval. She marvelled at Khalid Sharif's endless repository of strange and wonderful stories about India. She grappled with his descriptions of Calcutta, her orderly life unable to comprehend the enormity of the human chaos which was the heartbeat of the city he loved with such passion. But nothing intrigued and enthralled her more than when she heard about Munir. Zareen felt as if she had missed out on a soul mate in her grandfather's cousin whose pursuit of winged creatures, he claimed to be his friends, stirred in her a burning, primitive curiosity about supernatural and exotic beings.

The glitter of enthusiasm in Khalid Sharif's eyes betrayed the exaggeration of his narratives, but she enjoyed them even more for the dramatic dimensions he added to his stories. His knowledge of Islamic poetry and Indian history fascinated Zareen, and he captivated her with a diversity of yarns about his travels to the remote and exotic parts of the subcontinent. He was like a network of secret chambers crammed with treasures. Each one she entered revealed the riches of fabulous experiences, accumulated and stored with meticulous care.

Zareen was an imaginative girl who excelled in English and art at school. Her flair for those subjects isolated her at home where there was little scope for any form of aesthetic stimulation from the other members of her family. When he wasn't playing squash, Javed was constantly occupied with his computer and calculators. Shanaz, who worked for an international pharmaceutical company, constantly complained about the lack of time to pursue and develop the cultural side of her life, without ever making the effort to read, visit art galleries or attend concerts and the theatre. Her sole diversion was shopping—clothes, furniture, the latest in kitchen gadgets and anything that could demonstrate the family's affluence. As for Zareen's brothers—she no longer waited patiently for them to grow out of their obsession with computer games, their fanatical devotion to contact sports or their fixation with violent movies. Their adulation of macho sporting stars, whose glossy posters deified the walls in their rooms, had assumed the intensity of a religious fervour instead of indicating signs of a diminishing hero-worship.

Khalid Sharif drifted into the kitchen where Shanaz was chopping fresh coriander leaves with a mechanical slowness which suggested her mind was elsewhere. The herbal odour made him hungry. He dared to hope that there was something more spicy than a roast or a plate of pasta. Without even looking at her he sensed that she was struggling to maintain the facade of a normal demeanour. He patted her shoulders in a gesture of silent sympathy.

Shanaz looked up and smiled wanly. 'There is a curry tonight,' she said, feeling guilty that she had dragged him into the connubial argument to justify the accusations hurled at Javed. Her father-in-law was a kind and exceedingly generous man. Shanaz was genuinely fond of him. It was Javed's arrogant assumption, that it was his patriarchal prerogative to have his father live with them indefinitely, which had upset her. She had a right to participate as an equal in the major decisions which affected the family, Shanaz reminded her husband. Her monetary contribution to their living expenses was substantial enough to warrant a voice in family matters.

From her perspective, Khalid Sharif did not belong in these unfamiliar surroundings. It was far too late for him to adapt to an alien way of life. Shanaz didn't think that Khalid Sharif would be conscious of his loss of resilience. At his time of life, an unwillingness to accept the limitations of age was common. She remembered how her father had refused to give up driving until the accident which had landed him in hospital for several months.

Silently Khalid Sharif helped to lay the table. He set a place for Javed as if he knew nothing about the quarrel and his son's stormy exit from the house.

As Shanaz prepared the *raita*, Khalid Sharif made his way to Zareen's room. He knocked timidly on the door.

'What?'

The impatient rudeness in his granddaughter's voice made Khalid Sharif even more determined to coax her into eating with them.

He entered without replying.

Zareen was sitting at her desk, sketching distorted male faces in various stages of paranoid anger.

'*Kahnna, Begum Saheb!*' Khalid Sharif announced lightheartedly, bowing low with his hands held together in front of his face in a posture of obeisant respect. 'What do you think I said?'

'Dunno.' Mindlessly she shaded a corner of her sketch-pad with a pencil.

'Try.'

She shrugged her shoulders indifferently without betraying that she was intrigued by the sound of the words she didn't understand. 'Did you speak Urdu or Bengali just then?'

'Guess.'

Zareen swung around in her chair. 'Urdu?' she said tentatively, arching her eyebrows.

Khalid Sharif nodded. 'What did I say?'

'Something about not sulking?'

'No.'

'About being happy?'

Khalid Sharif shook his head.

'But that's what you always tell me.' Zareen brightened visibly, responding to the challenge of the mysterious words.

'It is related to happiness. It should be anyway.'

'What?'

'*Kahnna, Begum Saheb!*'

'Tell me!'

'Food, Lady Master! That is a close literal translation.' He held out his hands to her.

'Lady Master!' Zareen giggled and reached out spontaneously.

The voice came from across the fence like a reluctant emissary of time, reminding Khalid Sharif that a life cannot be entirely cloistered in memories. He turned around. A female's face was wedged in the opening between the trellises.

He attempted to get to his feet without pushing his hands against the sleeper to balance and steady himself. Stubborn male pride thwarted the dictates of caution. Khalid Sharif grunted and concentrated on directing all his strength to the lower part of his body. His legs failed him miserably. There was inadequate thrust to move upwards without assistance. He rose slightly, his buttocks wobbling like mounds of jelly, before the weakness of his lower limbs betrayed him into a painful and undignified landing on his bottom.

Khalid Sharif was acutely embarrassed that an elderly woman was watching him. He sat on the ground and inhaled deeply. Then, with his hands resting firmly on top of the sleeper, Khalid Sharif managed to push himself up to an erect position.

'Do you speak English?' The words were repeated. The woman spoke slowly, enunciating each word with a discernible movement of her lips.

Khalid Sharif's initial impulse was to stare blindly and fulfil her expectation that he was unable to comprehend what she was saying. The condescending patience in her manner of speaking prevented him from indulging in a playful silence of deception. He felt the pain of strained tendons in both his legs as he gingerly made his way over to the fence.

There came another voice from behind the woman. Khalid Sharif thought he heard a giggle. It was a child's squeal of mischievous delight.

'Black man! Black man! Black . . .'

'Adam!' the woman called sharply, turning to look behind her. 'Stop it at once!'

'I am sorry!' the woman apologised, blushing and looking agitated. 'That's my grandson. He isn't used to people from other cultures. I . . .' She paused to scrutinise his face. It gave her no assurance that he understood what she was saying.

Khalid Sharif matched her stare, his imagination peeling off the years until she was young again. He pictured her amongst a wild, tropical greenness, a nymph in the woods, an adornment on the Keatsian urn coming to life—passionate, teasing and elusive, her strong, sensuous body full of the mysteries of creation, her blue eyes shimmering like a midday sea.

'Yes,' he said tonelessly. 'I speak your language.'

She nodded, wilting under the intensity of his gaze. She was unable to place his accent. It certainly wasn't Indian. Perhaps he was one of those privileged subcontinentals with the benefits of an education in the United Kingdom. Her controlled hostility weakened. His eyebrows were unusually thick and furry. She favoured him with the faintest of smiles.

'I'm afraid my grandson has taken some plums from your tree without asking,' she confessed. 'He wishes to apologise. Adam!'

'Sorry!' The young voice chirped from behind her, the tone indicating that he was anything but contrite.

'Come here please!' Angela instructed. She stepped back to make way for her grandson.

A mop of uncut, brown hair surfaced over the fence. A freckled, unrepentant face confronted Khalid Sharif.

'Hello!' he greeted the boy.

'Hello,' Adam responded uncertainly, taken aback by the lack of reaction over the teasing and the stolen plums.

'Do you like plums?'

Adam nodded shyly, curious about the old stranger who displayed no temper.

Khalid Sharif reached above his head and plucked a handful of ripe fruits. He offered them to the boy.

In confusion Adam looked at his grandmother. She nodded her permission. He reached out with both hands.

'Adam!' Angela whispered fiercely.

'Thank you.'

'You are welcome,' Khalid Sharif responded warmly to the delight on Adam's face. 'Help yourself to the plums whenever you like.'

'That's very generous of you, Mr . . .'

'Sharif. Khalid Sharif.'

'Of course! Javed's father. I am Angela Barrett.'

'I know. My family has mentioned you.' Khalid Sharif turned his attention to her grandson. 'Do you know the best way of getting the ripe ones at the top?'

Adam shook his head.

'With a catapult.'

Khalid Sharif noticed Angela's mouth tightening and her forehead puckering into a frown of disapproval. One of those, he concluded. Propriety. Order. Great civic sense. One who measures out shares of daily fun. Uses her cutlery properly. Never speaks when she is chewing food. A tidy life. For no apparent reason he experienced a twinge of disappointment.

He turned to Adam. 'Do you have a catapult?'

'No!' The boy shook his head emphatically.

'Would you like me to help you make one?'

'I don't think that would be appropriate, Mr Sharif!' Angela intervened sternly.

'Grandma!'

'A catapult with soft, clay pellets won't hurt anyone,' Khalid Sharif said gently.

'That's right!' Adam concurred without knowing anything about clay pellets.

Angela caught the old man winking at her grandson. Adam grinned.

'Well . . . oh, all right!' she conceded, softened by Adam's enthusiasm. 'But nowhere near a house!'

'Yes!' the boy yelled, clenching his hands into fists and pumping them like pistons in the air. 'Yes!'

Khalid Sharif felt vaguely uneasy about the young fellow. He noticed the lingering shadows of sadness in Adam's eyes.

FIVE

The strain became unbearable. Letters jumped and words moved sideways. The vision blurred and his eyeballs ached. Irritably Khalid Sharif removed the rimless spectacles and closed his eyelids.

The world dissolved into specks of darkness.

Such moments were cruel reminders that old age was a dungeon without any means of escape. He was rotting away without the accompanying stench. Or could it be that he was beginning to stink? The possibility disturbed him. He lifted an arm and sniffed it suspiciously.

No discernible odour.

He wondered how long it was before a body decomposed completely in a grave. A year? Ten years? Of late Khalid Sharif had entertained the thought of cremation as a way of denying death its victory feast. His family would be horrified if he openly expressed his views. It was clean, quick, economical and, somehow, more dignified; not that it mattered, except for a logical satisfaction he derived from a practical point of view.

Death was an adversary, forever lurking on a misty horizon. Occasionally it appeared as a gaunt and dispassionate apparition with a monstrous appetite. Khalid Sharif had no desire to be generous toward an unfeeling conqueror. He could at least ensure that there was no flesh to nibble under the weight of the earth; no fat worms feeding remorselessly in the stifling darkness; no residue of bones and skull, with that grotesque grin mocking human endeavour to unscramble the elusive puzzle of mortality. Eyeless sockets that did not need sight to know. The remains of the dead had no purpose. They lay there for years, often as parts of history's insignificant and forgotten details, until a machine arrived to turn over the earth and smash the bones into minute fragments. Extinction is the most complete sense of the word. It made all the fuss over the end-of-life rituals comprehensively absurd.

Khalid Sharif resolved to talk to Ashraf. There was little doubt that his friend would babble to the younger Sharifs even if the solicitor was sworn to secrecy. The old man grinned wickedly. It had all the makings of a ripe scandal which would lend further credence to the growing perception of his unmanageable senility. Emergency family meetings. Overseas calls to Javed. Arguments. Tantrums. Strategies to combat old-age lunacy.

Khalid Sharif liked the idea of being placed at the pivotal point of so much fuss.

He roused himself from his lethargy and reached into the drawer of his side table for a magnifying glass to decipher the childish scrawl on the aerogramme. It wasn't only the handwriting, but Munir's unstructured language and dribbles of thought, frequently expressed in brief images of startling originality, which made it difficult to make sense of what he was saying.

Khalid Sharif was able to perceive Munir's anguish. His cousin was in trouble and seeking to justify himself. His plea at the end was the only clearly stated part of the letter. Khalid Sharif smiled indulgently. Munir was asking for more money.

Khalid Sharif had already received the solicitor's letter the previous week. The tone was indignant and Ashraf suggested a firm course of action. That was the awkwardness of having a solicitor who was also a close friend. Ashraf made no pretence of maintaining a professional objectivity in his dealings with Khalid Sharif.

Munir had spent a fortnight's money in a single day and was demanding more. In an extremely embarrassing incident, Khalid Sharif's cousin had travelled to Calcutta and turned up unannounced at Ashraf's office to frighten the secretary and a couple of waiting clients by carrying on an imaginary dialogue with *those who lived in the trees*. Such acts of madness could not be condoned, the letter warned. Some therapeutic measure was essential. Munir's lack of contrition, after being rebuked, had exacerbated the solicitor's annoyance. Munir had justified his reckless expenditure by claiming that his family was accustomed to a comfortable standard of living, and that the high cost factor had necessitated the fortnightly allowance to be spent in a single day.

What family? Ashraf wanted to know. Was Khalid Sharif hiding something from one of his most intimate friends?

There was no explanation, of course. None that would be acceptable to a solicitor accustomed to the restrictions of a logical cause and effect mentality. A family that lived in the trees? A company of winged creatures? Beings that only Munir could see? Preposterous! Madness!

In a good-humoured, condescending act of indulgence, Khalid Sharif had participated in his cousin's fantasy ever since they were children. His reward for spending time with Munir was a privileged insight into a secret world populated with invisible beings—*buraks* and *nagas*. *Djinns* and *pories*.

The introduction was quite sudden.

'Kha . . . Khalid, something else!' Munir whispered, one afternoon, after Khalid Sharif had allowed himself to be beaten in a game of marbles. 'We now play with *po . . . pories*. Come!'

'There's no such beings as fairies!' Khalid Sharif scoffed. Secretly he devoured stories about supernatural creatures.

Without too much protest, he tagged along behind Munir. It was impossible to gain an insight into what went on in his cousin's mind.

Munir did not react unfavourably to his friend's evident scepticism. He was loyal to Khalid Sharif with a fierce tenacity that stemmed from loneliness and the fear of rejection. Whenever the Sharifs were in Modhunagar, Munir stuck with his city cousin whom he trusted implicitly with a child's reliance for protection. Given the slightest opportunity, the village boys teased and bullied Munir. The nickname, *Pagla*, which Khalid Sharif thought was not only cruel but unwarranted, was a catalyst for the village's derision. The villagers were mindful of the power the Sharifs wielded in Modhunagar, and there was no blatant act of physical violence which could provoke a severe retaliation. They knew of Shahid Sharif's blind allegiance to each member of the family, despite his dislike of the bastard child who was a constant reminder of the secret shame that the head of the Sharifs had to bear. The mistreatment of Munir was restricted to snide remarks and verbal abuse.

Munir was not insane. He was devious and cunning. He pretended his speech impediment was related to a mental debilitation which prevented him from understanding instructions, especially when they entailed school work or domestic chores. Before Hasina died of a terminal illness, she lavished attention on her son, and spoilt him to atone for her misdemeanour which had resulted in Munir being deprived of a father's affection. Early in his life Munir realised how easily he could confuse adults into pitying him so that no expectations or responsibilities were thrust on him. He broke the shackles of time and spent his waking hours exploring the frontiers of an imaginative landscape denied to his envious peers.

'Come!' Munir encouraged Khalid Sharif who had stopped at the edge of the forest. 'Come! We go to an . . . another place. Fun! Much fun!' He gesticulated furiously with his hands. The conviction in his voice made Khalid Sharif even more wary.

It was accepted in Modhunagar that the forest was the abode of supernatural beings who were benign enough, during daylight hours, to allow mortals to benefit from the bounty of fire wood, wild fowls and fruits. They were even tolerant of the foul practice of men and women relieving themselves unashamedly under the trees. As for that ultimate human silliness—the below-the-navel game of hide and seek which often led to embarrassing consequences—there was no retribution. But daunted by stories of fierce, fire-exhaling monsters, with voracious appetites for young flesh, the children suppressed their curiosity and kept clear of the dark, dense foliage. The concealed lives of some of the more pious and respectable males in the village community thus continued to flourish.

There had developed an unstated communal understanding that the heart of the forest was to be left unexplored at all times. It was . . . the villagers often hesitated and thought hard before offering a vague explanation . . . well, it was where the *others* lived. It wasn't right to infringe on their exclusive territorial rights considering their magnanimity to the inhabitants of Modhunagar. Any incursion into the forest after dusk was, of course, out of the question. It was not even worthy of a fleeting moment of temptation in view of the terribly tragic tale of Modhumati's fate near the pipal trees, after her bold assertion that her beauty would prevent even the most ferocious spirits from harming her. To prove herself, Modhumati chose to enter the forest at night, a few days after her marriage to a landowner's son, never to return.

Her mangled body was recovered the next day.

And when did this happen? Certainly not in anyone's living memory. Long ago, the villagers patiently informed the upstarts from the Sharif clan of Calcutta. Some time in the past when all this talk of modernising the village, educating the young and making them ambitious had not corrupted the rural soul.

Unknown to the villagers, there was one, a mere child, in flagrant breach of the convention of respecting the rights of the *others*. No one could have imagined that Munir penetrated the depths of the forest and stumbled upon a world full of the mysteries of an existence as yet unproven by the rational mind. He seized the new life with a disdainful aloofness toward those who teased him and made him wretched. He began to smile and laugh when he was taunted. That was deemed to be further proof of his madness. How could any person bear such extreme provocation with the calmness he displayed? Even Khalid Sharif began to wonder about the startling changes in his cousin. Rumours. Gossip. Stories and lies. It was sad. So, so sad. The boy would have to be taken to Calcutta for treatment.

Soon they found themselves among the banyan trees. The day paled and appeared to drop off suddenly as though it was inadvisable to follow the boys any further. Overhead the sky darkened. Khalid Sharif looked up apprehensively. The interlocking branches were like the fingers of giant hands intertwined in mystical communion. Thin beams of white light perforated the leafy awning. He dodged the ghostly shafts, his mind shadowed by a fear of undefinable shapes writhing and twisting in a frenzied movement of a macabre celebration.

Ahead of him, Munir laughed. It was a loud sound of joyous recognition, its purity of happiness welling from a realisation that the uncertainty was over, that he was home. Munir sprinted toward a gnarled, old banyan tree, forgetting his cousin's presence behind him. He embraced the trunk, pressing himself against the wood, his hands rubbing its rough surface. After several minutes he moved back and stood under the branches which spread out symmetrically like the limbs of a Hindu deity.

'Zohra!' he called. 'Are you there? I brought a friend to play. Zohra?'

The clarity of his cousin's speech surprised Khalid Sharif. Normally Munir stuttered and slurred over the words he spoke, often trailing off into a confused silence without completing a full sentence. He called again. Anxiety had crept into his voice.

Khalid Sharif watched wondrously from a distance. He felt heavy, as if his entire body was bogged in mud. A breeze brushed his face.

The laughter was more intense. Munir began to skip around the tree with a gracefully coordinated movement of the hands, held high and swaying above his head as if he was in a trance, paying homage to an unseen force occupying the tree. He began to sing in a smooth voice. It was in a language that Khalid Sharif had never heard before.

The words didn't matter. The hypnotic drone transported Khalid Sharif into an unfamiliar state of consciousness. He found himself in a grove populated with the most beautiful females his young mind could conceive. They were, without exception, very small—no taller than his legs. Each of them was endowed with exquisite features as if a master sculptor had chiselled the face to a supreme standard of perfection. In every respect, except for the covered protrusions on their backs, they looked human. They came to him from every side to caress him with the gentlest of touches.

'Can you love without fear?' one of them asked. 'Without thinking of yourself? If you can love as innocently as he does, you can enter our lives.'

Khalid Sharif stared at them, mesmerised by their demands, unable to articulate a reply. Innocent love? Whatever that meant was beyond his capability.

They understood his silence and left him mired in his selfish world which had already taught him about the dark emptiness of the human heart.

He felt abandoned. Cheated. Angry with himself and his limitations which prevented him from reaching out to those who had offered him the richness of their lives.

The trees blurred. Dizziness conquered him.

Khalid Sharif felt as if he had awakened from a peaceful sleep. He hadn't moved. He was still standing on the damp, soft ground.

His cousin was sitting under the tree, staring at him.

'Munir? What happened?'

Munir shook his head dejectedly and threw a handful of leaves on the ground.

'Tell me!' Khalid Sharif insisted, moving toward him. 'What happened? It was all a dream, wasn't it?'

'You di . . . di . . . didn't play. Didn't see!' Munir accused him in a low, sullen voice. 'Now you can ne . . . never play with them!' He buried his face in his hands and wept.

What prevented Khalid Sharif from consoling Munir, in his customary manner of an intelligent superior, was his own confusion about an experience which could not be shared, nor simply brushed aside as a fanciful play of the imagination. It had an intense and all-absorbing quality of an empirical reality which chastened him into a bewildered silence. He could grasp the imaginative dimension of life, but it was confined to a comforting premise that it took a deliberate effort of the mind to conjure up events and beings that were essentially make-believe. Khalid Sharif couldn't decide whether to press his cousin for an explanation about the vision . . . the fantasy . . . the dream . . . and compromise the hold of infallible authority he enjoyed over Munir. Within himself, Khalid Sharif grudgingly acknowledged Munir's understanding of another world and those who lived there. He could quite possibly offer a satisfactory account if Khalid

Sharif humbled himself by pleading with his cousin. Arrogance battled curiosity for supremacy. The ego triumphed and Khalid Sharif remained silent.

As they crept back to the village without speaking, Khalid Sharif thought about his cousin with a respect that grew out of a sense of awe at Munir's astonishing powers. Despite his confused thinking, he concluded that somehow Munir was able to reach into other people's minds and implant worlds whose purpose could not be determined.

Later that night, as they sat in the kitchen and watched *chapatis* being made on a *tawa* over a charcoal *chula*, Khalid Sharif approached his cousin. The cook was too busy with the food and singing a *bahwaiya* about unrequited love to pay attention to the strange conversation between the boys.

Munir sat stiffly on a low stool as Khalid Sharif talked to him in a barely audible voice. 'Tell me what happened in the forest. What was there? Who did you talk to? What happened to me? Tell me!'

'You did not see,' Munir mumbled, staring at the flames. 'You spoilt it. You di . . . did not let my ma . . . ma . . . magic work. You did not . . . not wish to see.'

In frustration Khalid Sharif resorted to a form of crude and cruel blackmail he was never to use again. 'If you don't tell me,' he hissed venomously, 'I won't play with you! Ever!'

The ultimatum, with its future implications, was too fearful for Munir.

'You diddiddid not see!' Munir panicked. His teeth chattered as though he was unbearably cold. He beat the left side of his chest with both hands like a frenzied Shiite mourner in a Moharram procession. 'You did not see with your heart.' He shook his head dejectedly. 'You . . . you are like . . . like others. You do not see with your heart.'

'What?' Khalid Sharif could not make any sense of what he heard. He suspected Munir was being deliberately evasive by uttering meaningless words. 'How can you see with your heart?' He snorted, hiding his bewilderment behind a veneer of contempt. 'We see with our eyes, Munir. Eyes!' For emphasis he tapped his eyebrows.

His cousin's look of pity offended Khalid Sharif. He was unaccustomed to the feeling of inadequacy Munir induced in him. He felt slighted. Inferior. His education was in the best school in Calcutta, and yet he was made to feel ignorant by a virtual illiterate. The initial impulse was to reach out and grab Munir, shake him and tell him to stop behaving like a cheap prankster. But deep inside, there was a faint acknowledgement that perhaps there were things Munir knew beyond what Khalid Sharif learned at school. Knowledge beyond texts. Words outside the known languages.

'You did not see,' Munir repeated stubbornly. 'You did . . . did not see with your heart. You did not want to come to us. You . . . you were afraid.'

Khalid Sharif choked on a reply. He turned away under the flimsy protection of an embarrassed silence. *You did not see*. There was an implicit accusation of blindness and stupidity. A deficiency which marked his limitations. He was unable to muster a vigorous denial.

It took many decades for Khalid Sharif to understand, even faintly, what Munir had attempted to explain. And even then it was an incomplete intimation without the vision of experience, a revelation not to be shared. It lay palpitating in the remote corner of his memory.

The remembrance of his cousin's duplicitous behaviour, which warded off suspicion about his other life, amused Khalid Sharif. Only he knew how cunning the villager was. It was astonishing that someone as clever as Ashraf was confounded by Munir and sought to be dismissive by claiming that Hasina Sharif's son was mad.

'I warn you, Khalid Bhai,' Ashraf advised frequently. 'One day your protective generosity toward Munir will hurt you. Why don't you at least send him for treatment?'

Treatment? What treatment? Khalid Sharif fumed without expressing himself. *Let's seek a cure for his imagination. Drag him down to our levels of blinkered understanding. He has to conform to our perceptions of reality, doesn't he? We must destroy his sanctuary since we cannot get there. Let us deny him access to a world where he is happy. Doctor, cure this patient before he makes us see. His mind is too dangerous for us.*

Khalid Sharif's acceptance of his cousin infuriated Ashraf. If the elderly solicitor's loyalty to his friend had been any less fervent, he might have refused to pull Munir out of the embarrassing situations which were invariably detected and reported to the local *thana* in Haripal for police investigation.

Hastily Khalid Sharif scribbled a letter authorising Ashraf to send a substantial sum of money to Munir. Inevitably there would be an overseas phone call from the solicitor, demanding a valid reason for Munir's profligacy. Voyeurism, sexual harassment and attempted rape were very serious offences, Ashraf would remind him. There were only a limited number of loopholes in the law. The police were becoming increasingly difficult to placate. They kept asking for more . . .

It made Khalid Sharif uneasy to know that he could not offer a credible explanation to satisfy Ashraf. His stock response of cornered desperation—'It's my money. That is what I want done'—would have to rescue him again.

He checked the time. Too early to change. Perhaps he ought to lie down. Have a nap. But what if he didn't awaken on time?

'Come for tea if you like,' she had said, without specifying an hour.

He should have asked. Four? Five? Half-past four, he decided, before anyone was home. An hour earlier than he would have liked, but it would be far more convenient. He would avoid the scrutiny, the questions and the all-knowing grins of his grandchildren. He didn't particularly care to satiate their curiosity. The assumption that everybody had the right to know how and where he spent his time annoyed him.

Khalid Sharif enjoyed his own solitary presence in the house during weekdays. The solitude was not oppressive, but rather gave him an elated sense of freedom as though he had suddenly sprouted wings and learned to fly. Javed had expressed a passing concern about his father's loneliness, only to be assured that Khalid Sharif found it perfectly acceptable to be by himself. The emptiness of the house was conducive to the slow expansion of his reveries. He spent his time recreating the past as it should have been, without the monumental regret of the most significant year of his life.

Khalid Sharif wandered through the rooms, listening to his walkman, a gift from the family intended to discourage him from playing his strange music on the cassette deck in the lounge. Initially he had been sceptical about the *Welcome to Australia* present he received several days after discovering the power of the new speakers. But once he was introduced to the privacy of the earphones and the ridiculous ease with which he could move around without interrupting the music, Khalid Sharif was delighted. The walkman created a welcome barrier between the recollections of his memories and the dullness of an irritating reality which operated within the strictness of domestic routines established by Shanaz.

Khalid Sharif had brought with him a part of his vast collection of Indian music. Music was an undying passion, embedded in him since the day he entered the house of Tabassum Begum. The cassettes were neatly labelled and carried in a vinyl-lined box. The *ghazals* of Ghalib, Faiz Ahmed Faiz, Josh Malihabadi, Jigar Moradabadi and Sahir Ludhianvi were his inseparable companions. He scorned the new crop of trendy singers, influenced by pop culture and western instruments, who attempted to drag the purity of Urdu poetry into the mire of commercialism.

A worthy *ghazal* relied on two factors—the voice of the

singer and the quality of the poetry. A *ghazal* was intended to make the listener feel, and then think. A great singer had no need to hide his or her voice in a cacophony of instrumental sounds. A very gentle beat of *tablas*, an accompanying harmonium and the mournful strains of a *sarangi* were all that was necessary. It was the voice that seeped into the soul, like water entering a dry, porous soil. The voice and the words created the situation and evoked the yearnings and the passions. A *ghazal* sung by Begum Akhtar, Malika Pukhraj, Noorjehan, Farida Khanum or even Mehdi Hassan aroused a sleeping soul, soaked it in pathos and intensified feelings in a way that was rarely experienced in life. *Ghazals*, Khalid Sharif had concluded, were for dreamers who sought the stimulant of pain inherent in the impermanence of life and love.

The prospect of a cup of tea with Angela Barrett pleased Khalid Sharif. He had been flattered by the unexpected invitation, although it was casually extended and without any evident enthusiasm. Their regular across-the-fence conversations had revealed their polarised interpretations of modern Indian history, especially the partition of the country.

Khalid Sharif and Angela Barrett did not argue. Their attitudinal differences toward the Raj were implicit in their exchanges of anecdotal incidents about pre-partition life in Calcutta. Angela's recollections centred around the social life in British India, with marginally disapproving references to the political events which had ultimately reshaped the boundaries of the subcontinent.

Khalid Sharif was a polite listener. He was amazed by her accounts of a sheltered, young woman whose only obligation to life was to extend its more frivolous moments into a full-time occupation. Even her memories of Calcutta were confined to the house she lived in, the clubs and the shops on Park Street. She was crestfallen when Khalid Sharif informed her that the famous *Hall & Anderson* department store had closed down many years ago, and that Park Street was now flanked with uneven, broken footpaths crowded with litter and pedestrians, and lined with a variety of run-down restaurants patronised by middle-class Bengalis. Christmas and New Year were no longer celebrated with the opulence and gusto they both remembered. There were sporadic bursts of firecrackers to usher in the first day of January, and the blazing lights, which were once strung across the street like exquisite necklaces, were now feeble and sparse. Poverty and dilapidation reached out from every side. Park Street was no more than a skeleton of a vibrant body that the British had nourished.

Angela Barrett was obliged to listen to Khalid Sharif's narratives of riots and political agitation, hasty trials and lengthy prison sentences incompatible with the severity of the charges, and a crooked judicial system intent on subduing the natives with the strength of British laws. She remained silent when Khalid Sharif spoke about the independence movement, giving the impression that she politely accepted his graphic accounts of violent repression. In reality, her mind reshaped the events he described, deleted the excesses of his imagination, and obliterated and inserted words according to the dictates of her faded colonial conscience.

At one stage she expressed a mild desire to see Calcutta again—to picnic on the grounds of Victoria Memorial, enjoy a horse and carriage ride near the Hoogly River, stroll on the footpaths along Chowringee and shop at the New Market.

Khalid Sharif's amused facial expression offended her.

'Of course, I cannot afford to go,' she said frankly, staring back at him.

He shifted uncomfortably. 'Travelling is very expensive.'

'For me it is,' she responded calmly.

'It is best to leave Calcutta with our younger days,' Khalid Sharif suggested, his voice rouged with nostalgia as if he lamented the demise of a great city. 'That is where it belongs.'

Angela contained the sadness that welled inside her. She

had no wish to have her memories of the city modified by someone who lived there. She preferred to live with the comforts of her illusions rather than have them tarnished with Khalid Sharif's confirmation of what she had heard, seen and read in the media.

India was temporarily banished from their conversation.

Khalid Sharif wondered whether the invitation to tea was a gesture of gratitude for the time he spent with Adam.

Angela's grandson was far more docile, even cheerful and cooperative since the old man had willingly devoted a significant proportion of his days to him.

They had spent a couple of afternoons mixing clay, water and bits of straw and then rolling them into small pellets. Khalid Sharif promised to look after them and ensure that they were placed in the sun to dry and harden while Adam attended his new school. The following Saturday morning was spent in hunting for a sturdy, forked stick which could be shaped into a catapult. Eventually, when they found one that was suitable, Khalid Sharif cut off bits with a knife and smoothed the roughness with sandpaper. He tied a rubber band, inserted through a small piece of leather for holding the pellet, to the forks. He surveyed the contraption without much satisfaction. It was a clumsy job, one that would be barely functional.

The much-awaited plan to knock off the ripe plums from the top branches of the two trees was a dismal failure. They took turns with the catapult—five shots each. Their aims were woeful, and when the odd pellet accidentally hit a leaf or a branch, it plopped softly and disintegrated. When one of Adam's errant shots managed to hit the stem of a ripe plum, the fruit swayed gently without dropping off.

Disappointed with their lack of success, they sat on the ground to discuss the shortcomings of their arsenal of pellets.

'Too soft,' Khalid Sharif observed apologetically, squashing one of the clay balls flat between his thumb and index finger.

'Too soft,' Adam echoed.

'Too much water,' the old man added. 'The sun wasn't strong enough.'

Adam nodded vigorously with an air of wisdom which suggested that he had known all along that the entire project was doomed to end in a fiasco. 'Doesn't matter,' he said laconically, making a brave effort to sound like an understanding adult. 'We mustn't give up. That's what Grandma tells me when I can't do my sums.'

'Very wise lady, your grandmother.' Khalid Sharif was relieved that the boy showed no disappointment and did not intend to quit. 'We'll try making some more pellets. With less water this time.'

Solemnly they shook hands.

It was too hot for gardening. The boring prospect of facing the afternoon's empty hours unsettled Khalid Sharif. He felt guilty about denying Adam the privilege of an adventure he had himself enjoyed as a boy. 'Maybe . . . we could do something else today,' Khalid Sharif suggested hesitantly. 'Perhaps you could show me how well you ride a bicycle.'

Adam sighed audibly. 'Haven't got a bike. It was stolen.'

'That is very bad luck!' the old man commiserated.

'Mum says I can't have one before Christmas,' Adam said despondently. 'Grandma tells me to pray hard for a new bike.'

'Oh.'

Adam looked up sharply. 'Mr Sharif?'

'Yes?'

'Do you think God can help me to get a new bike if I pray every day?'

'Ah, I don't really know.'

'He could write to Santa, couldn't he?'

'I suppose he could. All depends on the mail service between Heaven and the North Pole.'

'Mr Sharif?'

'Yes Adam?'

'Does God listen to every prayer? There'd be millions . . . zillions!'

'He might be able to find the time. I am not sure.'

'You don't know much about God, do you?' Adam eyed the old man critically.

'No . . . no, I don't,' Khalid Sharif whispered, looking straight ahead of him. 'That is why I would make a good priest.' His faint smile confused Adam.

They sat in glum silence until Angela called her grandson inside to have a shower.

Khalid Sharif eyed his clothes with resentment. The pair of grey gaberdine trousers and the white shirt needed ironing. In Calcutta his Hindu *dhobi* would have attended to such an insignificant necessity of life. Momentarily he felt angry with Shanaz.

He picked up the clothes and grumpily headed for the laundry.

He grunted and strained. The steam iron hissed as he clumsily tried to glide it over the soft material. The end result was not pleasing. Inadvertently he had managed to add a few creases to the legs of the trousers. The shirt sleeves were no better. Impatiently he returned to his room.

It didn't occur to Khalid Sharif that a tie and a jacket might be too formal for an afternoon's chat over tea and cakes. He chose not to try and iron the jacket which appeared to be in a reasonable condition, despite its shapelessness. The tie was a new one which he had bought at a sale in a crowded Melbourne shop. Unintentionally he had wandered in to see what lay beyond the flashing red light and the young woman, smartly dressed in black, encouraging passers-by to stop and take advantage of the bargains.

He held up the tie near the window. The splotchy effect of the garish colours created doubt about the wisdom of a non-essential purchase. In the shop his vanity had been easily flattered by a persistent but pleasant salesperson who sibilated the right words about the compatibility of ties with individual personalities, and the importance of colours to enhance the aura of warmth that was intrinsic to sensitive people. Khalid Sharif had walked out of the shop, secretly pleased with the purchase, without being able to shake off the impression that twenty-five dollars could have been contributed to a worthier cause. Pure silk, the salesperson assured him. The man fingered the material tenderly as if to emphasise a bargain that no sane person could refuse. It was an offer never to be repeated. Khalid Sharif succumbed to his ego and the remnant of an acquisitive instinct that had gradually withered away after his wife's death.

He prepared himself with meticulous care. This was his first invitation in Australia and was more than likely to be his last. Trimmed fingernails and a second shave. A small pair of scissors jabbed cartilage and flesh as an unsteady hand snipped strands of hair poking out of his nostrils. He opened the packs of shampoo and special conditioner for thinning hair, bought at the local chemist's after a lengthy discussion with the patient, good-humoured woman who served him, and placed the containers in the shower recess. Earlier he had decided against the hair dye. He buried the striped white and orange paper bag under a pile of singlets. Wispy, black hair would merely serve to accentuate the clefts and ridges on his face.

Khalid Sharif loitered inside the walk-in wardrobe, unable to decide on the socks and handkerchief. He enjoyed the privacy of the enclosed space which was like a secret chamber where he could think freely and be himself. Here he sensed a security similar to the assuring knowledge, one takes for granted, that no other human is privy to the world one carries inside the mind.

A full-length mirror confirmed what he was reluctant to confront. Khalid Sharif stared at the reflection as if he was intent on bullying an adversary who had become unbearably provocative. Slowly, he ran the tips of the index and middle fingers of his left hand over his face. It was like taking a bumpy ride on one of Calcutta's broken-down roads.

It had been a passable face. Once. He couldn't really expect anything even bearable at seventy-six, he reminded himself. He looked closely and imagined what the face might have been without the dark spots and with a taut skin.

The hooked nose was a fraction too long, the lips thick and fleshy. The eyebrows remained bushy and unruly. They were indications of virility, he had once been playfully told. Under the chin there was irredeemable disaster. Flaps of skin hung loosely and extended all the way down to his throat on either side of his Adam's apple. They reminded him of a turkey's neck. He pinched and patted them without exerting any force. Khalid Sharif felt no resentment about his appearance, only astonishment that he was alert and reasonably functional despite visible signs of an imminent collapse. He poked his cheeks with his fingers. The skin and flesh were like soft earth. They sank under the thrust of the none too gentle jabs. Without his dentures he would look hideous.

He moved back a few steps.

'The rest?' He wondered aloud. 'It couldn't possibly look any better.'

Suddenly he became curious about a forgotten part of himself, one which had capitulated to the drowsiness of the creeping years. He peeled off his singlet and stepped back as though the sight of a barren, unattractive landscape had blunted the desire to explore it.

Khalid Sharif forced himself to look at the reflection of the bony torso with its ungainly bits protruding like mounds of earth on a parched stretch of land. He was mortified by the uneven colouring and looseness of the skin. The pronounced curvature of his belly wobbled like jelly as he probed the wrinkled skin covering the flaccid muscles. He scratched his navel and ran an index finger up to the hollow depression between his collar bones. Straightening the shoulders was an impossibly painful effort. It was a body which belonged in Calcutta—faded and broken, on the verge of collapsing. He was his own reminder of death, of decay and confusion. He stroked his eyebrows caringly. They had survived the onslaught of mortality and were his only precious reminders of the way he was.

Sharif Saheb, you look so dangerous . . . no, wicked . . . when you raise your eyebrows like that. She snuggled against his chest, clinging to him as she sensed that he was thinking of going home. *Stay another hour. Let me sing to you.*

And she sang in a pleasant voice that made him melancholic, for he knew that each passing evening brought him closer to the completion of a year and a parting from this orphan girl who revealed nothing about herself. She was meant to teach him about manners and behaviour, about love-making and its pleasures beyond the act itself. Instead, he learned about the vulnerability of the human heart and the way it defies reason.

Those were his early days in *Khush Manzil* when he flirted with fanciful illusions. He began to think of shaping his destiny. And her's . . .

His fingers fumbled with the knot of the *lungi*. A senseless act. Undignified. There was neither guilt nor shame. Notions of propriety were tossed aside by a crazy desire to confront himself as he was. The *lungi* dropped around his feet and left him without the coveted shield of respectability between himself and the link with his primeval heritage.

The patch of grey looked like a tuft of grass that had been hit by frost. And just below, like a shrivelled Lebanese aubergine clinging stubbornly to its stem, the uninviting sight of his penis. His hand travelled tentatively to touch its softness. An ancient power stirred faintly as though there still flickered the weak embers of a life that could be kindled into a fierce fire. Quickly he removed his fingers, simultaneously pleased and embarrassed by the sensations.

I am still capable, he thought proudly, defiantly aware of the condemnatory howls that would greet the revelation if, in his wildest moment of irrationality, he chose to disclose that his sexuality was not yet redundant. He thought of the cliches of vilification that would be hurled at him with a vitriolic savagery. *He's mad. Dangerous. Crazy, old ram! Had he no shame? Disgusting! He ought to be locked up!*

He looked without flinching. *Instinct doesn't die with age. We learn to subdue it. The world would have me feel guilty. Why? Should the proof that I am alive make me contrite and embarrassed? There is little that is left. Memory . . . lust and despair. What else do I need?*

Ponderously he entered the bathroom. 'What else indeed?' he reflected loudly. 'I shall have escorts all the way to the gates of darkness.'

SIX

Melbourne was in one of her sublime moods, inducing a forgiving forgetfulness of her winter tantrums. The benign face of the city's late summer strummed a faint chord of nostalgia in Khalid Sharif. It was the sort of day made to be spent near the sea in Puri, or on one of Darjeeling's hilltops from where one could have an uncluttered view of gaping horizons waiting to be smeared with budding hopes and expansive ambitions.

A lazy afternoon for dreams and rides on winged horses in a quest for immortality. Power. Money. Fame and love on a grand scale. To fill the bin of the future with an exciting array of possibilities, untouched by the caprice of time, was the special prerogative of the young.

That was all behind him.

All Khalid Sharif could now attain were touch-ups of the past to bypass the guilt and unfulfilled moments which lingered in his memory as shadowy regrets. His mind rebelled and refused to obey, whenever, in short-lived gasps of desperate optimism, he attempted to dip into the near future for a glimpse of what might lie ahead. Khalid Sharif's life was like that of an exhausted writer devoid of fresh ideas. He could envisage his future encompassed only within the proximity of a few months, and holding little beyond pain, medicine and hospital beds.

Before locking the front door, Khalid Sharif scrounged around in his pockets for the key and the pills his grim-faced doctor had prescribed in Calcutta. He checked the time, holding the watch close to his face for several seconds. He decided to allow himself half an hour's walk before turning back for Angela Barrett's house.

Near the nature strip he remembered the brown paper bag he had left behind on his bed. He hesitated, reluctant to go back inside. Perhaps it was just as well that he had forgotten. But at his age! Surely such a gesture could not be interpreted as anything but an act of friendliness, untainted by insidious motives? Angela had enthusiastically informed him that Judy would be there. It was the consideration of the daughter's presence that became the ultimate deterrent. The chocolates would not spoil. Some other time, perhaps.

The playground was only a few minutes away. He hoped to see Adam on the slide or in the sandpit with his toy tractor. He intended to take the boy for a walk further up the road, stopping at the milk bar to buy him an ice-cream.

The playground was deserted except for a teenaged couple locked in a serpentine embrace next to the swings, their arms and hands like eager tentacles—clutching, rubbing and probing each other without a care for the sensibilities of the rest of the world. There was something frightfully predatory about their youthful passion.

Khalid Sharif sat down on a bench under a gum tree. Shocked curiosity compelled him to stare at the couple. Their urgency for physical gratification appeared to have negated any tenderness of feelings. The boy's hands were vigorously kneading her buttocks as though they were lumps of dough. The girl stood on her toes and strained her body against him, moving her hips slowly and sensuously in a grinding, rotational motion. Her mouth was open, and Khalid Sharif thought he saw a part of the boy's tongue, like a fat, pink worm, burrowing restlessly into the opening as if it was desperately seeking a hiding place.

Khalid Sharif looked away. The blatant demonstration of sexuality was odiously foreign to him. It belonged to the world of painting and movies where such vulgarity could occasionally be excused as realism in art.

He wondered whether this was one of the manifestations of a selfish world which dedicated itself exclusively to reckless pleasures. Was it now a part of the accepted rhythm of life to which he no longer belonged? Could it be a form of honesty, an instinctive response to desires, unfettered by the conventions and nuances of social order? Was it that the West was entirely different from the world he knew? India, too, had changed, he admitted reluctantly. It was all for the sake of freedom and individual rights. He had grown accustomed to lengthy lectures from his daughters who were dismissive of his views on morality and unafraid to accuse his generation of hypocrisy and double standards.

He couldn't resist another sneaking glance. The teenager's hands had disappeared under the loose T-shirt the girl wore. The groping and the fumbling became more urgent. Khalid Sharif heard a moan. He was startled by its softness which was unexpected in the frenzy of the harsh foreplay. He pondered on the boy's age. Seventeen? Certainly not much older than eighteen.

Eighteen. It was the age when he experienced his first serious conflict. Spurred on by his academic interest, he wished to study at the university; but his father felt it was the ideal time for Khalid Sharif to make a transition into the family business. It was also the age of extensive *adda baazi* with his friends. Their fun was innocent enough. Games of carom, lengthy card sessions, cups of *chai* to stimulate their conversations about everything that was important in their lives. Khalid Sharif's overwhelming passion was kite-flying from the terrace of their house in Tengra. Most afternoons were devoted to aerial battles with neighbouring Anglo-Indian boys, their red and black kites tied to strings dried under the sun after being slathered with a mixture of ground glass and glue to make them sharp and stiff. Stories about Khalid Sharif's expertise and his magnificent collection of *lathais* and *munjas* bestowed on him the unofficial title of master kite-flyer.

At eighteen he was not acquainted with females outside his family. Girls belonged to an alien species, confined in strongly guarded domestic territories that were tacitly accepted as being sacrosanct. Despite the lack of contact between the sexes, a mild form of flirtation was prevalent. It entailed evening walks for Khalid Sharif and his friends, usually during *magrib* when most adults in Muslim households were occupied with prayers. In the narrow lanes, pedestrians offered some scope for amusement to the housebound females. Dressed in their best clothes, with hair tied back neatly with stringed tropical flowers, faces made up with powder and rouge, eyes decorated with *kajal*, the girls stood at the windows, giggling and commenting on the males who walked below them. Young men were pelted with dried fruits and the odd letter or poem expressing veiled amorous interests. The crucial part of the entertainment was not to be seen by the targeted males, since facial recognition could lead to awkward overtures of courtship. As soon as the missiles were thrown, the girls moved away from the windows, causing spirited speculation and light-hearted banter among the hapless victims. Exotic tales of romance emerged from these harmless incidents and invariably dominated the daydreams of the young men yet to experience love.

Khalid Sharif's male-oriented life began each day at the all-boys St Xavier's College and tailed off with a late dinner with his father, uncles and male cousins.

The dining table was an enduring symbol of patriarchal hierarchy, its ranking determined by age. The position of the younger males in the family was one of accepting subservience. They were expected to eat in respectful silence unless specific questions were directed at them.

Dinner was an elaborate affair with several servants waiting at the table which was covered each night with a fresh, white tablecloth that was ready for the *dhobi* by the time the meal was over. There was enough food to feed twice the number that were present for dinner, including the females who ate separately after the males had been fed. Wastage was never a moral problem. The excessive food was a confirmation of the family's prosperity. To be blessed with more than enough was a mark of Allah's favour. There was an obsessive family tradition never to allow a significant part of the table to be bare. That would have demonstrated a niggardly spirit, a meanness that was tantamount to a blasphemous rejection of Allah's generosity. The leftover food did not ever appear on the dining table for the next meal. It was distributed among servants, beggars and the fat, stray pye-dogs whose survival instincts had been dulled by the ready-made feast deposited outside the main gate of the house each day.

Dinner consisted of both *chapatis* and rice, *bhajis, dhal,* beef, mutton and chicken cooked in *ghee* with a rich texture of *masalas*. The Sharifs were reluctant fish eaters, and then only at lunch. It was a custom which originated from the fallacious belief that only the Bengali Hindus ate fish for dinner. The Sharifs, who prided themselves on their rather naive notions of cultural identity, spurned anything that was even remotely associated with the polytheistic believers of the land.

It was customary for everyone to be seated before Shahid Sharif entered the dining room to take his place at the head of the table. The freshly made bread, wrapped in white linen, was brought in from the kitchen, followed by the vegetables and lentil. Shahid Sharif was served first. He waited patiently until there was food on every plate.

Head bowed, he murmured, 'Allah *shukur.*'

The others repeated, 'Allah *shukur*.'

Slowly Shahid Sharif drank half a tumbler of water. Then, with the utmost deliberation, as if he wished to prolong the humble moment of thanksgiving to the Almighty, he tore a piece of bread with his right hand and wrapped it around a small quantity of steaming, spiced vegetable. He nodded as the first morsel disappeared into his mouth. It was the cue for the commencement of communal gluttony.

The conversation among the adults was slow to start, but once appetites were satisfied, the day's events were discussed animatedly. The night gradually entered a phase of light-hearted conversation which excluded the younger family members. It took anything between two and three hours before the *firni* or the sweetmeats left the table, followed by the bloated, good-humoured patriarchs. The men retired to the drawing-room to chew *sanchi paan*, puff on the *hookah* and discuss business matters for the following day.

The boys headed for bed.

It was only then that the women assembled in the dining room to eat and gossip.

Barring the political ripples of independence, which grew ominously stronger, the years passed uneventfully. The Sharifs continued to prosper. The rice harvests in Modhunagar were excellent. The city tenants were regular with their rents and the textile business boomed.

Toward the end of 1942, Khalid Sharif turned twenty-four. Much to Shahid Sharif's displeasure, his son had spent a little under two years in the family business and then had stubbornly chosen to continue his studies at Calcutta University.

'Philosophy?' Shahid Sharif snorted contemptuously when Firdaus conveyed Khalid Sharif's intention to pursue his academic interests. 'What good does it do to fill one's mind with ideas of no practical use to anyone? History also? Why does he wish to spend his time on the past? Talk to him Firdaus! Put some sense into his head.'

'*Bhai Jan*, I have spoken to him,' Firdaus responded respectfully. Secretly he was quite pleased with the prospect of a budding scholar in the family. 'But he is not interested in business at the moment.'

'Not interested?' Shahid Sharif shouted, gripping the arms of his chair and raising himself. 'Have I asked him if he is interested? Have I given him permission to loaf around with intellectual parasites at the university? Doesn't he feel guilty about wasting his time with obscure words? Hah?'

Firdaus remained silent, apprehending that any defence of his nephew would whip Shahid Sharif into a state of destructive and uncontrollable anger.

'Does he know what responsibility means?' Shahid Sharif continued to rail against his son. 'Can he be so selfish? Talk to him again, Firdaus! Why did I have to father such a foolish son?'

Further talks between the reluctant uncle and his nephew merely firmed Khalid Sharif's resolve to pursue a Masters degree. He loved luxuriating in the world of ideas where there was no necessity for the mundane and the trivial. He immersed himself in reading and dreaming of remote worlds ungoverned by conventions, practicalities and patriarchal figures of authority. He frequented the library when he should have been attending lectures, and one of his favourite pastimes was to walk along College Street, stopping frequently to browse in the makeshift bookshops which lined the footpaths. It was not uncommon in those days to find a first edition of a Victorian novel or a rare title among the books under the canvas canopies.

Khalid Sharif was not a model student. He missed tutorials and often handed in indifferently written assignments. His examination results were never better than average. But he could argue brilliantly and his interpretative skills impressed his tutors and lecturers. The library became his haven. There, he accumulated knowledge like a miser hoarding wealth in utmost secrecy. He never deliberately demonstrated to his peers the richness of a mind that floundered under the pressures of stringent academic requirements.

The strange passion of Khalid Sharif became the focal point of discussion among his father and uncles. They brooded on their miserable failure to persuade the young man to follow the established way of his cousins who were grafted into the family business as soon as they entered adulthood.

'The boy must be brought to his senses!' Shahid Sharif thundered late one night, his patience exhausted. 'He must learn to exercise some responsibility!'

An awkward silence ensued. Firdaus looked uncertainly at Rashid and then at Anwar. They nodded their approval.

'*Bhai Jan* . . .' Firdaus bit his lower lip and shot another glance at Rashid. 'He is old enough to be married.'

Shahid Sharif stopped puffing on the *hookah* and sat upright. The thought hadn't occurred to him.

Firdaus received words of encouragement from his brothers.

'*Mashallah!*' Anwar enthused. 'This is a divinely inspired idea!'

'The perfect way to thrust responsibility on him!' Rashid acknowledged, winking at Firdaus.

Shahid Sharif trusted the collective judgement of his brothers and their commitment to the family. 'When?' he demanded fiercely. 'When?'

'*Bhai Jan*, we must not rush into a quick decision,' Firdaus cautioned, uneasy at the prospect of upsetting his favourite nephew by destroying his world of endearing innocence.

'It is never too soon to cure someone's foolishness!'

Since Rashid, the second oldest among the brothers, thought that the entire scheme was his own idea, he felt obliged to defend Firdaus. He coughed politely. 'Firdaus is quite right. Nothing must be done too hastily. Khalid is very unripe.'

'He is not wise to the ways of the world,' Anwar asserted with an uncustomary firmness.

'At twenty-four?' Shahid Sharif shrieked in disbelief. 'I was a father at his age!'

'He is at a confused stage,' Firdaus said, buoyed by the support he was receiving. 'We must be cautious.'

'*Aarey bhai*, let us not avoid the main issue.' Rashid laughed as if he was amused by their coyness. '*Saheb zada* is probably feeling the itch in his groin and feeling embarrassed about it.'

An unexpected smile from Shahid Sharif prompted his brothers to laugh.

There were jokes about the predicaments they themselves had to confront as young men. Nostalgia and recollections of youthful sexuality were concocted into tales of heroic conquests until overworked memories and fatigued imaginations collapsed into a compatible silence with the stillness of the tropical night.

'Well, what is to be done about educating him?' Shahid Sharif's sombre voice brought them back to the problem they had anticipated.

'He could be sent to Shireen Banu,' Rashid suggested. 'Or Tabassum Begum. None of the others are worthy of a young man from a respectable family.'

'Shireen Banu does not enjoy a good reputation these days,' Firdaus claimed. 'Greed is ruining her.'

'Tabassum Begum?'

'Very much from the past,' Firdaus replied approvingly. 'She is a believer in upholding old traditions. She deserves our patronage.'

Shahid Sharif remained sceptical. 'I wish Feroza Begum was still alive,' he sighed. 'Can we find out which families have sent their young men to Tabassum Begum?'

It took Firdaus several days and visits to different parts of Calcutta to compile an impressive list. There were aristocrats and *nawabs*, friends of the Nizam of Hyderabad and families with impeccable credentials.

Shahid Sharif beamed with pleasure when he saw the names. Some of his friends and acquaintances were listed. He chose to visit one of his oldest friends, Quayyum Aziz, the renowned fruit merchant whose family came from Delhi and could trace its ancestry to a highly placed official in Aurangzeb's court.

Quayyum Aziz was effusive in his praise of his son's education. 'Reza is almost civilised now!' he gushed excitedly. '*Aama yar*, Shahid, it is money well spent! Before I sent Reza to Tabassum Begum, he was a *lafanga*—boorish, idle, uncultured and keeping bad company. Far too much *adda baazi* with the *chokras* of the neighbourhood.'

'That is one of Khalid's problems,' Shahid Sharif complained. 'Idle loafing and a mind loaded with foreign ideas. He reads books written by white-skinned people! History! Philosophy! Poetry! He prefers to dream rather than help us run the family business.'

Quayyum Aziz was considerably saddened by his friend's disclosure. 'Young men lack direction in life these days. But with Tabassum Begum's assistance, Reza now takes an interest in our culture. He has learned the importance of behaviour and manners. He will make a worthy husband for some pretty girl.'

Shahid Sharif came away satisfied.

Firdaus attempted to contact Tabassum Begum at her house, only to be turned away from her front door by an enormously built man. A formal application, accompanied by the names of three referees, was the initial step, Firdaus was courteously informed. There was no guarantee that Tabassum Begum would respond positively to the application. There was a long waiting-list of eager young men from some of the best Muslim families in Calcutta, Lucknow and Delhi.

On behalf of the Sharifs, Firdaus wrote an eloquent letter

in Urdu and read it to his brothers who made various suggestions about formalising it to the point of an obsolete, courtly starchiness. Several drafts later the final copy, accompanied by prominent names and addresses, was enclosed and sealed in a scented envelope. The letter was to be hand-delivered by Hamid, the oldest and the most trusted family servant.

Hamid was familiar with the subtleties of such conventions. As a young man he had been thoroughly instructed before being sent to the house of Feroza Begum with similar correspondence.

The envelope was placed in the centre of a large, oblong-shaped silver tray which had been polished until it gleamed with a tantalising radiance. Fresh fruits, flowers and *ladoos*, coated with thin layers of edible silver foil and sprinkled with chopped pistachios and almonds were arranged around the letter. Hamid was privileged with a horse-drawn carriage to take him to *Khush Manzil*.

It was several weeks before a messenger from Tabassum Begum arrived at the Sharifs' residence to deliver a letter on the same silver tray graciously left behind by Hamid. It was a brief, polite note requesting Firdaus to appear for a meeting with Tabassum Begum on the following Saturday afternoon.

That same evening an unsuspecting Khalid Sharif was bewildered and delighted by an unexpected invitation to join his elders in the drawing-room after dinner. Outwardly he retained his composure and walked slowly into the room. He was overcome by a nervous exhilaration, having suddenly risen to the ranks of the family gods. As he entered the room, accompanied by Firdaus, both Rashid and Anwar rose from their chairs to greet him warmly. He did not immediately notice the absence of his father.

They seated themselves comfortably. The *hookahs* were lit for the brothers. Khalid Sharif was offered *paan* and *supari*. He would have preferred a cigarette, but he knew too well that the expected deference for his elders could not permit such a heinous act of rudeness.

Khalid Sharif was puzzled and flattered by the friendly attention of the two older men. Firdaus was always informal, at times even flippant, with his nephew. On their own the two men talked without undue inhibitions, and their mutual behaviour suggested a tacit agreement to transgress the barriers imposed by their age difference and the nature of their relationship. Firdaus did not surprise Khalid Sharif. It was the absence of a cold, supercilious aloofness which he normally expected from his older uncles, as well as their unfamiliar verbosity, which were unnervingly out of character.

Khalid Sharif was encouraged to talk about his university life. They listened with an air of genuine interest. It was a world alien to them, irrelevant in terms of what it had to offer for enhancing the family's prosperity. In their view, education beyond school, where one learned to read and write, acquired enough skills in arithmetic to balance the books and keep the accountant honest, was a form of intellectual indulgence that demonstrated an inherent weakness of character. It reflected an unwillingness for hard work. It was a subtle form of cheating which sought to justify itself by claiming an expansive richness of knowledge and a broadening of perspectives. Of course it was essential to train doctors and lawyers rigorously. Tertiary education served a vital purpose in those critical professions. But a historian? A philosopher or a poet? Their achievements could be grudgingly acknowledged, even admired, from a distance. A cultured breeding manifested itself in behaviour, manners and the appreciation of the arts. That was quite different from actually having an artist or a struggling scholar, without ulterior motives for learning, in one's family. It was a grim sign to have one of those spouting obtuse words learned from obscure books while others, more conscientious and responsible, were actually working to make a living.

Rashid was a shrewd judge of character. He sensed that talking about his nephew had relaxed the young man. He was now suitably vulnerable.

'What you are doing is nothing less than noble,' Rashid commended warmly, disarming his nephew even further. 'But . . .' He exchanged a meaningful look with Anwar. 'But there is another side to your education which needs attention.'

'I know my examination results are not brilliant,' Khalid Sharif said quickly. 'But I am not doing too badly.' He wondered if his father had heard anything to the contrary and whether Rashid was about to reprimand him for a lack of application to his studies.

'It's not your university work, *baeta*,' Anwar assured him kindly. 'We know you are doing well there. But you are twenty-four now.'

The silence made everyone fidgety.

Firdaus scraped the floor with the toe of his right sandal. Anwar made an elaborate fuss about relighting the *hookah*.

'You are old enough to broaden your experiences. There is much more to life than books, words and ideas,' Rashid observed, his eyes on Anwar.

'A young man's life is like a flower bud. It must be given the opportunity to blossom.' Anwar smiled weakly, uncertain if his analogy made any sense to Khalid Sharif. 'It must be watered and nourished, otherwise it will wither and die without flowering.'

'Soon you must turn your mind to marriage.' Rashid glared at Anwar, unimpressed with his brother's effort to garnish the simple facts of life with superfluous words. 'To a family of your own.'

'But before you experience the contentment of a settled life, you must prepare yourself for the responsibilities you cannot avoid much longer.'

'You have to be exposed to the complexities of life. You must know what it takes to be a gentleman. A man of honour.

Cultured and wise about the ways of the world. You will have to learn as much as you can about women.'

'You will never be able to learn everything about them,' Anwar warned. 'They are . . .'

'There is no need to be worried!' Firdaus interjected, responding to the apprehension on his nephew's face. 'There are rewards and considerable pleasures ahead of you.'

'I . . . I don't know what to say!' a flabbergasted Khalid Sharif spluttered. 'I don't understand what I am expected to do!'

Rashid left his chair and walked over to his dejected nephew. He placed a comforting arm around Khalid Sharif's shoulders. 'It has all been arranged.' He winked at Anwar. 'Firdaus will explain everything.'

'Everything!' Anwar echoed, and then laughed softly.

'We have to see *Bhai Jan* about some business matters.' Rashid made a move toward the door, followed by Anwar. '*Baeta*, you will go upstairs and see your father later? He is not well today.'

Anwar thumped his nephew heartily on the back. '*Shahbash Sher* Sharif!'

Before leaving the room, Rashid paused to whisper to Firdaus. 'Will you contact a marriage broker?'

'After some months!' Firdaus replied indignantly. 'Give Khalid some time!'

There was a look of smug gratification on Rashid's face as if a business deal had been concluded to his utmost satisfaction. 'Now all that needs to be done is let the women prepare for the marriage.'

'He has no idea how agreeable education can be,' Anwar chortled, closing the door behind him.

It was with a touch of disappointment that Khalid Sharif realised that Adam would not show up. He derived an inexplicable satisfaction in taking the boy to the milk bar and watching him agonise over the choice of ice-cream. It was much easier for Khalid Sharif. He did not venture beyond a single scoop of mango in a small cone.

The routine began as an apologetic gesture from Khalid Sharif. Much as he tried, he could neither catch nor kick effectively what Adam insisted was a football. The old man had allowed himself to be dragged into an inconclusive argument.

'A football is round,' Khalid Sharif explained patiently. 'You are not allowed to catch it. Only the goalkeeper can use his hands.'

Adam turned his head in disgust and spat on the grass. He treated Khalid Sharif as an equal ever since he discovered that there was much that the Indian did not know. '*This* is a football, mate!' For emphasis he kicked the ball straight up in the air and caught it. 'Don't you have Aussie Rules in India?'

'We play football with a round ball,' Khalid Sharif persisted, ignorant of Victoria's winter fetish.

'That is soccer,' Adam corrected him calmly. 'Not as good as Aussie Rules.'

Khalid Sharif's sceptical silence confused the boy. He had half-expected a verbal outburst of temper.

'Soccer isn't as good as Aussie Rules,' Adam repeated provocatively. He looked up at Khalid Sharif, his jaws clenched and his chin thrust forward defiantly.

'I'll tell you what's best. No argument about it!' Khalid Sharif backed off with good grace. He looked at Adam over the top of his spectacles. 'An ice-cream! Better than any game!' He slapped his thighs with great relish. 'Don't you think? Let me get you one.'

The unexpected offer dumbfounded the boy.

'Well, do you want one?'

Adam nodded eagerly, his mouth watering at the prospect of a double scoop of strawberry ice-cream piled high on a large honey cone. The vision faded quickly. 'I can't pay you back. I don't have any money,' he murmured, bouncing the football on a bare patch of earth.

'What's money between friends? I have a whole bunch of coins. They are too heavy for me to carry around.' Without waiting, Khalid Sharif shuffled off in the direction of the milk bar. Out of the corner of his eye he saw the boy step forward and then hesitate. The old man stopped and turned around, as if something important had occurred to him. 'I don't know much about the types of ice-cream you get here. Can you help me to choose something nice?'

Head bowed, Adam followed.

The walk to the milk bar became an almost daily treat. There was a mutual realisation that it was a precious secret to be cautiously guarded. There was a childish thrill in the shared knowledge that they were hoodwinking Angela who would have never permitted such an indulgence. Khalid Sharif was still a comparative stranger, and to allow him to spend money on her grandson would have jarred her finely tuned sense of what was fair and proper. Angela was uneasy about allowing Adam to wander about the playground on his own. But ever since Khalid Sharif's offer to keep an eye on the boy during the course of his afternoon's walk, she had willingly agreed.

Khalid Sharif walked slowly across the playground. The path he followed was to take him past some dense shrubs and onto a back street from where it was a short walk to Angela's house.

He heard a rustling noise from behind a bush as if someone was trying to compress a pile of leaves. There was a faint moan which did not suggest any pain or danger. Snapping twigs cracked like pistol shots.

Khalid Sharif quickened his steps.

He felt as nervous as he had that afternoon when he reluctantly left the carriage and disappeared into the narrow lane. Firdaus had drawn him a detailed and clear diagram of the twisting, intersecting lanes and the direction he was to take.

He smiled wistfully at the memory of his confusion. Such great chunks of the world were hidden from him until that day. It was impossible to recall his state of innocence when life was weightless. And time? A motion forward without the echo of heavy footsteps . . .

Dressed in his spotless cream-coloured *achkan*, buttoned up to his neck, and white *chooridar* pyjama, specially tailored by *Kalim & Sons—Master Darzi*, Khalid Sharif walked rapidly, holding Firdaus' instructions in his right hand. His other hand sought the security of the *achkan*'s side pocket. He pressed the softness of the silk handkerchief and fingered the contours of the small leather pouches filled with coins. It felt as if the eyes of the world were focused on him. There were titters and provocative comments from the upper windows of the houses on either side of the lane.

Khalid Sharif was to go past the mosque and take the first turn to the left. He walked past the neatly dressed devotees filtering into the House of Allah for the afternoon's prayer. Near the steps he paused to figure out the distance before the turning. A bearded man inquired politely if he had lost his way. He was a young *mullah* with dull eyes and a serious face which suggested a state of mind that excluded everything humorous or flippant in life.

'The House of Tabassum Begum?' Khalid Sharif asked uncertainly. '*Khush Manzil?*' He looked at the piece of paper he clutched in his hand. Firdaus had marked the mosque in red pencil.

The *mullah* sprang back as though Khalid Sharif posed a grave danger to his well-being. His face distorted into a feral snarl. He muttered a string of words under his breath, puffed his cheeks and blew into the space separating him from Khalid Sharif. With a vigorous shake of the head, the *mullah* turned around and sprinted up the steps of the mosque.

Khalid Sharif was unable to guess the reason for the sudden change in the *mullah*'s behaviour. He thought he heard the words *Shaitan, Jahannam* and *aag*. It puzzled Khalid Sharif that a man of Allah should concern himself with the Devil and the fire of Hell so near to the time of prayer.

He turned left, past a group of squatting men smoking *biris*, and stopped to check the directions again. All he could see ahead was the lane narrowing and twisting sharply to the right. A fit of terror seized him. There was an overwhelming impression that he had been set up, that this was part of an elaborate hoax intended to make a fool of him and provide several evenings' entertainment in the family's drawing-room. He felt miserable and out of place in this unfamiliar part of the city, among the crowded houses without balconies and verandahs. His tight-fitting clothes were ridiculous and uncomfortable. Self-consciously he tore out the red rose bud from the button-hole and flung it into the open gutter.

'Sharif Saheb?'

He spun around.

The man had appeared from nowhere. He had probably been waiting in a house, watching Khalid Sharif through one of the open windows which resembled the hollow eyes of the dead. He was small and frail-looking, with effeminate features dominated by large, dreamy eyes. The smile with which he greeted Khalid Sharif appeared like a band of sunlight splashed across a dark landscape. There was a mechanical politeness about him, suggesting a rigorous training in courtly elegance, and which forbade even a modicum of feeling to influence him.

'Yes,' Khalid Sharif replied hesitantly, as if he was uncertain about his own identity.

'*Aadavarz hai!*' The man bowed obsequiously, touching his forehead with the fingertips of his right hand. 'Welcome!'

'*Shukuriya*,' Khalid Sharif murmured, unable to determine what he was being welcomed to.

'My name is Rizwan. I am to accompany you to *Khush Manzil*. Begum Saheba is eagerly awaiting your arrival.'

Firdaus had drummed into his nephew the importance of manners and behaviour. 'First impressions!' he had emphasised. 'First impressions will count for the treatment you receive. Often it is what you don't say that is crucial. Remember! Be shy. Speak eloquently when you have to say something. But *Khuda keh vasteh*, watch your manners! Act properly.'

Khalid Sharif remembered the advice. He reached into the narrow slit of the breast pocket and extracted a folded note.

Rizwan's right hand responded graciously.

'*Shukuriya*,' Khalid Sharif muttered again, careful to avoid a direct eye contact. 'I am indebted to you.' He managed to sound humble and grateful.

'*Jeeteh raho baeta*!' Rizwan smiled warmly, pleased with what he had seen so far. Here was a young man of pedigree, one who had been schooled in the art of gentle manners and conventions of *tahzeeb*. He was a rarity among the arrogant and rough males who entered *Khush Manzil* each year. But his grasp of Muslim culture? Rizwan wondered. How educated was this novice?

Khalid Sharif walked deferentially behind Rizwan.

The lane opened up unexpectedly into a spacious square fringed with houses and small shops. Khalid Sharif spied a narrow path squeezed between the high walls of two houses. Otherwise, they had reached a dead end.

From the centre of the unevenly paved area, a sprawling bazaar extended itself in clusters of makeshift stalls and glass-caged pushcarts. *Purdah*-clad women haggled aggressively over the afternoon prices of meat and fish with grubby, sweat-drenched butchers, wearing bloodstained singlets and *lungis*, and tired fishmongers who had concluded the bulk of their business by noon. The aroma of saffron wafted into Khalid Sharif's nostrils, only to be replaced by the more pungent smells of turmeric and garlic. He found himself amongst people bargaining spiritedly for rolls of dazzling coloured silk, rugs and cotton garments. He refused the offer of a shoeshine and turned away from a pavement barber. A fortune-teller, squatting on a straw mat, invited him to have his future revealed. A caged parrot, with its wings clipped, squawked as if it was desperate to sound a serious warning.

'The bird knows!' The toothless man grinned. 'Give me some information about yourself and the parrot will leave its cage and pick five cards,' he explained, pointing to the shoe boxes stacked with hundreds of yellowing, grease marked cards. 'Babu, know your life for four annas! Keep up with Kismet!'

Khalid Sharif felt the firm pressure of Rizwan's hand on his arm. They walked through the middle of the bazaar, stopping frequently for Rizwan to exchange greetings with the vendors he obviously knew quite intimately.

'Sharif Saheb, this is the house!' Rizwan pointed to a triple-storeyed building with its windows shut and its walls in need of repair. The heavy front door looked awkwardly out of place. It had been freshly varnished.

'Knock on the door twice,' Rizwan instructed. 'Pause. Then knock again, three times.'

A nauseous panic rippled through Khalid Sharif. 'Will you come with me?' Outwardly he remained calm, his voice betraying no anxiety.

Rizwan stifled a smile. They were all the same on the first day—charmingly innocent, shy and diffident. A year later, for those who lasted, it was entirely different. The final departure was marked by a swaggering conceit built on a dangerous confidence about the importance of their place in the world. They carried their elaborate illusions with them like prized trophies to jog their memories in a distant future when youth would suddenly depart and leave them to face the bleakness of mortality.

'This is as far as I go.' Rizwan laid a comforting hand on the young man's back. 'We shall meet again during the evening's *mahfil. Khuda Hafiz!*'

Despite the fierce heat of the infernal afternoon, a coldness crept up Khalid Sharif's legs. He felt weak. An indefinable sadness brushed him fleetingly, leaving a vague awareness of a loss that he was unable to identify. He sensed an imminent danger. It was as if the secure innocence of his life was about to be irrevocably changed and reshaped into a myriad of experiences smudged with shades of grey, replacing the easily distinguishable and simple priorities of youthful irresponsibility.

Reluctantly he climbed up the four cemented steps. In the corners of the landing were freshly watered pot plants reeking with tropical fragrance. The swirls of pink, white, yellow and red dazzled the eyes and prompted the imagination to search behind the forbidding door. The small nameplate aroused Khalid Sharif's interest.

TABASSUM BEGUM
TEACHER AND ENTERTAINER

An extraordinary person, he thought. Someone capable of imparting knowledge without drying up laughter and killing curiosity. He could faintly hear the rhythmic synthesis of the sounds of harmonium, *jumru, tabla* and *sarangi*. A muffled voice.

Timidly Khalid Sharif knocked. Twice. His mouth felt dry. He reached for his handkerchief and mopped his brow.

He knocked again. Thrice. Latches clicked. The door swung open. The light from the magnificent chandelier blinded him momentarily as he stood on the threshold of the entrance, unable to focus on the dark, formidable figure of the turbaned man who introduced himself as Rangeela.

'*Tashreef laiyeh* Sharif Saheb!' He invited the young man with the same courtesy that had characterised Rizwan's meeting with Khalid Sharif.

He entered the unexpected splendour of the foyer. The peacock blue walls were decorated with silk paintings, and a huge carpet covered most of the marble floor. The reality of time and place assumed an entirely different dimension. This was the fairyland of his dreams, a place where he could not be harmed. Suddenly his inhibitions were overcome by a giddy carelessness. He felt invincible. The consciousness of his apprehensive journey vaporised into the atmosphere of a timeless zone.

A controlled male voice cracked with authority. The music and the singing stopped. There were muted sounds of disagreement. A tense silence. The music began again. The harmonium and the *tabla* synchronised at a gentler pace, and the anklet bells of the dancer moulded into the pattern of a less frenetic sound. But it was the singer's voice, a female's plaintive utterance, which haunted him. It held a mermaid's irresistible attraction, inviting him to pleasurable dangers. The woman sang in Urdu. The pathos in her voice reached out like a gentle hand to stroke him and germinate sensations whose seeds had lain dormant somewhere inside him. He listened intently.

> *It's at such gatherings*
> *That lives are lost . . .*
> *For Beauty does not spare*
> *And Love does not*
> *Know economy . . .*

'The words of Mir Taqi Mir. One who does not pay homage to the great man is an uncultured brute, the poet Nasikh once said. Is Saheb familiar with the *ghazals* of Mir?' Rangeela inquired politely.

Mindlessly Khalid Sharif shook his head. He was desperate to meet this woman with the mournful voice. He imagined her to be very beautiful. Sad, misty eyes. There was suffering somewhere in her life. He experienced an inexplicable yearning to enslave himself to the cause of alleviating her pain. He resisted an overwhelming urge to burst through the door and announce himself as her saviour.

'Who is the singer?' Khalid Sharif whispered.

'Munni Bai. She is one of our senior courtesans and our best singer. Has Saheb read the poetry of Dard and Jurat?'

Khalid Sharif's silence confounded Rangeela.

'Ghalib? Momin? Dagh?'

'No,' Khalid Sharif confessed guiltily. For the first time in his entire life he felt inadequate and thoroughly ashamed of his lack of cultural breeding. Plato. Aristotle. Hobbes and Kant. Shakespeare, Pope and Tennyson. They were of little consequence here. This was meant to be his territory, but he did not know the landscape.

'Has Saheb ever graced a *mushaera* with his presence?'

'I . . . I fear I haven't.'

'Saheb must have listened to *thumris* and *dadras*?'

Khalid Sharif avoided Rangeela's scrutinising stare.

'Does Saheb know anything about the conventions of *kathak* dancing?'

'No.'

Rangeela turned away wearily. Each year *Khush Manzil* had to contend with an increasing ignorance among its newcomers. It was an alarming reflection of the cultural demise of Indian Muslims.

Angela Barrett was unprepared to receive Khalid Sharif. A white streak of flour over her left eyebrow made her look forbidding.

'Oh hello, Mr Sharif!' she exclaimed. Her hands slid back to untie the knots of the printed apron. 'I wasn't expecting you quite so early.'

Khalid Sharif looked at his watch. 'I . . .' He checked himself. 'You did say tea?'

'Yes . . . Oh!' Her hand flew to her mouth. Realisation dawned on Angela with an auroral flush which spread across her face. 'Come in! Please come in! It is entirely my fault. I owe you a huge apology! I should have explained. I wasn't thinking when I invited you. Tea here usually means an informal evening's meal.'

SEVEN

Those rare moments when Khalid Sharif was tempted to be censorious about the duplicitous behaviour of others were short-lived. On such occasions, the memory of what he considered to be his own act of betrayal surfaced to admonish him with a vigour undiminished by the intervening years.

He couldn't exactly tell how Nazli had been affected. There were no histrionics. Few words. A stoical acceptance of adversity which made his verbose self-justification all the more clumsy and insincere. He liked to imagine that she had been traumatised, that the pain had brought her close to tears. In the dimness of twilight he could barely see the outline of her face.

What he couldn't remember Khalid Sharif created, and inserted into the past to refurbish a time of his life he then used to torment himself. Remorse. Guilt. Self-recrimination. The years had been unflaggingly merciless in retaining their steely sharpness. In his mind an endless battle had raged since the conclusion of his year of enlightenment with Tabassum Begum.

He had abjectly caved in to his father's vitriolic demands. There was a brief period when he flirted with the idea that one's duty to family was of paramount importance in life. That did nothing to subdue the rebellious voices which clamoured their protest. Gradually they poisoned his notions of propriety and family honour.

Such ideals . . . do they shape us into civilised hypocrites? he often asked himself disparagingly. *Should we continue to accept the enormous gulf that splits us between the way we act and feel? Between what we say and think?*

He gave the impression of settling into the smoothly flowing mainstream of patriarchal life, unruffled by doubts or hesitations, devoted to the acquisition of money which ensured the security and survival of a Muslim family in an unstable India feeling the tremors of dismemberment. But there wasn't a semblance of a resolution to the problems which troubled him relentlessly.

Khalid Sharif became perceptibly quieter. Those who doubted his ability to survive successfully in a world of commerce were surprised. He demonstrated a shrewd business sense and expressed no desire to return to an academic life.

Shahid Sharif and his brothers were delighted.

'He has matured!'

'*Mashallah!* Khalid is no longer a boy chasing foolish dreams!'

'This is how marriage should affect a young man.'

Khalid Sharif overheard and ignored the comments, his mind grappling with the deficiencies he beheld in himself, his imagination recreating what should have happened had his courage not failed so dismally to fulfil a promise made in a naive earnestness.

The evening gave Khalid Sharif ample opportunity to visit the shadowy corners of the previous years. As he dined on rice and lamb *korma*, Khalid Sharif unfurled the past and imagined himself as a distraught suitor unhinged by *her* fickleness. What gave some validity to this recreation of events in *Khush Manzil* was a very faint doubt he had strictly prevented from growing any further. At no stage, during the year he spent at the house of Tabassum Begum, had Nazli ever revealed an indication of her feelings about him. Khalid Sharif had attributed her lack of verbal response to his own hyperbolic declarations of love as an innate shyness in her character.

Khalid Sharif was embarrassed by the candour with which Judy and her mother were discussing their intimate family problems. It was uncharacteristic for Angela to be so garrulous and demonstrative. He had a vague suspicion that her behaviour was related to the pre-dinner gin and tonic she had gulped down, and her fondness for the chardonnay Judy had contributed to the meal.

Both women accepted him as someone who did not gossip. He was an inconsequential presence. His age neutralised him in their minds.

Even without listening closely to what Judy was saying, in response to her mother's overbearing advice to be more receptive to Simon's overtures, Khalid Sharif was able to understand the reasons for their argument.

Simon's generosity in sending a card of apology to Angela had softened her into a defence of her son-in-law.

'Men are like that,' she observed benignly, ignoring her daughter's friendly caution to go easy on the wine. 'They are impulsive and prone to fits of temper which make them behave poorly. They are like children, angry and lashing out blindly whenever their pride is hurt.'

'Well, I don't wish to remain married to a child,' Judy retaliated.

'We have to be forgiving of their ways,' Angela slurred magnanimously.

Khalid Sharif poured himself some mineral water and avoided being dragged into the conversation.

'Bullshit!' Judy snapped in a fit of exasperation as her mother slid rapidly into a state of bovine inebriation.

Angela was prepared to forgive the entire world of the cumulative sins it had committed against itself.

'How can you justify the way Simon has behaved? Look at the way he treated Adam. His own son!'

'He has said he is sorry. Look at the lovely card he sent me.'

Judy reached out to pat her mother on the arm.

'So polite,' Angela droned. 'He even rang to ask if he could visit me. Deep inside he's a good man.' Simon was a proud man. Like Tom.

'It isn't about being good or horrible,' Judy insisted. 'We have nothing in common any more. I am not sure we ever did.'

Whatever the specific reasons for the relationship's breakdown, Judy bitterly regretted the explosion, in the ugly finale, that lacerated Adam with the shrapnel from an adult's dark world of brutality. The shock of the beating sent him reeling into a shell of silence for several days. When he emerged hesitantly, Adam was a sour boy, distrustful of adults.

Judy's gratitude to Khalid Sharif had not been directly expressed for fear of an explanation which may have unlocked hidden chambers and spilled the details of her personal life. After work, when she picked up Adam from her mother's, Judy sometimes lingered for a drink and a meal. Whenever she spied Khalid Sharif, she sought his company across the fence. He transported her to strange pockets of a forbidding country, made all the more enticing by what she remembered of her mother's account of an India that was simultaneously exotic and too terrible to behold.

'I would like to visit India some day,' she declared during one of their short bursts of conversation. 'All that is wonderful and tragic appear to coexist there. It would be a breathtaking experience.'

Khalid Sharif smiled wanly, as was his habit when confronted by innocent ignorance. To predetermine the nature of an unknown experience was to invite a crushing disappointment. India didn't respond to preconditioned notions about what it had to offer.

Why do you wish to experience more extreme forms of tragedy? he thought of asking. *Isn't there enough here?* His mind swept over the fragmented lives of Javed and Shanaz. He speculated about Judy and Adam without drawing hasty conclusions about their circumstances. Then there was Angela, not entirely conditioned to her loneliness, filling in the emptiness of her days with the faded dreams of a past that continued to throw up its ghosts to please her. Perhaps Judy craved sustained melodrama. Here it was the quiet, personal struggle of individuals against themselves, rather than the unremitting, noisy panorama of communal suffering that made it easier to be selective about what one chose to see.

It was ironic, Khalid Sharif mused, as he scraped the stray grains of greasy rice from the edge of his plate, that Judy should have spoken about the tragedy of India when her own life was evidently in turmoil. *One shouldn't have to contend with so much unhappiness.* His thoughts jumped to Javed.

From the distance of an uninterfering silence, Khalid Sharif had observed the frustration of his son. *He doesn't hide things too well*, the old man concluded. The paternal concern was tempered by what Khalid Sharif judged to be Javed's struggle to come to terms with an unfamiliar dimension in life—one which exposed those pitfalls of the human condition that could not be remedied by material prosperity.

He is experiencing conflict, Khalid Sharif deduced shrewdly. Whoever she was had managed to confuse and bleed him. But she had barely penetrated the toughness of his instinct for self-preservation. A few scars, perhaps. The occasional itch to remind Javed of his fallibility and the hazards of life's unexpected turns.

Not a bad thing to happen, Khalid Sharif said to himself with a degree of caution. *As long as he isn't seriously hurt, there is no harm in the suffering she is causing him. It will make him stop to think and measure life's non-tangible achievements.* It was the certainty that his son's unhappiness was a transient phase, destined to be buried and forgotten once he stopped smothering himself with self-pity and directed his energy and attention to his work, the stock exchange and squash, that made Khalid Sharif complacent about Javed's trauma.

What Khalid Sharif could not have guessed was that Javed's discontentment had also been triggered by another aggressive letter from his sister. Nasreen's accusations had enraged him into an imaginary verbal combat which ended with his sister in tears and Javed marching off triumphant, having extracted an apology from her.

He felt compelled to read the letter repeatedly. She had bluntly accused him of a sycophantic dawdling and a spineless inability to face their father and *thrash things out. We have heard nothing*, she accused him. *As the main beneficiary of an unjust and obsolete law, it is your responsibility and moral duty to talk to him and settle his future. Surely you are not afraid of him and the possibility of missing out on the odd bits of family jewellery* . . .

It was a coincidental misfortune that the letter arrived on the same day as his break-up with Theresa. Javed had driven to her flat straight after work, prepared and rehearsed to be suitably humble and contrite about their irreconcilably different circumstances which made it prudent for them to part, hopefully as good friends, without tarnishing the memories of their times together. He was fortified with a stock of conciliatory phrases intended to calm any outburst of grief.

Theresa turned out to be anything but helpless and tearful. Before Javed could sit down, she told him of her decision not to see him again. There was nothing in the relationship for her. He was deficient in every respect.

'Inadequate! Do you hear me?' she screamed. 'Unsatisfactory in all possible ways!'

'It hasn't been a bad relationship!' he protested, struggling to recover from the surprise attack.

'Relationship?' Theresa threw back her head and laughed bitterly. 'This was no bloody relationship! It was a one whore brothel for one arse-hole customer! Free of charge. *Be there! I shall come whenever my balls feel heavy!*'

'Theresa!' Javed cringed at her language. 'Please!' He had not imagined her to be capable of such crudity. The demure and softly spoken widow he had met at Steven's party now seemed to be a creature assembled in his nightmare. She was a hideous distortion beyond his control.

His shocked cry prompted her to continue. She stood in the middle of the room, enjoying the payback for the loneliness she had endured, the frustration of reaching out openly with her feelings only to find herself kept at a distance, groping among the peripheral trivia of a male world crowded with a thousand concerns among which she was incidental.

'You are shallow and cursed with a feeble heart! You are! And . . . yes, believe me, you are a lousy fuck! All that your dick deserves is a once a year jerk with sandpaper! Piss off and don't ever come back!'

Her language stung him into a paralytic silence.

'Go on! Get out!'

Javed went home in a daze and locked himself in the study where the day's mail awaited him on his desk.

'*Kutheeh!* Bitch!' he kept repeating to himself in a voice distorted with hatred. His emotions were like tight fists, hammering ineffectual blows on a fate that had sabotaged his reign over life. The relief of the desired end was insufficient compensation for being insulted and tossed aside without remorse. His battered ego leaned on self-pity and wept silently for several days, affirming his view of a world where only a male could be the initiator in the web of a relationship. That Theresa had usurped his destined role, and played it to a heartless perfection, made Javed feel guilty of a shameful weakness that disqualified him from the lofty ranks of men.

Had Khalid Sharif been fully aware of the intensity of his son's anguish and the exact circumstances which kindled it, he might have viewed the resulting domestic tension with more understanding. The old man wondered whether Javed's childhood, nourished in a patriarchal ethos, had straitjacketed him from adapting to a world forever seeking changes, a world that was intent on clawing down old structures and shredding traditional orders for purposes he could not determine.

One of the reasons for the widening cracks in Javed's marriage appeared to be his inability to accept Shanaz's dogmatic autonomy. Khalid Sharif was astonished at the changes he witnessed in his daughter-in-law. From the shy, diffident girl, who had rarely expressed an opinion, to the assertive, forthright woman, finely tuned to the social need for men's participation in raising a family, Shanaz had transformed into a person worthy of cautious admiration. Quite frequently she managed to confuse her father-in-law with her quiet self-confidence and her lack of inhibition about contradicting Javed in front of others.

Only once, in a rather mild, off-handed fashion, had Khalid Sharif made an effort to understand why she had altered her lifestyle to such an extreme extent.

'Don't you wear saris any more?' he had asked, after observing her in jeans, shorts and tracksuit pants at home, and slacks or skirts when she went to work.

'No. It's impractical,' she replied brusquely, and then realised that the question was merely one of harmless curiosity. 'Washing several metres of silk or chiffon would be a nightmare. And then the ironing! Besides, it's too cold here most of the time for saris.'

She smiled at the look of scepticism on his face and shook her head. 'No. Not practical at all.'

Shanaz did not venture to add that conformity in appearance was an essential prerequisite for professional acceptance and upward mobility. To be seen in a splash of draped colour among the austerity of grey and black would be seen as irresponsible and improper, deserving of a call to the top floor for a friendly chat. No threats. Merely a flattery of her professional competence and the possibilities it created for her. Teamwork. Image. That was what success was all about. Sticking together, working in harmony, following established conventions. Shanaz had worked long enough to know that big business had an unpublicised notion of propriety, pertaining to dressing and behaviour, which could not be flouted without harming one's ambition. And Shanaz was ambitious.

It struck Khalid Sharif how often Shanaz used the word *practical* in the course of her conversation at home. There was a hard-edged commonsense about everything she did. When feelings threatened to influence her domestic decisions, she allowed herself time for her rationality to rescue her, like a reinforcement unit bringing much needed relief to beleaguered troops.

It wasn't as if Khalid Sharif was unsympathetic toward the feminist movement; in fact he didn't know enough about it, nor did he think it necessary to educate himself about its social evolution.

It doesn't matter at my age. He excused himself whenever his daughters latched on to the anomalies prevalent in his views of gender roles and pounded him about the need to modify his attitudes. But his indifference did not desensitise him from appreciating Shanaz's pivotal role in keeping her family in some sort of running order. She was like a juggler in control of an act that required highly developed skills. The balancing feat between the unrelenting demands of her working life and the needs of the family was maintained, if at times precariously, with an unwavering sense of commitment.

Watching Javed and Shanaz over the weeks he had been

in Melbourne, Khalid Sharif was intimidated by the stress of western life, the combination of emotional and psychological strain that had a corrosive effect on personalities and relationships. An ever-expanding utilitarian obsession with life crowded out the open spaces where one could slip away in the company of dreams or reminiscences, and drift randomly in a contemplative mood, without being jostled by the demands that success breeds.

Despite the comforts they had bought for themselves, there was a dreariness in the marriage which concerned Khalid Sharif. When Javed and Shanaz were home, their evenings were punctuated with brief, passing colloquies involving pick-up times, shopping lists, payment of bills, school notices, banking and unavoidable social commitments which warranted the facade of togetherness. There was a routine precision about most things they did, and it appeared to Khalid Sharif that it was Shanaz who determined the order and pace of life in the house. Javed was an isolated presence who erupted sporadically into expressions of dissatisfaction, usually about his children who accepted his outbursts as a flaw in his temperament. They were casually conscious of his contribution to their lifestyle which could not be maintained with such thoughtless extravagance on their mother's income alone.

On those rare occasions, when Javed accidentally managed a prolonged conversation with his wife, the tone was singularly unvaried and marked by a distinctive note of critical urgency, as if their financial ruination was an imminent certainty.

Their similarity of views on economic matters created a fallacious impression of a reasonably compatible relationship cemented by a desire for security. The cost of educating children, stocks and shares, the property market, the fate of investments, tax benefits and retirement plans were topics of sufficient mutual interest to sustain rational discussions devoid of the dampness that had seeped into their marriage. Their lives were dominated by a search for an elusive future shimmering with a promise of a tranquil prosperity. The present was a sacrifice essential for the attainment of an old age ideal.

The past doesn't exist for them, Khalid Sharif concluded sadly. *It is a dry, abandoned well incapable of nourishing the spirit. There is no stable sanctuary where they can drop anchor for renewal and fortify themselves for what lies ahead.*

He couldn't resist comparing Shanaz with Nazli and wished that she had possessed his daughter-in-law's resilience and mental toughness. But that was another age when it was assumed that female love was purely a matter of the heart, unencumbered by reason and the desire for self-survival.

Khalid Sharif wondered if men had changed or still continued to be deceptive, heartless and irresponsible with women, as he had been in the way he misled Nazli and abandoned her.

An unfortunate weakness in the formative stages of a young man's character, Ashraf consoled Khalid Sharif years later when the solicitor discovered the strength of his friend's guilt which had not been expiated by marriage and four children. *Aama yar, Khalid, the family's izzat was in jeopardy. You would have been completely ostracised! An outcast shunned by family and friends. The shame would have killed your father. There was no choice. What you did was the only honourable way out.*

Honour? There was no honour in what he had done, Khalid Sharif felt obliged to remind himself occasionally. In a strange way there was a brief revival of his yearning for the young courtesan after he observed the way Shanaz conducted herself. If only Nazli had not been quite so helpless! He would have been comforted had she shrugged him off as an immature profligate, a self-centred rogue incapable of fulfilling his commitments, a weakling in love and entirely unworthy of her.

He looked up to see Angela looking confused and close to tears.

'Mum, I'm okay!' Judy attempted to convince her mother. 'I'm learning to overcome my loneliness by finding out about myself. I am meeting all these strangers inside me. I am not about to feel guilty about my decision to leave Simon simply because you feel that Adam should have a father or that Simon deserves another chance.'

'Such a shame!' Angela sniffled into a tissue.

'That's the way it is meant to be.' There was a calm finality in Judy's voice, an inadvertent fatalism that surprised Khalid Sharif.

He winced at her choice of words. Memory was still capable of delivering some surprisingly painful blows.

Judy turned to Khalid Sharif and apologised for their rudeness. 'We didn't mean to embarrass you. Sorry.'

Sheepishly Angela mumbled similar words.

'Not at all,' he assured them, mulling over what Judy had said to her mother. 'Not at all.'

The women made a move to clear the table for dessert. Khalid Sharif's token offer of assistance was politely refused.

He sat at the table, wondering.

That's the way it is meant to be.

He could see her face in every detail as though it was suspended in time under the glare of bright studio lights. He had never been able to determine her age or detect changes in her moods. Was she at all susceptible to the vagaries of emotions? The question obsessed him as the year progressed. The voice was soft with a melodious lilt that calmed the most agitated of men. She was always there, willing to talk and listen, comfort and advise. But that was the extent of her involvement with the males who gathered around her. Men bet and lost large sums of money on her.

Tabassum Begum was untouchable. Beyond temptation. Outside their reach. She was attainable only in the fantasies of men made to feel humble and inadequate by her decisive rejection of their overtures. The politeness which controlled her behaviour was like an impenetrable shield, deflecting those who were charmed by her aura of mystery and sought to know her intimately.

Tabassum Begum possessed the uncanny knack of deflating male egos without creating the noise of a bursting balloon. She was renowned for her ability to control guests when their behaviour became unacceptably unruly. She could outstare the rowdiest of men into a contrite silence, keeping Rangeela hovering outside the door in a state of perpetual disappointment. Rarely was he summoned to exert any physical force to remove a client from the house.

Khalid Sharif remembered the owner of *Khush Manzil* as she appeared on his first day there.

Rangeela led him up the clean, wide stairs to a small waiting room without furniture. Khalid Sharif was politely asked to remove his shoes before he stepped on the blue Kashmiri carpet patterned with floral designs in gold, red and white. Huge bolsters, covered in maroon satin, were symmetrically arranged to indicate the seating area. He stood awkwardly, gawking at the china blue distempered walls adorned with tapestries and silk paintings of royal hunts and the gaiety of court life in Moghul India. They were gifts from appreciative guests, he was later informed. Curiosity prompted him to move to the solitary window grilled with iron bars. He thought he heard a female giggle from the courtyard below.

'*Bhateyeh Saheb!*' Rangeela's voice was respectful and yet demanded an unquestioning obedience. He hovered outside, his imposing figure extending beyond the wooden frame on either side of the door.

Meekly Khalid Sharif lowered himself on the carpet. Self-consciously he leaned back with his left elbow resting on the top of the bolster. It was a sophisticated posture, he decided, one which would hide his trepidation. He was desperate to appear suave and confident, a man with very little to learn and familiar with the ways of elegant manners. He was, after all, a university graduate.

The jingling sound of bangles announced a new arrival. An attractive girl, with mischievous eyes, stood at the door with a silver tray. Rangeela had moved to one side and was whispering in her ear. The girl nodded several times before entering the room. She was dressed in white *chooridar* pyjama and a red *kameez* flecked with gold sequins. A green *dupattah* covered her head, its ends hanging over her breasts.

With the tray held firmly in her left hand, the girl curtsied. '*Aadavarz hai*, Sharif Saheb!' She greeted him shyly, her eyes fixed demurely on the carpet.

Khalid Sharif scrambled to his feet. Her suppressed giggle told him of his glaring error in standing up. He swallowed hard and raised his right hand to his forehead. His legs were leaden. He imagined how an ox stuck in deep mud might feel. He sat down once more.

The girl placed the tray on the carpet in front of him. He envied her grace and the elegance of her movements. She curtsied again and walked backwards to the door.

'*Shahbash!*' Rangeela commended her as she left the room.

Khalid Sharif stared at the gleaming tray with an awed curiosity. He was unaccustomed to this kind of stylised refinement. A filigreed plate was piled with *ladoos* and *peras*. Next to the plate was a tumbler filled with a pale orange sherbet, its surface crowded with blanched almonds and strands of saffron. A matching silver bowl, resting on a white napkin, was half-full of scented warm water. Half a dozen red rose petals wavered like empty barges on the Hoogly River.

Khalid Sharif was hungry. His stomach growled rudely as though it was intent on embarrassing him. He reached for a *ladoo* and bit into the moist, granular texture of the yellow round. It was delicious.

Another female voice outside the door. Rangeela spoke circumspectly and then disappeared.

Khalid Sharif stuffed the rest of the *ladoo* in his mouth and choked on it. A fit of coughing seized him. Hastily he gulped the sticky, sweet drink and wiped his mouth with the back of his hand. Before he was able to immerse his fingers in the bowl, Tabassum Begum had bounded into the room.

Her radiant smile dispelled his apprehension of their first meeting and dispensed with the formalities of the greeting he was dreading.

'Sharif Saheb!' She exclaimed warmly, her face reflecting a genuine pleasure in meeting a newcomer. 'Welcome! We are honoured to have you in our company. *Mashallah!* What a generous family! Your uncle is a rare gentleman.' She spoke with a note of warm approval in her voice.

Tabassum Begum knelt on the carpet and rested her forearms on a bolster.

Khalid Sharif couldn't help staring at her. He was mesmerised by the deep darkness of her eyes that reflected the sadness of her bruising encounters with life. At once he apprehended that he was a novice in a complex world of experiential learning, someone who had been unexposed to the pains of emotional scalding. He felt inadequate and inferior. His education was narrow and negligible compared with what this woman knew. It was an intuitive appraisal, but one that proved to be accurate.

It was unusual for Khalid Sharif to listen to a stranger without interruptive questions. Mere acceptance of factual details was not in his character, especially when it entailed conformity to an alien mode of behaviour. Yet he listened to Tabassum Begum without any outward sign of dissent or dissatisfaction. Her close presence had an enervating effect on his ability to concentrate.

He struggled to assess her looks and reached the reluctant conclusion that Tabassum Begum was not beautiful. Her face was too fleshy and the nose protruded like a mountain peak. Her thick lips scared him, even as he was attracted by them as though they were a deadly trap waiting to suck him into a furnace.

Many years later Khalid Sharif readily admitted to himself that he had been drawn to Tabassum Begum with a fierce passion that had sprung up like a gust of wind, only to disappear with an inexplicable suddenness.

'Sharif Saheb! You are not listening!' The ever-present smile removed the sting from the rebuke.

'Ma . . . maaf keh . . . kejeah, Begum Saheba!' Khalid Sharif stuttered an apology, his mind forcing its way through a swirling mist to grasp her words.

'Sharif Saheb . . .' She sucked in her breath and scanned his face. A momentary uncertainty clouded her eyes. She sensed a rebellion lurking behind the polite exterior. He could be one of those who made it a point not to leave quietly. 'Sharif Saheb, you must exercise some self-discipline here. This is not any common house of pleasure. I am obliged to emphasise that! You have to learn to treat us with respect. Act properly. Follow our customs and obey our rules. You will find us caring and generous. Please don't abuse our hospitality. Between us there are barriers which must never come down. You see, we belong to a different world. Ours is hidden in the shadows, behind the great banner of an easily proclaimed morality which upholds the respectability of a family like yours.' She laughed gently at his perceptible discomfort. 'It's all right, Sharif Saheb. Eventually we must all accommodate hypocrisy in our lives. Used properly, it can be quite a useful tool. At the appropriate time we hope you will be able to leave with our goodwill, without hurting us or yourself. Our farewells are final. When you have finished here, you will be expected to leave nothing behind. A name in our register that will be stored away at the end of the year. You may take only your experiences of *Khush Manzil* with you. If we are to exist in your memory, it must be as a distant illusion in a remote corner of your mind. Keep it hidden. You cannot reveal us to your wife or children. Perhaps you will suffer the torment of isolation, of having known what cannot be shared with those you will come to love. I doubt it, though. Most men manage to exclude us from their nostalgic reminiscences.' Tabassum Begum laid a hand on his arm and shook him. 'Do I make myself clear, Sharif Saheb?'

He nodded cautiously.

She understood his confusion and guessed some of his unasked questions.

'Circumstances, Sharif Saheb! Circumstances in life are never entirely to our satisfaction. Occasionally we may risk bypassing them recklessly as we seek a meaningful end. But otherwise we are bound to accept their restrictions and the unhappiness they bring. That is what kismet has decreed for most of us. That is the way it is meant to be.'

Tabassum Begum spoke authoritatively as if she was Fate itself, unwilling to change directions and alter the course of destiny. 'Come!' she invited him. 'Now I would like you to meet Nazli.' There was a slight note of reluctance in her voice as though she knew she was in the process of committing a significant error. 'Come!' She held out her hand. 'We have to teach you to become intimate with life, love it and be pained by its whimsical betrayals.' She looked at him broodingly and shook her head in disbelief. *Not so young*, she thought. *And yet so innocent. Much too innocent.*

Tabassum Begum led Khalid Sharif into another room.

'Mr Sharif!' Judy's hand was on his shoulder. 'Tea or coffee?'

He thought her voice was unnecessarily loud. 'My hearing is not impaired,' he said mildly.

'Sorry! But you didn't seem to be listening.'

'Uh . . . no . . . no, I suppose I wasn't. Just thinking about something you said.'

'What did I say that was so profound?' Judy asked playfully.

'Doesn't matter,' he replied tersely, his tone signalling his intention not to discuss it any further.

'Tea or coffee?'

'Nothing. Nothing at all, thank you.'

EIGHT

Well, what is it that troubles me?
Khalid Sharif had never allowed himself to forget Levin's introspective question toward the end of *Anna Karenin*. It was the ultimate probe, the decisive determinant to gauge if a person was morally alive. He had fiercely embraced Tolstoy's words to prevent a recurrence of the crippling indifference which had blighted the most important year in his life.

1943. The year of the great famine in Bengal. The war drew closer from the east.

More, many more than a million starved to death that year. Nearly half of Modhunagar's population perished despite the efforts of Shahid Sharif and his brothers.

There were unimaginable tales of suffering in Calcutta. A post-mortem on a man, found dead in a street, revealed undigested grass in his stomach. Bodies of malnourished children, partly eaten by dogs and foxes. Some were still alive when they were found. Infanticide and a thriving trade in selling children for paltry sums of money. Cholera, dysentery and diarrhoea.

Death. Suffering. Death. Suffering. Death. Death . . .

And he didn't care. Nothing troubled Khalid Sharif.

It was a year when a young man's passion kindled into

flames to fire his imagination and melt his conscience. Khalid Sharif was a man smothered by the selfishness of his desires, unable to feel the turmoil of a wider world.

Self-fulfilment became an obsession. Love, an excuse.

He watched intently.

Viewed in colour, the greatest of catastrophes lacked the bleakness of despair and the intensity of monumental suffering.

The grim images from Rwanda tunnelled him back to the guilt he had deliberately kept alive for over half a century.

The impeccably dressed newscaster played his part. Of course it was neither possible nor desirable for him to shed the appearance of prosperity in order to become the harbinger of such titanic disaster. After all, the ratings had to be considered. But he did manage to look suitably serious and concerned. His teeth did not flash in a rehearsed smile of a cheery facade, and the tanned cheeks were not ridged into dimples of seductive charm.

'Oh, he's gorgeous!' Zareen had summed up the man with a teenager's frankness, on that first evening of her grandfather's arrival, when Khalid Sharif had settled down in the family room to watch the news.

The description puzzled him. *Gorgeous*. Men weren't supposed to be gorgeous. He looked up the word later. *Richly coloured, sumptuous, magnificent . . . strikingly beautiful.* He could think of other, more appropriate words. *Suave. Sophisticated. Handsome.* Certainly not *gorgeous*.

His grandchildren spoke another language.

Gorgeous faded away.

A different world.

Reality from a comforting distance. Gripping TV coverage. Beyond touch or smell. Sanitised misery without the stench of decomposition, stale urine and diarrhoea.

Tearful children, without the energy to vocalise their anguish. A half-naked woman. Ageless. Ribs, despair and faded eyes. Nipples barely protruding, like sultanas on a parched, crinkly sheet of black paper. Attractive to flies.

A stagnant puddle of filthy rain water. Withered, trembling hands of dying hope scooped up the snotty green surface scum. The odds were against finding a dead insect.

Enough details. The impatient camera swept over the human chaos. A reporter's articulate voice reiterated what the eyes could see.

Nearly two minutes . . . There were other pressing matters.

The ads intervened. Immediate transportation back to the relief of a make-believe world. *Follow our example.* Attractive young men and women flashed past with brief messages, waving the wand of consumerism. Inducements to easy living. Buy . . . enjoy . . . experience happiness. Life was about sustaining illusions.

Khalid Sharif jabbed the volume button on the remote control.

A muffled laughter?

He was meant to be around. Monitor their behaviour. Controlled romance. *Moderate your passions children. I shall tell you when the thermometer rises to an unacceptable level. You are too young to follow the dictates of instinct. A dark, predatory jungle where you can be hurt . . .*

But then he was not supposed to know about such matters.

The conversation in the kitchen had been within his hearing. He continued to deceive everyone with the hard-of-hearing act.

'Not much point in asking Papa,' Javed had argued. 'They'll get around him easily.'

'His presence will be enough. Javed, she is not a child any more.' Shanaz was determined to discourage furtive meetings between Zareen and Aldo. It was at her suggestion that the shy, young Italian had been invited to the house to work with Zareen on a history project.

'I don't like it!' Javed frowned without an outright rejection of Shanaz's proposal. 'Papa is far too naive about teenagers.'

Shanaz's patience crumbled. 'For God's sake, get rid of your subcontinental hang-ups!' she snapped. 'Listening to you outside this house, one would immediately think of you as a liberal, tolerant man. Talk of double standards!'

Inwardly Javed cringed. He shot a quick look at his wife. Was there more to what she had said? Could she possibly know anything? Was she suspicious? He withdrew into a pacifying silence, anxious not to be drawn into an argument that might inflame tempers and betray him into injudicious revelations. He was wary of Shanaz. She had the knack of goading him until he burst into a careless retaliation.

Zareen accepted their condition with a sullen reluctance.

'Here, on the kitchen table!' her mother insisted. 'There's enough space to spread out your work.'

Zareen's distorted facial expression and her mumbling infuriated Javed who found it difficult to cope with the gender gap and its resulting hostility.

'Where you can be seen!' Javed chimed provocatively, ignoring Shanaz's glare. 'Dada will keep an eye on things.' He nodded emphatically, as if Khalid Sharif had already agreed to be the definitive control over Zareen's behaviour.

'Why don't you invite Aldo to the cricket with us? Your project is not due until the end of term.'

Shanaz's tentative question did not ease the tension. Zareen remained unmoved, allowing her wilful silence to develop into a scornful rejection. When the duration of the pause had stretched into an obvious embarrassment, she turned defiantly and walked out of the kitchen with clenched fists.

Her parents braced themselves for the door to slam. Shanaz laid a firm, restraining hand on Javed's arm.

There was not even an audible click.

A moment of parental relief. They exchanged empty smiles

and shared the same thoughts. There wasn't any need to speak. Zareen was maturing, learning self-restraint.

Javed exhaled noisily. 'I wish we were all going!' He could find no valid reason for his father's refusal to accompany them to the day–night game at the Melbourne Cricket Ground.

'It's too tiring at my age,' Khalid Sharif had said by way of an explanation. Never again would he intrude and inconvenience the family outings, he promised himself.

The previous weekend in the Grampians had made him aware of his nuisance value and his catalysing effect in provoking disharmony. There were brief outbursts and terse exchanges. For a start both the cars had to be taken, since Khalid Sharif was the sixth person. One too many, he deduced later.

Before they left, an argument erupted about who would ride in the car with Javed and Khalid Sharif. Javed insisted that one of the boys accompany them in the back seat of the station-wagon he was driving. Asif and Safdar grumbled and argued. The impasse was broken with Zareen climbing impatiently into the wagon. Her brothers' triumphant grins provoked a stinging response. It was audible and rude enough to draw a sharp rebuke from her father. Shanaz sprang to her daughter's defence, and the driveway quarrel ended with Javed almost reversing the car into a man delivering junk mail.

The tension lingered, even in the tranquillity of the countryside. There were disagreements about meal times, the types of food ordered ('Nothing with ham in it!' Javed had warned his children beforehand), the walks and the drives. Javed and Shanaz insisted that the weekend was essentially for Khalid Sharif's enjoyment. His needs and wishes were to have priority.

'We will do things as a family,' Javed declared sanctimoniously when they reached Halls Gap. His sudden resolution stemmed partly from the relief of escaping Theresa. Her savage mauling of his self-esteem had driven him to a determined effort at being a worthy family man.

The weekend didn't work out the way Javed had intended.

Khalid Sharif was no longer fit for uphill walks. The trek to the top of Mount William was abandoned after about a hundred metres. The abdominal pain, Khalid Sharif had nursed throughout the car trip, worsened. His legs were weary. He insisted on limping back to the car without assistance. That evening he was unusually quiet and moody, hardly touching his dinner at the restaurant. He did not respond to his granddaughter's efforts to cheer him up.

'What can I do?' Javed addressed himself exasperatedly, after they returned to the motel. 'Very little pleases him.' He had noticed how withdrawn and reticent his father was. It seemed that there was a preoccupation within Khalid Sharif, a locked world forbidden to others.

Shanaz continued to dab her face with cotton wool.

'Everything must be so strange to him!' Javed brooded. 'He is lonely and out of place.'

'At his age it is not possible to adapt to such a different environment,' Shanaz agreed.

'Yes . . . yes, it must be!' he said quickly, gratefully seizing on the rigidity of old age to calm his uneasiness about filial negligence.

Javed suffered bursts of guilt about neglecting his father. He experienced a sadness at the gulf he had discovered between Khalid Sharif and himself. He pondered on the polarisation of their cultural circumstances and concluded that the despair, created by distance, was inevitable. Javed had to admit that it was a sense of obligation, rather than any spontaneous love, which controlled his responses to his father.

It wasn't as if Khalid Sharif had neglected his son when Javed was young. The old man had been a patiently caring father who responded sensitively to his son's developing perceptions of life. Never at any stage was there an imposition of the rigid notions of manhood which the Sharifs felt compelled to instil in the male members of their family. Above all, Javed remembered his father as a kind man.

The hunting incident epitomised Khalid Sharif's protective love for his son. Javed was ten. He had pleaded with his father to be taken on a tiger hunt. The *shikar* was an annual event of male camaraderie initiated by the Sharifs, and undertaken by about twenty male members of the family and their close friends, toward the end of December.

They assembled at Gosaba and made their way east to hired launches which took them south through the network of canals to the dense interior of the Sunderban jungles. It was an elaborately planned expedition with the comforts of servants, cooks, guides and supplies to make life easy in the unfriendly terrain.

In the evenings they camped by the waterside, eating roasted venison and wild fowls. A roaring fire was fuelled all night by vigilant servants and coolies who took turns to guard the sahebs against the wild animals lurking in the vicinity. It was an adventure without the excitement of unpredictability, a hunt conducted in the utmost safety.

It was after the fourth day of travel that one of the guides found a fresh set of a tiger's footprints. Three *machans* were erected on the sturdy branches of mangrove trees and equipped with bedding, guns, food and hot drink. Before the launches were steered further down the waterway and anchored with most of the servants and coolies on board, an early meal was concluded and the campsite cleared before dusk.

Javed was confounded by the sight of goats tied to the trunks of nearby trees. A guide casually informed him that the animals were live baits to attract the tiger.

'Will the tiger kill the goats?' the young boy inquired

apprehensively, his eyes widening with concern for the hapless animals. 'Will they feel pain?'

'One or two will possibly die,' the guide replied nonchalantly, his attention on one of the ropes he was tightening around the trunk of a tree to stabilise a *machan* above him. 'Depends on how well the sahebs shoot.'

Javed's imagination was seized with scenes of unbearable and prolonged suffering. Ugly claws and deadly fangs tore at the goats while his father and uncles sat on the platforms and laughed at the spectacle. The rapacious beast satiated its appetite before a single shot was fired. When the guns finally boomed, the bullets missed the target and the big cat wandered into the surrounding mist, unharmed.

The inordinate cruelty and the unfairness inherent in the scenario led to an extraordinary confrontation.

His eyes brimming with tears, Javed found his father and accused him bluntly of perpetrating the savage killings of harmless animals.

The directness and the force of the condemnation stunned Khalid Sharif into a paralysed silence. It felt as if his son had plunged a sharp knife into an unhealed wound and exacerbated a pain that had subsided into a dull throb.

Men turned away. Such an open display of ill-mannered anger toward one's father deserved the harshest of punitive measures. The boldness of the boy!

Khalid Sharif's meek surrender lowered him in his friends' esteem. How could he? they asked later. How could a man let his dignity and authority be trampled by his own son? The shame of it!

Even the mangrove trees murmured their disapproval.

Khalid Sharif turned to the guide and instructed him to untie the goats and lead them back to the launches.

'But Saheb!' the man protested. 'Without the goats there is almost no chance of tempting the tiger. It can drink anywhere along the canal.'

Khalid Sharif's stare was enough to prevent any further remonstrances. He had already made up his mind to pay for the entire cost of the *shikar*.

As darkness descended, with the weight of a profound fear on a pristine imagination, Javed clambered up a tree, helped by his father. Khalid Sharif wrapped several blankets around his son to keep him warm. The cold dampness of the alien night blossomed with the noises of its unseen inhabitants. The boy shivered, partly because of a residual fear of his impertinence, wary of his father's attention. The expected reprimand had not eventuated. There wasn't the slightest hint of anger in his father.

Javed struggled to stay awake. The intimidating roar of the tiger remained in his imagination. The animal was now the hunter, stalking Javed in search of revenge. Claws dug out his entrails, canines sank into the neck. His father stood by helplessly. Some time before midnight Javed fell asleep, his thoughts trapped between the nightmare of a mauling and the heroic world of Jim Corbett's rivalry with Javed Sharif, the famed Indian hunter.

It was daylight when Javed awoke. He was snuggled against his father who was sipping a mug of tea.

'Did you kill the tiger?' the boy cried excitedly, rubbing his eyes. The slowly rising mist made it impossible to see what lay on the ground below. 'Where is it?'

Khalid Sharif looked at his son with amused tolerance. 'No,' he replied indifferently. 'We didn't get the tiger. It didn't come.'

'Oh. Oh!' Javed sounded crestfallen and contrite as if the hunt had failed miserably because of him. 'Oh! And was it all my fault?' he asked tremulously.

Khalid Sharif put an arm around his son and drew him close. He felt Javed shaking against his chest. Calmly he continued to enjoy his tea.

* * *

The silver-haired weather man smiled and conveyed the good news. Rain in dry areas.

A burst of unrestrained laughter.

He would not check on them, Khalid Sharif decided. Zareen's curiosity was insatiable. Sometimes it made him uncomfortable.

Dad says you were not allowed to go out with girls.

It was different in those days.

But you sneaked out, didn't you? Come on, Dada! You can tell me.

It was not acceptable.

What was it like to be in love?

Pain and yearning whenever he was away from *Khush Manzil*. The stretches of time he spent in Nazli's room did not please Tabassum Begum. Afternoons and evenings. Late into the night.

He was never comfortable with the casual ease with which she undressed and slipped into bed. He found it awkward to take off his clothes in her presence.

Nazli was the initiator. Her hands and lips stroked away his shyness and evoked exciting sensations. She was like a goddess charging him with life.

Later they lay in bed without speaking. The world was a sanctuary for lovers. Words were not immediately necessary to communicate the intimacy he felt. He pressed himself against her back and listened to her gentle breathing. Eyes closed, he inhaled the fragrance of perfume from her neck. He was blessed with the knowledge of Paradise. The calmness made him complacent.

And when he spoke, she listened quietly, her hands caressing the back of his head and neck as if to tone down the extravagance of what he said. He talked about contentment. Peace and permanence.

What was it like to be in love?

She was too young to understand. An exhilarating journey

through the colours of the universe . . . a song of the eternal mystery.

Gingerly he moved sideways in his chair. The pain was bearably persistent.

The craggy old specialist had been kind and pretended as if time had little bearing on his professional life. They had coffee and cream biscuits. A chat about India. Alan Gibson had been there several times, both as a tourist and in a professional capacity. Goa, in particular, fascinated him.

'A region of immense charm,' he reminisced. 'The ghosts of Europe linger there.'

'Nothing very charming about ghosts,' Khalid Sharif growled. 'The British continue to haunt us.'

'Ah, but the Portuguese! They were different.' Alan Gibson did not miss the disapproval in Khalid Sharif's voice. 'Sensuous and exotic. They had a tropical temperament, unlike the British.'

'Arrogant and vindictive,' Khalid Sharif retorted. 'Thought they'd last forever. Same as the British.'

The Australian's memories of Panjim, Mardao and the stretches of white beaches where the Goans strolled, dressed as if they were on the way to a formal party, were untainted by the blots of colonial excesses. He had read about the Portuguese soldier, Afonso de Albuquerque, who annexed Goa for the Portuguese empire in 1510, and thought of him as a great adventurer.

'Amazing place,' the specialist continued, recalling the cathedral of old Goa where Francis Xavier was buried. The neglected old buildings on Mandovi River captivated him. They stood like silent orphans without hope, heartlessly abandoned to the corrosive effects of the passing years. He looked mischievously at Khalid Sharif. 'The influence of Christian civilisation is very evident there.'

'Goa was liberated only in 1961. Give it another hundred years.'

'Of course. All traces of any civilisation must ultimately disappear.'

'The unbending rule of history—the conqueror must himself be buried.'

'More coffee?' The specialist's hands rested causally on the manila folder in front of him.

Khalid Sharif frowned and shook his head.

Ruefully Alan Gibson rubbed his chin. He wished he had something more positive to say. Some doubt. Even after the experience of more years than he cared to remember, he dreaded such moments. He eyed the Indian critically. Strong. Not the demonstrative sort. But he had been wrong before. Professional integrity demanded an exposition of facts without distortion. Perhaps it was heartless to stick too strictly to that aspect of medical ethics.

'Now!' Gibson steeled himself and made an effort to sound vigorous and businesslike. 'The reports on the test are . . .'

'Nothing encouraging,' Khalid Sharif interrupted confidently, as if he knew what the specialist was about to say.

'Well . . .' Gibson smiled with relief and a little envy at the old man's calmness. The Indian was more intent on enjoying the biscuits than in listening to the medical report. 'I'm afraid the specialist in Calcutta summed it up pretty accurately. Mind you, there hasn't been a significant change in your condition.'

'How long?'

'Pardon?' Gibson leaned forward, conscious of the importance of answering each question tactfully, but without distortion.

'How long do I have?' Khalid Sharif asked between mouthfuls, brushing the crumbs from the lapel of his jacket.

'Difficult to say.' Gibson hesitated. He passionately hated predictions about the longevity of life. The human will was capable of the most astonishing miracles. 'No reason why you shouldn't enjoy another couple of years. Maybe more. Without too much discomfort.' He did not feel as confident as he sounded. The tests had revealed enlarged supraclavicular nodes. The liver had hardened and was enlarged by metastases.

'Will the pain increase?'

'There are pain-controlling drugs.'

The silence denoted Khalid Sharif's dissatisfaction with the reply.

'I would like you to come back in about three weeks.'

Khalid Sharif rose from the chair. *There must be summative questions to ask oneself before the finish. Is there a God? An afterlife? The two most common ones, I suppose. I am too close to the answers to make them challenging. Is there one that . . . Yes, it has to be dragged out from all that I will leave behind. What have I lived for? That would have to be it. A final evaluation of this grand illusion that has created meaning and offered solace. I have done everything—been happy, made monumental errors, loved, hated, lied, suffered, been selfish, dreamed, fooled myself and sometimes led a sightless existence guided by the dictates of greed. For what purpose? What have I lived for?*

'Will you come back for some more tests?' Gibson handed him a prescription. Normally it wouldn't be a diffident question, but a polite assertion of medical expertise. But this fellow . . . he was somehow different. 'It will mean a couple of days in the hospital.'

What for? The sap has drained from the soul. The flame flickers timidly, without warmth. And in the song-haunted twilight, what else is left? The husk and the staleness of time-nibbled dreams. The growing blindness and the confusion of rasping whispers . . . 'No.' He did not feel the need to offer an explanation.

Gibson nodded and opened a drawer to put away the folder. 'I'll see you out. I take it you are going back to India?'

A rhetorical question.

They shook hands with an understanding that required no words.

Khalid Sharif looked at the specialist with gratitude. A younger man might have been more difficult. That was the benefit of acquired wisdom. You knew when to let go.

The receptionist was surprised to see Alan Gibson.

'The next appointment is not for another ten minutes,' she reminded him.

He nodded. 'I might just see Mr Sharif to the door.'

It is now an unwinnable game played in the shrinking spaces of time. The outcome is inevitable. But when? Will I have tied up my business with the world? Foolish man! To think you can ever be totally prepared! Isn't there always something left to be accomplished? Now I must be content with a quiet place in the deepening shadows that have devoured me. And yet the desires! Montaigne was so detestably perceptive. Damn him for knowing! Our desires incessantly grow young again. *How pitifully indecent, this longing for the sun. From this wreck a voice calls not to give up. And how will I be judged? The settlements won't please them.* Someone should have advised Papa more forcefully. Who could have possibly known how far gone he was? Toward the end he became utterly irresponsible. *Now my responsibility is to the past. If I could only pluck out the one doubt . . . She never did say even once. Her emotional inhibitions were too great . . . Wouldn't it be blissful without regrets . . . Oh, the virulence of guilt! Its power to plunge me into hell . . . There is no one to say sorry to . . . I cannot apologise to my memory . . . How does one atone? I have been stung into numbness. Isn't that enough? Wouldn't it be convenient if memory collapsed and left me with paltry recollections? I could rearrange the way it all ended . . .*

He was powerless against her disruptive presence. Whenever he attempted to tamper with the past, she never failed to burst into his consciousness from somewhere in the dark pool inside him, her silent presence admonishing him. She was beyond the manipulative grasp of time. Forever young. He often recalled Tithonus' lament. She, too, held him in the

East, her *rosy shadow* dragging him back to the way it had been . . .

There was an antechamber next to Tabassum Begum's room. He was told to wait there. Through the small window he watched the sun sink into the folds of the tropical dusk. The fading light touched him with an uneasy sadness he did not quite understand. His life had suddenly turned a corner, leaving behind the pastoral simplicity of an uncluttered youth for the crowded and insidious network of adult experiences.

Gradually noises and voices filtered into the room as if an entire population was in the process of a nocturnal awakening. A *tabalchi* exhorted a dancer to quicken her feet movement. The faint sound of running water. A male voice inquired about the number of guests expected for dinner.

The door opened noiselessly. An elderly man entered, dragging a huge candle stand with two dozen holders arranged in three layers of concentric circles.

The melancholy sound of the *azan* wafted in through the window, loitering in a forlorn echo before dissipating in the deepening darkness of the warm evening. The servant lit the candles and asked if a prayer mat was required.

Khalid Sharif gaped at him and then slowly shook his head. The old man frowned, curtsied elegantly and left.

The muezzin's voice called again, beckoning the faithful for *magrib's* prayer. An awed quietness crept across the evening. The house fell silent once more, as if in tacit submission to Allah's Will.

A nervous anxiety and the afternoon's searing heat had fatigued Khalid Sharif. He found himself hovering between a surreal consciousness of his surroundings and the blankness of a deep sleep.

His cousin waited in the heart of the forest.

The banyan tree had been crudely chopped down and the trunk and branches carted away. Only a stump stood as a reminder of the tree's presence.

'The tree? What happened?' Khalid Sharif was unable to apprehend a bewildered and pained sense of loss. It felt as if a part of himself had been amputated.

'Go . . . gone,' Munir whispered. 'Nev . . . never to grow again. We do not be . . . belong here now.' His voice trembled and he was close to weeping.

'The tree, Munir!' Khalid Sharif demanded, dissatisfied and irritated with his cousin's vagueness. 'Who cut it down? Where is Zohra?'

'Zoh . . . Zohra?' Munir looked blankly at his cousin. 'Who is Zohra?'

'Your friend! The . . .' The look of incomprehension on Munir's face made Khalid Sharif think. It didn't seem appropriate to use the word . . .

'My friend? You . . . are my only friend, Khalid.'

'But what about Zohra?' A desperate anger filtered through the voice.

'Zoh-ra? Zohra . . . who?'

'The *pori*!' Khalid Sharif yelled in exasperation. 'You know, that creature you said could be seen, but not with the eyes!'

'*Pori*? Zohra *Pori*! Munir shook with laughter. It became a high-pitched, uncontrollable noise. 'That is fun . . . funny! Zohra *Pori*? Who believes in her now?' Just as suddenly as the laughter had begun, it stopped. Munir looked confused. 'Gone . . . gone . . .'

'Gone where?'

'Gone back in . . . inside. To die?'

'Where?'

'Inside . . . killed. She died inside.'

'Inside? Inside what?'

'Dead inside,' Munir said dully. He bent down to feel the top of the roughly hewn stump. 'In . . . inside, Killed.' Abruptly he straightened and clutched the left side of his chest with both hands as though he had discovered the reason for Zohra's death.

'These games are for children!' Khalid Sharif yelled. 'We have grown up! The forest is not the place for us any more . . .'

The gentleness of the touch startled Khalid Sharif into an embarrassed awakening. He raised his head from the bolster and managed to mutter a terse apology. His hands felt clammy and his forehead and the back of his neck were wet with perspiration. Even in the confused daze, which marked his instant return to the sticky heat of the poorly ventilated room, Khalid Sharif detected a glint of amusement in Tabassum Begum's eyes.

'Sharif Saheb,' she addressed him with a professional respect in her voice. 'I have brought someone to meet you. This is Nazli.'

The light from the candles threw gaunt, mutable shadows on the walls and enhanced the impression that he was meeting an apparition. Khalid Sharif avoided staring at Nazli. It was impolite, he had been instructed. Her face was covered with a thin *duppatta* which silhouetted an oval-shaped face. There was a sense of unreality about her presence, as if she had been conjured up by a trickster's sleight of hand, destined to disappear without a murmur of dissent.

Tabassum Begum's right hand was around Nazli's shoulders as though guarding a precious possession.

Clothes rustled. There was a jingle of jewellery as the women seated themselves on the carpet.

'Nazli has only been with us for two years, Sharif Saheb,' Tabassum Begum explained, her tone imploring him to be gentle and patient.

With a deft flick of the hand, she threw back the covering from Nazli's face.

Khalid Sharif looked toward the solitary window in the room. He had missed the transience of twilight. Apprehensively he looked at the darkness of the upturned bowl outside. It denoted fear. Mystery. Uncertainty. The imponderable facets of life itself. *The world has spilled into space from a freak accident,* he thought phlegmatically. *We are a part of that inexplicable disaster which perpetuates itself in chance occurrences.*

He heard a shy, whispered greeting.

'Sharif Saheb?' Tabassum Begum's voice cajoled him to look at the girl.

Nazli was attractive without being strikingly beautiful, but the vulnerability and the hint of a permanent sadness in her face induced Khalid Sharif to endow her with the attributes of a fictitious character in an ancient romance, cleansed of all the imperfections of life. At once she became the centre of an impulsive obsession, graced with a celestial purity, the nucleus of an innocent and timeless fantasy world where decisions, actions and consequences blended into a harmonious synthesis of lasting happiness. It was a young man's instant love with an illusion he created and imposed over a disquieting reality.

'*Aadavarz hai!*' His voice trembled with intense anxiety as he raised his right hand to his forehead.

The conversation was fatuous and awkward, punctuated with lengthy periods of silence. Nazli was stocked with an endless supply of innocuous questions. Khalid Sharif told her about himself without a reciprocal response.

'I am here. That is all that matters,' she said with an unexpected firmness when he pressed her about her past.

There was a tap on the door.

'It is time to join the others,' Tabassum Begum announced. 'We must go downstairs, now, Sharif Saheb. You can talk later.'

Tabassum Begum continued to be uneasy about him. He was different . . . very different. Gentle but intensely passionate. Idealistic and stubbornly committed to causes. He was the type who was capable of transcending the ephemerality of hedonistic pleasures for the nobility of something more permanent. The poor fool! A rare male, but one who could also prove to be difficult and exceedingly stubborn.

The *mahfil* was a lavish induction for newcomers. The hall was like an imperial *durbar* shimmering with the careless opulence of a Moghul court. Here, it was easy to forget the choking poverty which surrounded *Khush Manzil* and appeared to be pressing ominously closer each year.

The air was thick with the fragrance of rose water, *attar* and incense. From the blue-coloured walls hung tapestries and large, rectangular mirrors fitted with candle stands. Huge candles lit the room which was manned by eight turban-clad servants dressed in white. They fanned the air with hand *punkahs* crafted from peacock feathers.

At the far end of the room, a raised platform, draped with carpets and ringed with satin-covered pillows and bolsters, was reserved for the established and more affluent members of *Khush Manzil*. Here, in the company of nearly a dozen elderly men, Tabassum Begum presided over the evening gatherings with the imperial mien of a queen. She sat in the company of *nawabs*, *nizams* and wealthy imposters who claimed to be the descendants of titled aristocrats. They were expatriates from Lucknow, Aligarh and Delhi, now reluctantly settled in Calcutta for reasons unknown to Tabassum Begum. Their backgrounds and their dubious claims to the imperial Moghuls did not concern her. They were moneyed people, cultured and sophisticated, with a superb command of Urdu, the only language Tabassum Begum permitted to be spoken in her house.

Inside *Khush Manzil*, Calcutta was a distant city inhabited by aliens with strange customs and a language foreign to Muslims. Such misconceptions guided Tabassum Begum's rigorous screening of the families who wished to send their young men to *Khush Manzil* to broaden their life experiences and seek an education that was beyond the scope of conventional institutions. What some families lacked by way of their pedigree could, naturally, be made up with additional contributions to promote excellence, and ensure the maintenance of the high quality of service she provided. In Tabassum Begum's world of lofty ideals, there was adequate space for honourable compromises.

The appalling circumstances through which she had dragged her young, orphaned life had inculcated in her a firm belief in the gains to be made by exploiting wealthy, ageing men who were unable to reconcile the virility of their fantasies with the diminishing prowess of their sexuality.

When Tabassum Begum was fourteen, a rich businessman, renowned for his generous contributions to charity, had bribed one of Calcutta's orphanages to part with her and burn the records of her existence. After nearly four years, when the rotund and balding businessman reached the conclusion that the ageing process was irreversible and that it was no longer possible to revitalise himself with his mistress's youth, his conscience intervened and led him back to his wife, children and a life devoted to charity work.

Tabassum Begum's compensation was two hundred rupees and an introduction to Hamida Begum, an elderly lady who was forever eager to employ young girls in her entertainment business.

Little was known about Hamida Begum. She was a small, frail woman with aristocratic manners and a foul temper. She spoke Urdu fluently and wrote volumes of poetry which was appreciated by those who attended her *mahfils*, but never quite interested the publishers in Calcutta or Delhi. She was from Shahjehanbad she boasted, refusing to use the name Delhi. She traced her lineage to a royal Moghul family that had been cruelly treated by the British and had fallen on hard times.

'My dear child,' Hamida Begum explained to the bewildered girl, 'a woman is blessed with great powers. Use them! Your job is to create a world where men can deceive themselves that they are happy, where time is not an enemy and they feel like giants. When they leave this house, they should be convinced about their invincibility the same way children believe in stories. This is *Khush Manzil*—the house of happiness. Let them play here and delay the discovery of their growing limitations in a one way street called life. Indulge them . . . teach them to dream.'

The young orphan girl became her confidante and the daughter Hamida Begum never had. When the old woman eventually died, her flourishing business passed on to her favourite protege. By this stage of her maturity, a hardened cynicism had convinced Tabassum Begum that an indulgent self-survival was the only moral imperative in a world where charity, without ulterior motives, was an exceptional human attribute.

It wasn't as though Tabassum Begum herself was uncharitable. But her generosity was rarely spontaneous, and was measured by the extent of the benefit to be derived for herself. She looked after the women under her care. Those in their late twenties and older were not abandoned. They were provided with free accommodation in small, airless *havelis* fringing a square courtyard behind the kitchen, and were used as domestic helpers in return for a paltry remuneration. They cooked, cleaned, tutored the girls and were free to marry and leave at their discretion. Such departures were rare. Having discovered the fickleness of men and the hollowness of their extravagant promises, usually whispered in the billowy heat of a horizontal turbulence, they chose the security of *Khush Manzil*.

Tabassum Begum used her considerable charm and acumen to expand her business. Two rival houses of some reputation, in nearby areas, were compelled to sell out to the ruthless new woman whose considerable negotiating skills were matched by her ability to attract men, not only from distant parts of Calcutta, but from other Indian cities as well.

Early on, through her enjoyment of the power that was thrust upon her with the ownership of the business, Tabassum

Begum made a crucial discovery. She found that it was possible to fabricate an insulated microcosm for herself among the web of illusions that her chosen clients sought with a tenacious desperation. With great deliberation, she formed a network of efficient men who dealt with the tedious business matters of the outside world. She herself began to live as a recluse, rarely venturing outdoors, content to dwell with idyllic dreams of bearable sadness, her evenings embellished with poetry and music, in the cloistered sanctuary of *Khush Manzil*.

Private tutors were employed at considerable expense to initiate her into the details and ways of high culture. Tabassum Begum was curious by nature and felt that there was more to learn than Hamida Begum had taught her. Her perseverance and willingness in pursuing a selective knowledge, compatible with her idealism of a fairytale past, astonished her learned tutors who had been reluctantly seduced by her monetary offer, rather than by the challenge of a sharp, academic mind.

She struggled with the diverse complexity of Islam's history in India. Details about the waves of invasion and their impact on political and social changes bored her. She chose to ignore the cruel excesses of Mohammad Bin Tughluk and some of the later Moghul emperors. Tabassum Begum almost fainted when told about Aurangzeb's treatment of his brother, Dara Shukoh. The image of Shukoh's severed head being sent to his father, and the likely reaction of the broken, old Emperor, haunted her into spending sleepless nights, raging against the heartless culprit. She hated the last of the great Moghuls as if he had inflicted a grievous wrong on her. To ban music, dancing and poetry from the court was an inexcusable moral offence, she concluded indignantly. To imprison the soul in a dark dungeon of ignorance, depriving it of vital nourishment, could only be the fiendish act of an uncultured tyrant. Her way of retaliating was to dismiss Aurangzeb from her mind and banish him to the pages of history texts.

Tabassum Begum distilled the essence of nobility and aesthetic achievements from history, discarding its darker side as an inconsequential deviation from the mainstream glories of an era she upheld as the high note of Indian civilisation.

In her spare time, Tabassum Begum lavished her imaginative energy on creating her own private myths about Akbar, the torrid but tragic affair between Prince Salim and the courtesan, Anarkali, the magnificence of Shahjehan's court and his undying love for Mumtaz Mahal. At one point the history tutor's payment was withheld for several months because he had the temerity to insist that Shahjehan had maintained a crowded harem for his own pleasures.

Tabassum Begum's competence in Farsi and Urdu enabled her to devour the *Ain-i-Akbari*, *Akbar-nama*, *Tuzuk-i-Jahangiri*, *Shah-Jahan-nama* and the poetry of Sauda, Jur'at, Dard, Mir, Zauq, Ghalib, Momin and Miran. Anecdotes from Ferdowsi's *Shah Nama* were painstakingly memorised, and narrated with a scholarly conviction to the admiring guests at the *mahfils*. The details of acceptable courtly behaviour, for Moghul gentlemen in the mid-seventeenth century, were culled from the *Mirza Nama* and impressed on the newcomers as a model to be emulated, without the slightest concession for nearly three centuries of social evolution.

Such was the contrived cultural ethos in which Khalid Sharif had his initiation in the ways of a suave Muslim gentleman. He felt inferior to the other men present at the gathering. An ignorant, bumbling, uncouth male. He sat entranced by a foreign world of cultural sophistication which synthesised learning and pleasure into an elixir to enrich the entire being. His own learning was dry and unstimulating. The formal education was no more than a quest in a vast desert. The worlds of history and philosophy were as far removed from the excitement of his present circumstances as snatches of vaguely remembered dreams.

Nazli's close presence was the only stabilising factor in the confusing flux of the evening's entertainment. It was too noisy to sustain a conversation, but not for a moment did he doubt her sympathetic and complete understanding of his bewilderment. Frequently her hand reached across to stroke his arm and back to assure him that this was no elaborate hoax of the imagination.

The evening began with a lavish feast. It was a superb spread with exotic offerings of rice, bread, meat and sweets piled on glistening silver plates and bowls. There were ample servings of *kakori* and *bhoti kababs, nargisi koftas, sheermals, murg musallam, rumali rotis, chicken korma, mutanjan* and *pulao, mash ki dal, kheer, halwa* and *muzaffar*. The aroma of pure saffron, spices and rose water lingered in the air long after the dishes and the finger bowls were taken away and the *sanchi paans, peek-daans* and the *hookahs* brought in.

The singers, who had assembled to provide a dreamy vocal backdrop to the dinner, were now joined by several dancing girls. The seductive skills, with which they flouted their art, mesmerised Khalid Sharif. The playful sound of *ghungroos* was quite distinctive from the mournful blending of the harmonium, *sarangi* and *sarod*. All forms of contemporary music were strictly forbidden by Tabassum Begum. The singers evoked the past in plaintive tones which mourned the transience of everything noble and sublime in life. The *ghazals* were unfamiliar to him. None of the songs ended happily. Khalid Sharif was struck by the melancholy that enveloped the room. He listened attentively, imitating the behaviour of the more experienced men, shouting '*Wuh! Wuh!*' whenever a clever or a poignant phrase was voiced with a modulated subtlety. He remembered the leather pouches, crammed with coins, he carried in his pocket. He watched the established patrons and then timidly flung a bag intended to land at the feet of one of the singers. His throw was hopelessly inaccurate. It landed near the *tabalchi* who frowned at the clumsy, ill-mannered novice and continued to pound the drums. Khalid Sharif glanced at Nazli. She smiled an encouraging approval. He tried again. And again.

Some time before the lightness of dawn, a tired voice signalled the end of the *mahfil* with a *ghazal* that reconciled man to the finiteness of love and the ephemerality of his passions. Man was a tragic creature, doomed by the dictates of his instincts. Such was life's imperfect story, the singer concluded to a scattered applause from those young men who were still awake.

A gloomy silence descended as the dreams ended. The room emptied as the participants staggered away under the burden of the night's indulgences.

Khalid Sharif staggered to his feet and lurched toward a back door, guided by Nazli. His temples throbbed with the pain of a savage headache. The drink from the silver goblet had made him dizzy.

A room. A bed. Nazli's presence—her voice from a distance, her breathing and the deft fingers. He wanted to protest, to say that he had to go home. But there were irresistible powers that whisked him to enchanted realms of silken touches and whispered words.

So, that is why I was sent here. Death is peaceful, he thought. He shivered as a faint breeze caressed his skin. There were weights on his eyelids. He remembered the words of a *ghazal* he had heard earlier in the evening.

This little space of time they call life—we have
Accomplished it, dying every moment.

'I . . . I have to go.' He sounded sluggish and unconvincing. 'It is very late.'

In the darkness he could not see her smile. 'Or very early, Sharif Saheb.' Nazli drew him closer. 'Dawn is the time of love.'

He stopped struggling. Burning sensations. Pleasure could not be distinguished from pain. He was not alone, Khalid Sharif consoled himself. Not alone.

Suddenly the fall.

He was plunged into a euphoric darkness where his life dissolved and reshaped itself.

No sensation. Only the awareness that there was a new self to grieve about.

NINE

The relief and yet the regret.
She had the house to herself again. But . . . loneliness stalked Angela Barrett like a silent predator.

Listlessly she tiptoed around the kitchen in her faded dressing-gown and bedroom slippers, mildly irritated by the dullness of the quiet order that had reimposed itself.

The back of her neck was sore, and she felt the heaviness of a lingering depression that had kept her awake most of the night. A sense of purposelessness created a frightening void within her. In its darkness she allowed herself to drift through the open spaces which Khalid Sharif had exposed.

His words echoed ceaselessly in the stillness of the night, swirling around her, forcing her timid imagination to grapple with their unpalatable implications.

The future? Its stench tells me it is dead. Don't you know that at our age the present is a state of paralysis? These days I can only feel the virility of the past. And how true is the past? How much of it do we create as we grow older?

Angela was convinced that there were occasions when Khalid Sharif deliberately set out to upset her by proposing outrageous alternatives that threatened and sometimes drowned her own comfortably structured views of life. Her Christian ideals insulated her from despair and were mostly unaffected by age or periods of melancholic ponderings on an existence over which she exercised limited control. There were times when Angela did not fully understand what he said, but nevertheless felt threatened and hurt, as if Khalid Sharif had penetrated the shield of faith and stabbed her with his words.

The robust morning did nothing to enthuse her into changing for the customary walk to the milk bar. She was quietly surprised to realise that she missed Adam's morning unruliness. The acrid smell of burnt toast that led to an examination of the garbage bin. Her natural thriftiness could not tolerate the sight of several pieces of blackened bread resting under crumpled serviettes and bits of paper towel. The kitchen bench was usually dotted with breadcrumbs and roughly ground cornflakes. The marks of a wet sponge, tracing random arcs on the vinyl floor, were telltale signs of careless attempts to wipe up spilled milk and orange juice.

Now everything was in its proper place, the kitchen prissily clean and lifeless.

With clenched dentures, she put the kettle on to boil as a first step toward a self-directed recovery.

Against her judgement, Angela struggled on to reconcile herself to Judy's pursuit of life as a single parent. She found it impossible to understand her daughter's perceptible relief, and even a hint of elation. As if to prove that her intentions of terminating the marriage were earnest and irreversible, Judy had gleefully announced that she had rented a flat only a few minutes drive from her mother's house.

There had been a flurry of sudden activity with bits of furniture and boxes of unused kitchen items—cutlery, pots and pans, cups and plates—being carted off in the boot and back seat of Judy's car.

As she made inquiries about solicitors and their fees, Judy found it essential to choke her pride and accept her mother's offer of a sum of money which was to be paid back in instalments over the next couple of years. They also agreed that after he finished school for the day, Adam should walk over to his grandmother's house where Angela would babysit him until Judy finished work.

Even a second cup of tea did not brighten Angela. What burdened her gloominess was a swelling anxiety about Khalid Sharif's absence. Inexplicably he had failed to appear for several days. She missed their afternoon chats over cups of tea and freshly baked cakes. He had ceased to be a visitor responding to casual invitations.

Angela thought of phoning him, but propriety cautioned her against such a display of foreboding. He was looking gaunt and weary the last time she had seen him.

I am now a prisoner of mortality. Every dawn that passes brings a momentary relief. But as the day progresses, there is only one stupendous question: will the hangman turn up tomorrow?

She tried not to take his words too seriously.

Angela continued to sit at the kitchen table with a feeling of irritable dissatisfaction, without being able to identify the cause. She resented Khalid Sharif's influence on her. He made her think too much about the problems associated with age. With consummate ease he implanted grotesque shadows of uncertainty in her. Although she was uncomfortable with the clashing impressions of light and shade that flickered in her mind after their conversations, she could not deny the stimulus they provided for her imaginings.

'Thinking is a free wonder drug,' Khalid Sharif said to her one afternoon. 'It can do many things, from providing pleasure to the constant assurance that we are alive. The human mind is the greatest power in the known universe.'

She was surprised by the flat note of conviction in his voice. He sounded as if he was in possession of irrefutable proof to vindicate his claim.

'You sound very sure about that,' Angela responded irresolutely, reluctant to contradict him with her fortified belief in the omnipotent power that guided life.

'Absolutely.' His eyes twinkled briefly. 'After all, it created God.'

'You *do* believe in God!' she snapped. 'You yourself said that you fasted and prayed.' Her resolution, not to be baited into one of his obtuse arguments, was breached by his outrageous claim.

'Of course. In here.' He placed a hand across his chest. 'In here.' Moodily he turned to look at her. 'But does He believe in me?'

'But . . . but,' she stumbled, unable to determine if he was serious or merely indulging in one of his straight-faced games intended to fluster her. 'You are a Muslim! You must believe in Allah!'

'Yes,' he said nonchalantly. 'At most times I tend to respond instinctively to my cultural conditioning. I cannot change that. It is only in my very private moments that sharp-toothed doubts nibble at my pillar of security. When I get down to thinking seriously about it all, the odds appear to be against what I have been taught to believe.'

'Do you think there is an afterlife? A heaven?' Angela gripped the arms of her chair in apprehension.

'The thought tires me,' he replied seriously. 'Fancy going through another dimension of consciousness in the company of celestial beings. What is one to do in the company of creatures without fallibilities? I cannot think of anything more boring.' He watched her closely for a reaction. 'Have you never doubted your beliefs?'

Angela rose from her chair. 'I shall make a fresh pot of tea,' she announced.

She stretched her time in the kitchen—throwing the used tea-leaves in the bin, rinsing the pot, washing spoons, cups and the strainer with a slow deliberation that allowed her to regain her composure. She wished Khalid Sharif would refrain from asking her about matters she had no desire to confront. Some things in life were best left alone. She had reached an age when only those questions that could be answered without anguish were worth considering. She wiped the wooden tray and laid out fresh cups and saucers.

Khalid Sharif was sensitive to her frame of mind when she returned with the tray.

We are such misfits in a life that constantly adapts itself to suit the young. We have outlived our purpose in this dark shell crowded with fear, anger . . . hurt. Without a glimpse of a future, a stark bleakness pervades our lives. I must not destroy the past for her.

And yet he wanted her to know that behind her illusions lay the wounded India, hurt by the rampaging outsiders who had brutalised the land for their selfish needs.

Silently she poured him another cup of tea.

'Do you remember the New Market?' he asked awkwardly, hoping to strike a less discordant note in her memory.

She brightened immediately. 'Oh yes! It was such an ugly building, but with so much character. Hogg's market, we called it. I loved shopping there, especially during Christmas when there were all those makeshift stalls crammed with trivia. The bargaining was so much fun. And the sound of the big clock on the front tower! It could be heard even in Free School Street!'

'The back of the New Market was damaged in a fire some years ago.'

Her anguished 'Oh!' conveyed the same crippling feeling of loss that he had himself experienced when he saw the smouldering ruin of charred bricks, timber and ashes.

'That's awful! I wish you hadn't told me.'

Khalid Sharif hadn't anticipated her pained reaction.

'The fire destroyed the shop where I was first supposed to catch a glimpse of my wife. I didn't know about it at the time, but it had been arranged by my youngest, uncle. As it turned out, Jahan Ara was in *purdah*, and I didn't get to see her face.'

Angela was fascinated to hear about the events that had preceded his marriage.

Khalid Sharif omitted even the slightest mention of the crisis, and its reverberations, that had precipitated the frantic search for an eligible girl.

A *dalal* was employed to scour the city for reputable Muslim families with repositories of good-looking young girls. Times were difficult, the *dalal* warned the Sharifs. The war had made people cautious, and there was a noticeable reluctance to offer generous dowries. What did the Sharifs have in mind by way of a settlement?

'Only the girl matters!' Firdaus Sharif responded indignantly. He was repulsed by the mercenary transactions which were becoming commonplace among Calcuttan Muslims. 'An attractive Muslim girl, domestically competent, is all that we want. And yes, she must be from a reputable family.'

Shahid Sharif's wife proved to be particularly difficult when it came to a final choice from the four families thought to be worthy of a matrimonial alliance. Shahid Sharif favoured the landowners from Rajshahi. In addition to his *zamandari* wealth, Amir Hafiz was also a lawyer with a thriving practice in Calcutta. He was a man noted for his professional integrity. He was the first male in his family to break away from the tradition of making a living off the land.

'An enterprising man!' Shahid Sharif enthused. 'And his daughter?'

'His youngest girl, Sharif Saheb!' the marriage broker, Lamba, reported. 'Beautiful, well-mannered and gentle. She can cook and sew, reads the Holy Koran and is very religious.'

'Have you seen her?' Firdaus demanded, sceptical about the glowing description. He was familiar with the tendency of brokers to exaggerate.

'That is impossible, Saheb! She is in strict *purdah*!'

More information was painstakingly gathered and presented to Shahid Sharif. He had several discussions with his brothers without being able to extract their unqualified support for the family of his choice.

A family from East Bengal . . . Was that wise? The possibilities in Calcutta had by no means been exhausted. East Bengal . . . It might be advisable to scrutinise the other families more closely.

Impatiently, Shahid Sharif sought his wife's opinion. With her backing he felt he could enforce a decision without appearing to be a patriarchal tyrant.

Mumtaz Sharif was distraught by what her husband had to say. 'But Amir Hafiz's daughter is a *Bangaal!*' she protested fiercely. 'Our daughter-in-law must be an Urdu-speaking girl! The family must have some connections with Delhi or Lucknow. Or even Aligarh!' Mumtaz Sharif insisted in a display of high-spirited stubbornness, contrary to the customary deference with which she spoke to her husband. 'I want the best for our son! *Sunyeh jeh!*' She softened her tone. 'I was thinking about Mir Murshed's youngest daughter, Jahan Ara.'

'Do you know her?' Shahid Sharif said coldly, angered by his wife's impertinence.

'Intimately! Her mother is a friend of mine. I taught the child how to sew and knit. *Mashallah*, she is a very accomplished girl! Very pretty and well-mannered.'

'Her education?'

'She has been tutored at home. She can read the Koran Sharif fluently. She is an excellent cook and capable of running a household.'

Unable to find a flaw with the account of the girl, Shahid Sharif focused his attention on her father. 'It is rumoured that Mir Murshed is in debt. Do you know anything about that?'

Mumtaz Sharif shook her head firmly and claimed no knowledge about such vulgar matters which were not the concern of women. 'The family is from Lucknow!' she sighed.

'The girl speaks Urdu the way it is meant to be spoken. They are cultured people.'

'Cultured people from Lucknow and Delhi seem to make it a habit to be in debt,' Shahid Sharif snorted contemptuously. 'They recite poetry and behave with great civility, but they demonstrate no business skills or commonsense! They have scant respect for those who make money.'

'Such charm and good breeding!' Mumtaz Sharif continued, indifferent to what she thought was her husband's extreme and unfounded prejudice. 'She will have a calming influence on Khalid. Recently his behaviour has been very odd. For almost a year he has been like a stranger, looking quite lost and rarely speaking to me. I can never find him at home. The other evening he suddenly walked into our room and informed me that he was going to Modhunagar for a few weeks. Why? I wanted to know. He simply turned around and walked out. He has never been so rude to me before. Something must have happened. He worries me.'

Shahid Sharif dismissed her concern with an impatient wave of his hand. He was anxious to keep his wife ignorant of the disaster that could have been perpetrated by their son's mad selfishness.

'Young men often tend to be moody and erratic in their behaviour,' he explained. 'It is usually an indication of their readiness for marriage. Very well! Since you are so certain, the matter is settled. We will send a proposal to Mir Murshed. But remember! The success of Khalid's marriage is your responsibility.'

Shahid Sharif could not believe that he was caving in to his wife's snobbery about such a crucial family affair. But secretly he viewed her as his cultural superior, since she had been brought up in the old parts of Delhi where the descendants of Moghul royalty were still to be found, languishing in dilapidated houses crammed together in foul-smelling, narrow lanes.

The next morning a sullen and reluctant Lamba was briefed and sent to Mir Murshed's house in Zakaria Street. In anticipation of a quick, affirmative reply, the Sharifs cancelled their business engagements and stayed at home. It was a day wasted in the unfamiliar frivolity of card-playing and swapping *shikar* stories.

By the time the *dalal* returned, the brothers had disappeared for the evening prayer.

The house reverberated with the howl of Shahid Sharif's anger. His brothers rushed to the study where Lamba stood in petrified silence near the door.

'Who does the man think he is? An emperor?' Shahid Sharif roared, his queries not directed to anyone in particular. The clenched fingers of his right hand held a letter which he waved in front of him like a *punkah*. 'What insolence from a man who doesn't even own a second house!'

He scanned the letter and read parts of it to his brothers.

Mir Murshed gushed mellifluously for several paragraphs, as though he was a courtier buttressing an imperial ego with hyperboles before risking an unpalatable truth.

The Sharifs, Mir Murshed wrote, were well-known among the Muslims of Calcutta, and their success was a model for aspiring businessmen. Their family credentials were impeccable. Where Mir Murshed begged to differ was in the assumption that a matrimonial alliance between the two families was desirable on the strength of a religious commonality, important a link as that was.

> . . . *There are significant differences between us, Sharif Saheb, despite the fact that we both belong to the large and blessed family of Islam. We Mursheds proudly represent a tradition that is the noblest expression of Islamic culture in India. Our existence is dedicated to the preservation and nourishment of a unique way of life and the maintenance of the purity of our language, Urdu, as it is spoken and written in Lucknow. I need not remind you that we Muslims are a*

minority in this country, and any compromise with our ideals can only result in an adulterated weakening of our culture. Not even in my worst moment would I think of offending your much esteemed family, Sharif Saheb, but I fear that you have little to offer us by suggesting this marriage. May I be forgiven for drawing your attention to the regrettable fact that Calcuttan Muslims have been unduly influenced by other religions? I am reluctantly led to believe that in your family the learning of Farsi is non-existent, and that Gulabi Urdu, *with smatterings of* Bangla *and* Angrezi, *is spoken at home.*

Your ways, outlook and priorities are different from ours. A marriage between our families would require an unacceptable degree of adjustment for my daughter. I have no desire to put her through a trial that is likely to become a cause of regret and ill-feeling in the long term . . .

'Bastardised language?' Shahid Sharif screeched. 'Little to offer? We could buy that man several times over!'

The quick-thinking Firdaus calmed his brother and suggested an appropriate rejoinder to embarrass Mir Murshed.

'He sounds like a very proud man,' Firdaus observed. 'A snob of the worst kind. Perhaps a grand gesture to challenge his honour might humble him.'

Firdaus unravelled a plan which met with silent scepticism.

'That particular bank account doesn't have much money in it,' he argued. 'Should Mir Murshed decide to abuse our trusting generosity, he will be exposed as a greedy, dishonourable man, unworthy of further attention.'

'There is no harm in trying, *Bhai Jan,*' Rashid admitted after thinking about the scheme. 'Some subtle form of rebuke is necessary.'

Anwar nodded his agreement.

Shahid Sharif instructed his youngest brother to ensure that only a few hundred rupees were left in the account that was to figure in Firdaus' design to humble Mir Murshed.

Equipped with an Urdu dictionary and a book of Urdu and

Persian phrases, Firdaus Sharif stayed awake until after dawn to compose a letter of great ostentatious charm, mined with satirical barbs directed at snobbery, arrogance and cultural decadence. The letter revolved around what the Sharifs had to offer, and the seriousness of its content was underlined by the signed blank cheque that was enclosed in the envelope.

> *. . . It is true that there is little that we Sharifs can offer the mighty Mursheds, who have left the rich and exotic cultural ethos of Lucknow for the barrenness of Calcutta, except a happy home for your daughter, should you wish to reconsider our proposal. But, as a humble offering of our goodwill, please accept this small gift on our behalf. Feel free, Murshed Saheb, to fill in an appropriate figure which may appease your doubts about our ability to take care of your daughter . . .*

The sealed envelope, addressed to *Janab* Mir Murshed, was placed on a silver tray decorated with roses and marigolds and piled with *barfees* and *balushahees*.

Firdaus himself delivered the tray to Mir Murshed's house without seeking to meet the man.

The Sharifs waited, suspended between a niggling doubt about the wisdom of their action and a self-righteous certitude that the response was a justifiable retaliation provoked by Mir Murshed's unpardonable arrogance.

Three days later a servant arrived with a reply from Mir Murshed. Pinned to the letter was the cheque that had been sent to him.

'A man of character and honour!' Shahid Sharif beamed. 'He has been shamed by our trust in him. He is heroic enough to ask for our forgiveness. We have been invited for dinner.'

Shahid Sharif called for his *hookah* to be taken to the bedroom. There were reasons to celebrate. He was full of forgiveness and reconciliation. His son could now be allowed to return to Calcutta. The unfortunate business with the *tawaif* would soon be forgotten. Unknown to his brothers, he made plans for Tabassum Begum. She should have exercised more care in looking after his son . . .

He thought of Khalid Sharif with a forgiving affection. A young man's heart could not be trusted to guide him into maturity. It was now the family's responsibility to lead his son gently to a recognition of his duties and mission in life.

Shahid Sharif permitted himself a smile of satisfaction. Life was once more in his control.

Khalid Sharif's return to Calcutta was not a happy occasion. It was characterised by his disdainful aloofness from the inmates of the house and a lengthy period of silent hostility between father and son. He avoided Rashid and Anwar on the valid assumption that they had collaborated with Shahid Sharif's hysteria in sending him to the village. Grudgingly, he permitted only Firdaus to converse with him.

Brimming with impotent anger, Khalid Sharif disciplined himself to listen to his uncle's pleas for conformity, and the supreme necessity of maintaining the untarnished family image.

'You probably think we have treated you very badly. Well, we have,' Firdaus confessed. 'But consider our position. No family can allow one of its own to seek self-destruction without intervening. You gave us no choice. You wanted to marry a courtesan . . . all right, all right!' He held up his hand to placate his nephew. '*Aarey baba,* so she was gentle and honest, kind and loving . . . whatever you say. There must be some exceptional *tawaifs*. The fact remains that you were compromising our *izzat* and rushing yourself toward ruination.'

'Why?' Khalid Sharif demanded belligerently. 'Why all these assumptions? Wasn't she human? Is it impossible for a courtesan to love? What gives you the right to assert that family honour is more important than my happiness?'

Firdaus avoided his nephew's glare. There was a frailty in the older man's demeanour and a glimmer of sad wisdom in his eyes, as if he knew about the sham and the crookedness of a human system that preened itself on hypocrisy and managed to win in the end.

'Life does not run on love,' Firdaus reflected wistfully. 'That's the stuff for poets and novelists. It is the substance of daydreams. We all have them. Love is harmless as long as it does not kidnap you. When you realise that we live in a world full of deformities, one which seeks to hide its ugliness behind platitudes and moral righteousness, you will have matured. You will stop swinging blindly at an invisible enemy who cannot be hurt. Passions will cool and rebellion will die. We are here to help you to lose your individuality and encourage you to become dull. You must adopt our sterile views of family respectability, be responsible, work hard, have children, become a grandparent and . . . and look back with regret at what you should have done and die. It cannot be any other way.' His voice suddenly hardened with bitterness and an unforgiving condemnation of Khalid Sharif. 'Why didn't you have the courage to go off with her? Or didn't you have enough love to live on for the rest of your life? Did selfishness make you give in? Was the prospect of a life without the comforts you enjoy too daunting to consider?' He paused briefly. 'I, too, made the same mistake once. "A crime," your father called it. I fell in love with an older woman. A widow. Duty, honour, commonsense . . . they had to win. I sentenced myself to bachelorhood.'

Firdaus' revelation, coupled with the accusation of cowardice, blew down Khalid Sharif's defence of anger. Self-deception was a fatal casualty, leaving him exposed to his own cowardice. There was no space to manoeuvre. Abjectly he surrendered. His mind crash-landed to a base reality that made him feel mean and flawed.

'I wish to go back to the village,' Khalid Sharif whispered. 'I want to live by myself for some time.'

Firdaus nodded sympathetically, hating himself for acting as the cruel agent who exposed his nephew to a fundamental weakness of character. 'That will not be a problem,' he promised. 'Take as much time as you need. But when you decide to return, the past must be put aside. You will have to move forward.'

Modhunagar was like a healing chamber where Khalid Sharif struggled to recover. He fought to accept the severe limitations of social circumstances. Painfully, he began to attune his personality to the needs of the family, and drew up the parameters within which he could operate without hurting himself. Khalid Sharif spent most of his time in reflective solitude, reading voraciously and manipulating his mind to distance itself from the events of the past year. He failed in his efforts to treat *Khush Manzil* as an exotic creation of a fertile imagination. His persistently aching memories of Nazli made it impossible to brush it aside as an episode of little consequence in his life.

This is her revenge, he told himself grimly in a state of superstitious despair. There were moments when he thought he glimpsed her in the village. At times he swore he heard her voice . . . her footsteps following him as he walked in the fields. It was impossible to discipline his mind and contain her in the past. Like a dictator, unable to control his most rebellious subject, Khalid Sharif willed a vast prison deep inside himself and jailed her there, vowing that she would torment him no further. There, in the dungeon of his psyche, she languished, as he strove to become a responsible and respectable adult.

This arrangement with his past lasted only a couple of weeks until, one night, she broke loose and climbed back to the surface of his memory. Khalid Sharif gave in meekly to the turmoil of his inner world. From that point Nazli was free to roam his conscience, plucking its strings to sound a discordant crescendo of regrets whenever he became careless enough to think that the spectre of *Khush Manzil* had been dispelled.

Despite the preoccupation with his affairs in Calcutta, Khalid Sharif was alert enough to sense that the villagers kept an evasive distance from him. It was most unusual. They may have heard about *Khush Manzil*, he speculated in a moment of improbable imagining. It delighted him to be left alone. There were no territorial disputes to be sorted out. No complaints about stolen animals or nocturnal raids on orchards. Wife-beating and adulterous affairs were not reported. The problems of the village were not brought to Khalid Sharif for resolution.

His only companion was Munir who was impossible to avoid inside the house. Even when Khalid Sharif went outdoors, Munir tagged along as if he was employed as a bodyguard. The intense irritation of a hovering presence faded quickly once Khalid Sharif deduced that Munir, in his clumsy fashion, was merely demonstrating a concern for his cousin's despondent presence in Modhunagar.

Most of Khalid Sharif's evenings were taken up with Munir's outlandish stories of village gossip. A mild, absent-minded amusement was replaced by disbelief when Munir finally revealed the outrageous scandal that had left Modhunagar without a caretaker for the mosque.

The passion of the village *mullah*, Shawkat Rahim, for the young daughter of Malik Huda, the local barber, had shocked the village into an ominous conspiracy of silence. What could possibly have prompted the model man of Allah to behave in such a despicable manner was a matter of heated and violent arguments. It wasn't that the age difference between a fifty-three year old widower and a girl of seventeen made the liaison sordidly unacceptable. Such affairs and the resulting matrimonial compromises with the village's honour were not uncommon in Modhunagar. But a *mullah*, known for his gentle goodness and moderation, trampling on the trust of the entire village to satisfy his beastly carnality! *Che, che! Lojja!*

Shorom! There was unanimous condemnation and a vociferous demand for justice.

Before any punitive measures could be contemplated, the offending couple absconded.

Gossiping tongues unleashed the most lurid stories with a malicious vengeance. There was an underlying assumption behind the deadly rumours.

It was the Devil's work, of course. Or was it a wicked *djinn*? It didn't matter as long as there was a supernatural force to add a fearful dimension to the nefarious deed of Shawkat Rahim and his young whore.

Tauba! Tauba! Astakfirullah! the villagers repented. Such a monumental shame had to be purged with special prayers and the obscenity of the entire episode buried under a communal silence.

But there was such richness in the newly concocted brew of scandal that the storytellers and the song-writers could not be cajoled or threatened into anaesthetising their imaginations. The thriving oral tradition ensured that the event was treated merely as a spool of multi-coloured threads from which a variety of dazzling fabrics of the most intricate designs were spun.

The fabulists converted the *mullah* into a fox, a serpent, a wolf—anything cunning or insidious—to deliver an unambiguous moral message that a heinous crime could not escape punishment. The song-writers were more merciful. The *jarigaans* were captivatingly melancholic in their treatment of forbidden love that was doomed to a tragic finale. Since their lyrics did not condemn the transgression of certain social norms, the village singers were discouraged from public performances and strongly advised to take their talents to the city.

It was, however, the showman who suffered the most. Before the puppet show could cash in on a new story, the puppeteer was warned against any act that might lower the moral tone of Modhunagar or have a corruptive influence on children. Being a man of initiative and imagination, the puppeteer created a fairy tale in which a pious man was possessed by an evil spirit and led into sinful ways until a young woman's love saved him.

Those children, privileged enough to see the first and only performance, were enthralled by the sight of the climactic fight between the forces of good and evil. They clapped and whistled their approval of the final scene in which the ardour of two embracing puppets was fascinating enough to overcome the minor disaster of the flimsy curtains collapsing. The standing ovation was spontaneous. Unfortunately the sprinkling of elderly adults in the audience was not entirely appreciative of the show. The puppeteer was summoned to appear before the members of the newly formed council for administering morality, and ordered not to repeat the performance. To present a redemptive and happy conclusion to what was essentially the story of an evil man was unacceptable. It could only set a poor example to youngsters. As compensation, the puppeteer was given a goat, several hens, a sack of rice, *dhal*, sugar and dried chillies to prevent his family from starvation until he produced another show.

In the confusion and tension prevalent in Modhunagar, the one person who knew more than any other about the sorry affair kept himself outside the glare of suspicion cast on the creative types in the village. A chance meeting trapped him into disclosing what he really knew.

Late one night, Khalid Sharif tiptoed to the kitchen for a drink. He decided not to grope his way about in the darkness to reach the earthen pitcher resting on a ring of coir on the floor.

He lit a match.

The suddenness of the spurting flame startled the intruder who was busily filling a hessian sack with food from the meat safe. Without hesitation, Khalid Sharif pounced on the crouched figure.

Darkness enveloped the room again. Whimpering noises accompanied a brief struggle.

'Kha . . . Khalid!'

Khalid Sharif sprang back in surprise. The shock of Munir's thievery was odious and beyond comprehension. Grabbing his cousin by the shirt collar, Khalid Sharif dragged the passive culprit to the backyard. He made Munir empty the sack. There was enough food to feed a small family for several days.

'Kha . . . Khalid!' Munir trembled. 'It is for them!'

'More fairies? Have you increased Zohra's brood of winged creatures?'

Munir burst into tears of humiliated frustration. He was immune to everyone's mockery except his cousin's.

'Na . . . na! Kha . . . Khalid!' He shook his head in a vigorous denial. 'Food is for Shaw . . . Shawkat Rahim and . . . Bath . . . Bathasha Bibi.'

Munir's complicity in the sequence of events unravelled in a torrential confusion of broken sentences. Early one morning, he had stumbled across the fugitive couple hiding in the forest. Hunger and tiredness had not broken them. They were unrepentant and stubborn, with no intention of returning to Modhunagar to seek forgiveness. Munir had guided them deep into the forest with assurances of their safety. Together they made a shelter with branches and leaves.

Back in the village that night, Munir stole clothes and food for the runaway couple.

'Why did you do it?' Khalid Sharif's anger was overtaken by a curiosity about his cousin's motive. 'Why did you steal? Shawkat Rahim is not your concern!'

'Steal?' Munir squeaked, unable to understand the reason for such a serious accusation. He became belligerent and waved an index finger in a vehement denial. 'Na . . . Na! I did not steal! I . . . I am no th . . . th . . . thief! It was to help. Love needed help.' His voice changed. There was a deep note of satisfaction. 'It needed me.' He thumped his chest with immense pride.

For no apparent reason Khalid Sharif felt bitter and crestfallen. He sensed his cousin's triumphant grin. 'So you helped love, you think?'

Munir giggled with a childish pleasure. 'Beau . . . Beauti . . . Beautiful! It is all beau . . . ti . . . ful!' He bobbed his shoulders up and down as if he was being tickled. 'They loved so much!' He clapped his hands in enthusiasm. 'So brave! So bold! Khalid?'

'What?'

'I . . . can never love. Can I?'

'Why not?'

'I . . . I am too ugly.'

'Will they be safe in the forest?' Khalid Sharif asked hastily. He felt an urge to protect the couple. For a fleeting moment he imagined himself stranded in the forest, among the dense foliage, with Nazli.

'Of course!' Munir went down on his haunches and began to fill the sack again. 'Zoh . . . There are others to pro . . . protect them. I have to go now.'

Noiselessly Munir disappeared across the brick wall.

So brave. So bold. The words rubbed against Khalid Sharif's wound of failure. He ran to the wall and called Munir. His voice reverberated across the darkness and buried itself in the vast graveyard of the tropical night. He heaved himself to the top of the parapet. The sound of unseen insects and the croaking of frogs deterred him from following. He did not know his way in the forest. The darkness would engulf and disorient his sense of direction even before he reached the edge of the dense band of trees.

It was not in Khalid Sharif's nature to take chances. This was as far as he could go. Once seated on the flat hardness of the bricks, he lost the desire to go back inside. There was a seductive force in the expansive solitude of the universe. It split him open and sent his memory spiralling out of control. The dream-crossed night lacerated him with fragments of his exploded utopia. Among the *ifs* and *buts* of possibilities, he relived the sadness of dusk's uncertain minutes.

By design they were left undisturbed in the small courtyard.

She sat still without uttering a sound, her face impassible as ever. It registered no surprise or sorrow, as if she had known all along that his rash undertakings could not be seriously believed. Reluctantly, she had helped him to draw up the blueprint of a future because of the irresistible enthusiasm of his convictions. All dreams had their endings. This was the inevitable conclusion of a clumsy transgression. Despite the rigidity of her conditioning, Nazli felt a ripple of sadness for this foolishly honest and well-intentioned man. She had nothing to regret. Others in her situation would endure the aching barrenness of their lives without the brief, redemptive experience that had given her a glimpse of what might have been.

The following week she was to return to the *mahfil*. Without memories. Without yearnings. Another introduction awaited her. She was curious. Even excited. A *nawab*'s son. Educated. Rich. Good-looking. She was to feel privileged that Tabassum Begum had chosen her. Nazli reached behind her to pluck a large, red rose from one of the three bushes near the wooden bench.

He continued to talk incessantly about family loyalty, expectations and responsibilities. He would support her, he swore, and live the rest of his life as a celibate bachelor.

The tired day decided to quit and sank under the gloomy stillness of a hazy dusk.

His extravagant claims prompted a tremulous smile. She twirled the flower in her right hand.

Sharif Saheb, men rarely understand feelings the way women do.

You like the sounds of noble words and adopt them. Love. Affection. Loyalty. Trust. *In some ways the women here are like men. We use language as a tool of enchantment. Without meaning. Sometimes without intention. Don't you realise that we are taught not to feel? It doesn't always work. Occasionally the heart refuses to be sedated. But if we are to succeed for the miserable few years of our lives while the skin is taut and the sheen remains . . .*

His pleas did not draw her out of her silence. She knew that a solitary pair of eyes was watching through a chink in one of the shuttered windows. Slowly Nazli began to tear each petal in a mindless act of destruction.

The words ran out. Darkness covered him with silent accusations. There was no place to hide. He was a weakling and a cheat, the evening voice whispered. A gutless, whimpering sycophant, unable to stand up to his father. He had retreated and surrendered after a feeble resistance.

She took his hands and presented him with a gift of the torn petals.

The house had echoed with the rumble of a titanic anger the night Firdaus broke the news to Shahid Sharif.

'*Bathazeeb!* How dare he?' Shahid Sharif screamed, his voice reaching the corners of the house and sending the inmates scuttling into their rooms. 'Has he no shame? No honour? Am I cursed with a mad, immoral son? Like my sister?' In his maniacal fury he hurled the *hookah* against the wall and kicked a chair, sending it tumbling to the other side of the room.

'I have already told him what is to be done.' Firdaus made a feeble effort to placate his brother from near the door of the study.

'I shall cut out the tongue that gives sound to such profanities!' Shahid Sharif raved. 'I do not wish to see him again! Let him go to the other end of the world to live with his whore! Firdaus, this is the darkest day of my life! Oh, that I had no son! The ungrateful wretch!'

Another chair went hurtling across the room and smashed into a table.

Firdaus gulped, undecided between silence and the impotence of words. There was no knowing what other damage could be inflicted by the searing heat of his brother's wrath.

'Well? Say something!'

'*Bhai Jan* . . . *Bhai Jan!* Calm yourself. He is only a young man who does not think sometimes. We have all suffered from moments of madness when we were young. Love never agrees with reason.'

'Love!' Shahid Sharif barked, ignoring his brother's call for temperance. 'He will love the girl we want him to love! He will obey me if he has any intention of remaining a part of this family!'

Firdaus sensed a slight lessening in the intensity of his brother's rage. 'There is no need for alarm. I shall speak to him again. He shall not see her.'

'Can we be sure of that?'

'*Bhai Jan*, leave it to me. You have my word! It is best that he spends some time in the village, sorting himself out.'

Shahid Sharif grunted, his mind leaping to the ruination of Tabassum Begum.

It was several days after Khalid Sharif came across Munir in the kitchen that the self-appointed village *sardar* visited him. Tariq Mia was a robust man, well-built and unusually tall for a Bengali. His physical stature had given him the undisputed right to designate himself as the local constabulary and chief meddler in everyone's affairs, a man who was also available for bullying and damaging property if a frustrated villager sought to address a grievance. By all accounts he was well off, far more prosperous than the income from his rice crops could have made him.

They sat on the front verandah, soaking up the morning sunshine, drinking tea and eating *notun gur er shondesh*.

Tariq Mia had carefully planned the conversation. After

nearly half an hour of trite pleasantries, he thought it appropriate to raise the matter which affected the honour of the entire village.

'Sharif Saheb,' he gloated. 'They have been captured.' He looked coyly at Khalid Sharif, expecting immediate commendation. It was premature to angle for a *baksheesh*. '*I* trapped them.'

Khalid Sharif was startled. 'Who has been captured?' His voice bristled with hostility. Immediately he thought of Munir in one of his bungled attempts to lure a girl into the forest.

'The girl and that wicked man.' Tariq Mia reached for the last piece of sweetmeat on the plate with the air of a man who deserved a small reward for divulging the important information.

'Which wicked man?'

'Shawkat Rahim, Sharif Saheb!'

'Oh!' There was a mixture of relief and disappointment in Khalid Sharif's response. At least Munir had managed to stay out of trouble. But the *mullah* and the girl . . . His battered romantic impulse had fervently hoped for their undetected escape from the forest. He had given Munir a hundred rupees to help the stranded couple. 'Oh, I see.' His lack of enthusiasm was evident enough for Tariq Mia to look sharply at him.

'The honour of our village has been violated by that Devil's son!' Tariq Mia asserted savagely. 'We all looked up to him as a pious man. But he betrayed us. The entire village demands justice.'

'What kind of justice?'

'They must be tried and punished.'

'Only if they have committed a crime.'

'Sharif Saheb!' Tariq Mia stared in disbelief. City living had weakened the Sharifs into spineless, indecisive people with a blurred moral vision. They were unworthy of the respect they commanded.

'Yes?'

Tariq Mia swallowed and cleared his throat. 'I have been asked by the council to request you to hear the charges and decide on the punishment. The members have expressed the opinion that you should not be too lenient.'

'Me?' Khalid Sharif laughed at the absurdity of the proposition. 'I have no qualifications to be a judge.'

'In your father's absence you are the village head as long as you are here,' Tariq Mia said dutifully. 'It is your responsibility to see that justice is done.'

'You really don't believe that. Do you?'

'Am I to assume, Sharif Saheb, that you will not accept the responsibility?'

Tariq Mia's eagerness made Khalid Sharif hesitant. If he refused, the trial would proceed and the *mullah* was certain to be humiliated and severely punished. And for what? His so-called crime was to rip off the facade of piety that the village had erected for him. In a wild moment of impulsive honesty, he had flouted conventions and scared people by releasing his emotions and floating high with them. How madly brilliant! Khalid Sharif thought enviously. How wonderful to be able to leave the ground and soar among the eagles, just that little distance closer to Allah. If ever Shawkat Rahim faced his Maker, he could unflinchingly claim a true adherence to Divinity's most precious gift to mortals—instinct.

Khalid Sharif was dismayed by his own failure that had doomed him to the flat terrain of a family-directed life. He could only hope to look up and envisage the likes of Shawkat Rahim, with the strength of their passions and the foolish courage of their convictions, roaming the more ethereal spaces, unfettered by the impositions of moral fanaticism.

'Sharif Saheb?' Tariq Mia managed to sound patient. 'I shall be happy and honoured to do the job, if you please.' He leaned forward in anticipation.

'No,' Khalid Sharif responded, deriving a modicum of

perverse pleasure as he watched the confident smirk fade. 'I must do it. It is a family duty. I have to be responsible.'

Tariq Mia sat frigidly, confused by the mixture of authority and bitterness he perceived in Khalid Sharif. He could think of nothing that might alter the decision. The villager excused himself, bowed low and *salaamed* before heading back to report to the council.

It was rumoured that the trial was to be held in the front yard of the mosque, attended by those who wished to be present. Khalid Sharif was in no doubt that most of the village, as well as people from the outlying areas, would turn up in their best clothes, expecting a severe condemnation of the couple and a suitably austere sentence. A day of fun and fermentation of gossip.

The next day Khalid Sharif summoned Tariq Mia to convey his intention to hold a closed, informal meeting among the members of the council, the accused couple and himself, to thrash out the unfortunate affair.

There was much consternation in the village and muted expressions of anger. Men flocked to the tea shop and critically discussed the casual manner in which Khalid Sharif had chosen to deal with such a grave offence. Underlying the communal resentment was a strong feeling of deprivation. The villagers were to be denied the opportunity to participate in an issue of the utmost moral importance. The popular view was discreetly and euphemistically conveyed to Khalid Sharif by a quietly militant Tariq Mia.

Khalid Sharif remained adamant.

The new venue for the trial was to be one of the two tin-roofed classrooms that had been recently added to the school. Khalid Sharif decreed an unscheduled holiday to celebrate the end of the famine. Students were bribed to keep away from the vicinity of the school with promises of free sweetmeats the following week.

In making the necessary arrangements, Khalid Sharif met

with a singularly tedious failure. He was unable to persuade Munir to stay at home on the day of the trial. The strength of Munir's stubborn refusal surprised his cousin. Munir affirmed his right, as a member of the Sharif family, to be involved in the proceedings. Khalid Sharif compromised grudgingly. Munir could attend on the condition that he revealed nothing and sat quietly as an observer.

'No talking! Not a word. Agreed?' Khalid Sharif bullied his cousin. 'Otherwise you don't go.'

Munir nodded, murmuring vague promises of good behaviour.

On the morning of the trial they set out together on the short walk to the school. Much to Khalid Sharif's annoyance, Munir insisted on walking a step behind his cousin with a vertical index finger pressed firmly against his lips. Within minutes they reached the old *neem* tree, the abode of many a spirit and unseen beings according to Munir, which marked the corner of the narrow dirt track that turned left toward the school.

That was where the accident occurred.

Out of nowhere, as if it had been let loose by a malicious *djinn*, a huge, black bull charged around the corner and headed straight for Khalid Sharif.

The unexpected attack paralysed him into a state of defenceless inertia.

Khalid Sharif stood transfixed in the path of the bull, watching the animal rushing toward him. At that precise moment he had no thought or feeling, except a vague awareness of a quick movement from behind him.

With startling speed, Munir managed to get between the bull and its intended victim.

Munir's bare hands were no match for the rampant animal. The pointed tips of the horns burst through his fingers and gored him in the abdomen. He was carried half the length of a paddy field before being flung into a patch of wild grass.

Snorting and shaking its massive head, as if in agony, the bull continued to pound along the dirt road.

There were noises and *lathi* waving as several farmers, led by Tariq Mia, appeared in pursuit of the animal.

'It will be captured and killed, Sharif Saheb!' Tariq Mia panted, his eyes wide with terror. 'It broke loose from a farmer hitching it to a plough. *Allahar Kosom!* We beg your forgiveness!'

What Khalid Sharif was never to discover were the traces of red chilli paste mixed with ground black pepper that had been rubbed into the ulcerous wounds on the animal's flanks.

The bull was hacked to death and skinned immediately.

Munir was conscious when Khalid Sharif reached him. The front of his *kurta* was soaked in blood. He made a weak attempt to raise his head. A tremulous smile broke across the pain on his face. 'Kha . . . Khalid . . . I tried . . . I tried to save you,' he gasped. He squeezed his cousin's hand.

Khalid Sharif was shouting instructions to Tariq Mia.

'Not guil . . . guilty,' stammered Munir.

'What?' Khalid Sharif bent down near his cousin's face.

'Not . . . guil . . . guil . . . ty. Not.'

Khalid Sharif stroked Munir's head. 'Not guilty,' he confirmed in a gentle whisper. 'Not guilty.'

It was a slow journey on a bullock-drawn cart to Haripal and then by train to Calcutta.

By the time Munir was admitted to a hospital, he had lost enough blood to be in a critical state.

Shahid Sharif and his brothers arrived several hours later and used their influence to transfer Munir from the ward to a private room.

'He may have to be in hospital for some time,' a doctor warned.

'As long as it takes,' Shahid Sharif said firmly. His son had given him the details of the accident. 'Spare no costs.'

Three weeks later, when Munir was able to hobble around

on crutches, Khalid Sharif went back to Modhunagar. On the day of his arrival in Calcutta, with his injured cousin, Khalid Sharif had had the foresight to send a servant with a stern message to Tariq Mia, directing the villager to ensure that the *mullah* and the girl were not harmed or badly treated.

At the gathering in the school room, Shawkat Rahim defended himself stoutly. He regretted nothing, he said defiantly. He was human and prone to the same weaknesses as those other men who were dishonest enough to carry on clandestine affairs despite being married. He paused and looked knowingly at the villagers sitting on either side of Khalid Sharif. The men gulped and shifted uncomfortably. The chairs squeaked. The villagers stared at their feet or looked out of the windows.

The girl, hidden behind a makeshift curtain, was equally unrepentant. She loved Shawkat Rahim, Bathasha Bibi declared, for his kindness and the attention she received. She would leave the village with him if Sharif Saheb was merciful.

Fear and a self-righteous anger loosened an avalanche of fanatical arguments from the villagers. Initially their moral indignation demanded death by stoning. By early afternoon, after the *mullah* had indicated that he was privy to information which might embarrass the more prominent members of the council, the men were reluctantly prepared to settle for corporal punishment followed by permanent banishment from the village.

It was nearly dark when Khalid Sharif pronounced his judgement.

'Unhappy as some may be, it is not in my power to punish the accused,' Khalid Sharif ruled. 'What is their crime, anyway? A *mullah*, in his fifties, has fallen in love with a young girl. That isn't supposed to happen. Why not? Where is such love forbidden in Islam? It will be a catastrophic day for all of us when conventions, notions of propriety and envy thwart human feelings.' He paused awkwardly, feeling like a prime hypocrite prone to sanctimonious speeches. 'They have not hurt anyone. The girl is old enough to decide her fate. I find the couple not guilty of harming the village or violating any law. They must get married. But it up to them to live here or leave. There must be no coercion to influence their decision.'

There was an outraged silence in the room. Somewhere outside, a fox howled. For the first time in his life Khalid Sharif enjoyed the power his family commanded.

If only he could have borrowed Shawkat Rahim's courage . . .

* * *

It was nearly noon.

Angela rose determinedly from the chair. The housework could no longer be neglected. She had to vacuum the lounge, tidy the laundry and bake a batch of biscuits. But something had given way inside her. Her routine had been derailed and she didn't care. There was no guilt or any great urgency to get on with the chores. She wandered over to the sink.

Mindlessly she cast her eyes on the backyard. The window . . . she would clean the spots when she felt like it. The lethargy was a lovely sensation. No anxiety. She was free from the dictates of time.

Angela smiled contentedly.

Near the fence, Khalid Sharif had stopped raking the leaves. He was scrutinising a flower on a rose shrub.

TEN

Even in his state of agitated confusion, compounded by the pain in his arms and legs, Khalid Sharif made a concerted effort to grapple with Javed's unasked question. He didn't exactly know *why* he had intervened. He had a vague idea, one which he had no intention of divulging to his son. It would require too much explanation. Even if he tried to make it sound credible, the regrettable episode from years ago would sound far-fetched, and vulnerable to moral judgement.

The playground incident had been an impulsive act, weak but effective, without even a fleeting consideration of the likely consequences.

'Nothing to worry about,' the doctor assured Javed. 'The bruises are superficial. They look far worse than they are. The X-rays revealed no broken bones. The swellings should go down in a few days.' He turned to Khalid Sharif and placed a comforting hand on his bony shoulder. The bland smile and the gentle touch were a part of the new professionalism that demanded a more humane approach to patients. In this instance the gestures were also intended to be an effective substitute for the clinical remoteness of the words which the old man would not understand.

It was the doctor's unfounded assumption that English was not included in the patient's linguistic repertoire. He did not wish to stress the injured man any further with questions related to flexibility, movement and levels of pain. He directed the inquiries to Javed who, despite his irritability, managed a mischievous grin and translated them into Urdu for his father.

Khalid Sharif was reminded of the times he exasperated the British by refusing to answer the prosecutor's questions about seditious and treasonable activities in English. The *Angrez* magistrates, with their posh accents and supercilious manners, often resorted to dismissing the charges as a way of catching up with the more serious and provable cases that awaited trial.

Khalid Sharif firmly refused Javed's suggestion of a wheelchair and insisted on walking to the car. His calf muscles ached and the hamstrings felt sore. Outside the hospital building he reluctantly accepted his son's helping hand and limped his way to the car.

The drive home was slow, with stops at nearly every set of traffic lights which turned teasingly red as they approached the intersections.

Khalid Sharif was mildly amused by Javed's fidgety impatience with the traffic.

Don't rush life. Learn to adapt yourself to its changes of pace. Stay behind it. Let it lead you. That way you can see where it is going. Give yourself time and room to turn those sharp corners . . .

The old man continued to look ahead in contemplative silence.

Despite taking the morning off work, Javed looked frequently at his watch as if he was late for an appointment. As he stopped at the intersection, he drummed his fingers nervously on the steering wheel, waiting for the traffic to begin its sluggish crawl again. He was preoccupied with how he might respond to Theresa's unexpected overture. The note was tantalisingly brief:

Could you please call me at home in the evening some time

in the next couple of weeks? I think we should talk. I am sorry about my outburst.

Javed mustered up a well of frothy anger to prevent himself from an abject reply of surrender. Silence, he figured. A mysterious, prolonged silence that would prey on her patience. That would be an appropriate revenge—subtle, yet unambiguously insulting. He savoured the thought of her wilting by the phone as she waited in the evening's gloomy loneliness. His triumph would be her futile wait, signifying that he was beyond her temptation.

And yet . . . and yet . . . He shuddered involuntarily. The memories and the imaginings of the leaping flames in the bleakness of Melbourne's desolate winter. Those Wednesdays when he was supposedly playing squash and topping off the midweek exercise with the boys at the pub. Javed cursed himself for entertaining ideas of reconciliation. He felt a current of eagerness surging through his fingers as he imagined unhooking the bra and reaching out from behind her to cup the roundness of her breasts. It was that infernal body of hers, with the sparkle of a thousand demons between the smoothness of the avocado fleshed thighs.

The jaws of hell, he often joked as she softened like melted wax and spread herself for him.

Don't be pathetic! he chided himself.

The lights stopped him once more.

He closed his eyes to cut out the visual boredom of the line of cars in front of him. Darkness was conducive for conjuring up special memories. Strangely enough the writhing images faded, and it was their time after the bedroom romp that lingered in his mind and made him feel wretched and lonely. He missed the spicy meals and the cups of percolated coffee in front of the television before they made love again, simply as an act of greed.

The car behind honked a reminder for him to move along.

'Get stuffed!' Javed muttered under his breath. He shifted

into gear and fell behind a small truck. He stifled a yawn with the back of his hand. The pungent, lingering smell of tobacco on his fingers made him look longingly at the glove compartment. Hurriedly he had hidden the packet of cigarettes before helping his father into the car. The addictive desire for nicotine added to his irritation.

What a stupid fucking custom! he fumed, casting a quick glance at his father whose stuporous, unwavering stare at the road in front of them gave the impression of a state of mental paralysis. *An obsolete, alien convention that has no place here. And I give in to it!* Javed raged helplessly within himself, knowing that nothing could induce the courage to break the conditioning and enable him to light a cigarette in front of his father.

He turned to Khalid Sharif. A note of caution had to be sounded. 'Papa, you must never interfere in other people's affairs. It is not accepted here. You could have been very badly hurt.'

The old man remained silent. He bit his lower lip in a voiceless disagreement with his son's cautionary advice.

'They were school kids fooling around. No one was going to be hurt.'

That wasn't the way it happened. They were big boys ganging up on a younger lad. His cries were genuine howls of pain. One of the boys carried a baseball bat.

The incident had erupted quite suddenly.

Three o'clock. The playground appeared to be deserted. Khalid Sharif sat in his customary spot on the bench shaded by a gum tree. The flavour of the mango ice-cream wasn't as distinctive as he was accustomed to in Calcutta, but he still relished the treat. It had been a fulfilling morning.

The best you have, he had said. *It is for an eight-year-old boy.*

The salesperson was most helpful and had shown him the entire range of the most expensive mountain bikes with alloy wheels, Shimano gears and brakes, cotterless cranks and speedometers. The accessories would entail additional costs, the man explained sympathetically. Another grandfather willing to spend beyond his means to please his favourite grandson, he deduced. The man eyed Khalid Sharif with the acumen of a seasoned professional. There was nothing he saw to suggest an early morning's sale. An ordinary white shirt and a pair of ill-fitting, black trousers. Grey tweed jacket with a missing button and a faded, brown stain on the left lapel. Golf cap. A cheap pair of black shoes, worn and unkempt.

'Perhaps the speedometer and the odometer could be left out,' the man suggested politely.

'Everything,' Khalid Sharif insisted. 'Please add everything you have.' He knew what was likely to convert the obvious scepticism to a burst of enthusiastic efficiency. 'I shall pay the entire amount in advance.' A wad of fifty dollar notes appeared in his hand.

Khalid Sharif left specific instructions about the date, time and place of delivery.

'We cannot promise to get the bike there at that specific hour,' the man apologised. 'It will certainly be on that day.'

'Can you arrange a special delivery?'

'Yes . . . but . . .'

The salesperson had more money thrust into his hands.

'Is that enough?'

'Well, yes! I'll get you a docket.'

'I want it to be a surprise birthday present. It has to be hidden until that day,' Khalid Sharif emphasised. 'Could you please ensure that it is wrapped in plastic?'

A piercing cry penetrated the haze of reminiscing. Startled, Khalid Sharif looked around him.

A bush rustled.

His immediate impulse was to ignore his curiosity. But the fear and the plea for help, implicit in the sound, dragged Khalid Sharif to one of the lowest points in his life, on a hot day in 1947.

Calcutta was a dangerous city that year. Carelessly, it had

armed the barbaric instincts of its citizens with prejudice and given them the freedom to destroy life and property with impunity. The uncaring representatives of the tottering Raj chose to make a token show of enforcing a lawful order on a riot-torn city. The *Angrez* were too busy finalising their withdrawal to care about the land they had rapaciously plundered. India was no longer their responsibility.

For over a week the Sharifs had voluntarily imprisoned themselves behind shuttered doors and windows, listening uneasily to distant noises of mob fury, peeking through chinks to watch columns of smoke whirling in the air, eating, sleeping, arguing and playing cards. Their grave demeanours expressed their concern for the city. Park Circus was considered to be a safe area for Muslims. Close relatives had been urged by Khalid Sharif to stay in his sprawling house until the crisis was over.

The ancient animosity between Islam and Hinduism had peaked in a frenzied display of savagery. To maim and kill simply because people practised another religion became a self-righteous imperative. The injustices of history were capriciously manipulated and personalised to anaesthetise sanity and fuel tribal primitivism for territorial supremacy. Arson, looting and rape were the tangential spin-offs of religious fanaticism.

A burning Friday afternoon. Khalid Sharif had retired to his study to read *The Rise and Fall of the Roman Empire* and to contemplate the possible business opportunities likely to present themselves to Muslims in the new country to the west. The rest of the family had retired for an uneasy slumber after a modest lunch of rice, *dhal* and *bhaji*.

The privacy of his ground-floor room was a sanctum of solitude for Khalid Sharif. It was large and square-shaped, cluttered with antique furniture, books, files and *objets d'art* whose value had not been assessed.

Mounted on the white walls, stuffed buffalo and deer heads

hung among the nailed tiger skins which were a source of great pride to the men. Each animal was a victim of the predatory instinct which the Sharifs traditionally accepted as a legitimate manifestation of a desire for power. They hated uncertainty. The hunts were organised without too many doubts about the outcome. There wasn't the same degree of surety in ruining business rivals and expanding their own empire. The *shikars* were a more exhilarating form of patriarchal domination which the Sharifs wished to assert on all forms of life around them.

As he accepted more familial responsibilities, Khalid Sharif became conscious of the silent disapproval of the older men. They could not fault the thoroughness with which he conducted the business affairs of the family. But the thrilling feel of naked power, which culminated the achievements, had disappeared. He was too lenient with people. He instigated a system that enabled bankrupt rivals to retreat with some hope and dignity instead of being permanently crippled.

'It is a great weakness in his character,' his father had observed sadly, shortly before his death. To give an adversary the opportunity to survive also provided a platform for launching a future revenge against the Sharifs.

The study was a well-lit room with large, western facing windows overlooking the property's boundary wall. A narrow, cemented path, which curved and broadened in front of the main entrance, separated the wall from the side of the house. After returning from work, it was customary for Khalid Sharif to take a leisurely bath, drink several cups of tea and retire to the study. With a stoical resignation he spent the early part of the evening with paperwork related to business matters. He brightened visibly during dinner and spent some time in his wife's company, pretending to take an interest in the domestic life and general gossip which were an integral part of Jahan Ara's day.

Khalid Sharif was rarely rude or abrupt with his wife. He

conveyed the impression that whatever she had to say was of the utmost importance, warranting his undivided attention. His ability to remember even the most trivial of domestic details with an unflagging patience convinced outsiders that Jahan Ara was the pivotal factor in his life, loved and esteemed beyond measure by a devoted husband. Khalid Sharif was a spendthrift where she was concerned. His extravagance with gifts and money elicited the opinion that she was a fortunate woman. It was impossible for friends and family members to deduce that his generosity was a form of compensation for the tormenting guilt of being an unloving husband.

The marriage was an obligation he had fulfilled as an intrinsic part of his familial responsibility, but there was no love or joy or even moments of intense pain to define his relationship with Jahan Ara. It was legalised cohabitation devoid of emotions. Khalid Sharif thought of himself as a dry well—dark, deep and empty. A redundant presence. His caring attention to his wife flowed from his sense of righteousness which sensitised him to her state of innocent happiness within the framework of an arranged marriage. She demanded nothing from him. Her contentment, circumscribed by the unchallenged domestic authority she established in her new house during the first year of their marriage, contrasted sharply with Khalid Sharif's muted dissatisfaction with the predictability of the course of life that had been determined for him. His life was not for him to steer and control. As the children came along, he wondered if the exclusive purpose of existence was to live for others and perpetuate a harsh self-denial for the sake of family cohesion.

As an established practice, Khalid Sharif was able to slip back to the study for a few hours after dinner. Behind the locked door he shed the mask of calm rationality. This was a precious sliver of time when he was able to turn to the wisdom of great writers who stimulated him to reflect on the vagaries of a life that had mercilessly torn apart his feelings, and yet continued to grace him with all the visible trappings of prosperity.

The communal riots paralysed Calcutta and closed shops and businesses indefinitely. Compelled to stay at home, Khalid Sharif indulged himself in the luxury of free afternoons when he could embrace solitude, instead of being dragged into noisy and tedious transactions over tea and sweetmeats. He found the unexpected respite extremely agreeable.

On this particular Friday he read for almost an hour before a heat-induced drowsiness tempted him to lie down on a straw mat that was spread on the mosaic floor. He was weary.

The lunchtime chatter had incensed him into an uncharacteristically vitriolic outburst. Ramazan was due to begin shortly. There was a state of panic about the scarcity of food which threatened to doom the holy month into a prolonged period of joyless austerity.

Everyone had an opinion about how the difficulties could be overcome. The babble peaked to such an intolerable level of self-concern that Khalid Sharif felt an overwhelming necessity to express himself on their myopic views.

'Ramazan is a time for moderation and restraint. It is not an invitation to gluttony,' he said in a tone of exasperated sternness.

A silence of sulky indignation settled over the table.

'We eat far too much between the hours of fasting,' Khalid Sharif observed. 'The kitchen is busy all day preparing for *Iftari* and then dinner. And as if that is not enough, we make it a virtue to wake up before dawn, cook again and eat *Sehri*. More money is spent on food during Ramazan than at any other time during the year. We are supposed to be exercising self-discipline and striving for righteousness. Do we ever consciously think about the significance of the holy month? That is asking for too much, isn't it? But then, thinking on a full belly is an impossibility.'

Without waiting for a reaction, Khalid Sharif pushed back his chair and left the table. His stinging rebuke sparked off a heated argument about a lifestyle that might be compatible with the religious ethos of Ramazan. There was a self-defensive agreement that Khalid Sharif had been unfair in his condemnation of the family.

'Were *Bhai Jan* alive, he would be saddened to see his son being so uncharitable to his family,' Anwar huffed. 'There is a strange bitterness that prevents Khalid from appreciating our family strengths.'

'The strength to hurt people,' Firdaus murmured under his breath as the others voiced their agreement with Anwar.

Khalid Sharif was aware of the dim noises in the distance. Fanned by hatred, chaos was engulfing Calcutta. Drowsiness endowed him with wings. He migrated to another land in another dimension of time.

The pattering of playful feet. *Ghungrus* jingled to drown out the sound of the muezzin's sombre call for prayer.

The distraction of vendors and the gaudy colours in the bazaar.

Candles and lamps illuminated the past that Tabassum Begum insisted could be lived as the present.

Even the aromas of rosewater and saffron were as real as though he was inside *Khush Manzil*.

He had meant to go back . . . just for a glimpse from the outside. Stand under the shuttered windows, just as he had done every day for a month that year.

His eyelids snapped open. He felt contrite. Ruefully Khalid Sharif recalled his testy diatribe against the family's unthinking self-indulgence.

His own behaviour had been infinitely worse during the holy month in 1943.

Tabassum Begum's announcement came as an unexpected blow. Its implications plummeted Khalid Sharif into an abyss of depression.

He was enjoying the fierce argument between Nur Mohammad and Rafi Murtaza. Both the elderly men had managed to attract Tabassum Begum's attention during the evening.

Nur Mohammad had been particularly chirpy and hopeful since Tabassum Begum chose to sit beside him during a sequence of Ghalib's *ghazals,* sung with a haunting pathos by Munni Bai. As one of the courtesans in her forties, age had made Munni Bai professionally redundant. She was relegated to a *haveli* and assigned to domestic work. It was her singing voice which frequently brought her back to the *mahfils*. When she sang, men leaned back on their bolsters and refrained from conversation. In *Khush Manzil*, Munni Bai was the only person who had the temerity to defy the mistress of the house. Despite Tabassum Begum's pleas, Munni Bai made no effort to make herself attractive. She looked haggard and much older than her age, but her voice . . . what a voice! It seduced men's imaginations and caressed their loins.

If only she was young and pretty as she was once! the men lamented.

Munni Bai's love songs made them melancholy and full of drunken sentiments.

Khuda key Qasam! *I would have given up everything and married her!*

Ama yar! *Imagine a wife who could sing like that every night! A good cook too, from what I hear.*

Worth all the fortune and the reputation in the world!

Munni Bai heard snatches of such careless dialogue and scorned their insincerity.

'Men!' she was known to have said once. 'They deserve to be treated as play things. Women should hold them in the palm of a hand and listen to their pitiful lies. Once the amusement is over, they should be slipped over the edge of the fingers.'

Eyes closed and his head swaying sideways in appreciation

of the singing, Nur Mohammad listened to Ghalib's lyrics, his mind formulating a bold strategy.

The period of joy was all too brief like
  the dance of a slaughtered bird.
It was not commensurate with the extent
  of my desires . . .

'*Wuh! Wuh! Bohath Khoob!*' Nur Mohammad called, and casually slipped an arm around Tabassum Begum's waist. Cautiously, his fingers began to knead the rounded flesh on her hips. She did not flinch or move away. Passion flared in him like a stray ember on a stack of dry hay. His breathing became laboured and noisy. He leaned toward her and rested his chin lightly on her shoulder. A sliver of pink darted out from his mouth like a startled lizard but failed to make contact with the back of her neck. Visually, he measured the distance and moved his face closer. The tip of his tongue slathered his lips with saliva. Her bejewelled ear was a more achievable target. His arm tightened around her waist. But before he could commit his potent facial arsenal to a quick attack intended to conquer with surprise and passion, he felt a sharp pain in his ribs. He withdrew his hand in an immediate retreat. His head lolled to one side and he gasped for air.

'*Maaf key jeah*, Mohammad Saheb!' Tabassum Begum apologised with a gracious smile. She withdrew her elbow which had rammed into him like a solid tree trunk battering the front gate of a fortress in a medieval battle. Solicitously she stroked the back of his neck as he coughed and spluttered into a spittoon an alert servant brought to him.

Tabassum Begum signalled for a pitcher of water. A number of concerned young women surrounded Nur Mohammad and began to fuss over him. Tabassum Begum slipped away to the far end of the *takht* where Rafi Murtaza's fury had been whipped up like a monsoonal storm, as he watched Nur Mohammad's surreptitious attempt to ingratiate himself with the mistress of *Khush Manzil*.

'Murtaza Saheb!' Tabassum Begum extended her hands to him. The promise in her voice coaxed away his anger.

She smiled coyly.

Rafi Murtaza slid to one side to make room for her. He felt alert and virile.

By the Grace of Allah! Maybe tonight . . . he hoped. His legs twitched in anticipation.

Later that night, Nur Mohammad and Rafi Murtaza shared a *thal* of *sanchi paan* and a *hookah* in a mutual but guarded sympathy of failed objectives. They eyed Tabassum Begum with a venomous hatred, heaping abuses and curses on her.

'May her breasts become as sour as unripe tamarind!'

'The worms shall nibble those unkissed lips!'

'May her pubic hair turn to fish hooks!'

'Cheap flirt!'

'Bitch!'

On the other side of the room, Tabassum Begum was engrossed in a conversation with a group of newcomers.

Five months after the initiation in *Khush Manzil*, Khalid Sharif was honoured with the privilege of a place with the *hopelessly permanent*, the phrase affectionately used for the rich, old patrons of Tabassum Begum's house.

Khalid Sharif was unable to figure out the exact nature of their relationship with the inmates of *Khush Manzil*.

'And the women?' he asked Nazli. 'Surely they don't have to . . . with them?'

She laughed at the incredulity in his voice. 'Very rarely, Sharif Saheb. By the time the night is over, they are too drunk for anything but sleep.'

'Then why do they come here?'

'To talk and eat, drink and listen to music. Recite poetry. Watch the dancing. But most of all to remember, as you may some day in another house when you are very rich and no longer young.'

The wistfulness in her voice made him suspicious. 'Remember? I have no desire to languish in the past.' He grasped her hand and raised it to his lips. 'It is the present I live for . . . and the future.'

'Have you read Zauq's poetry, Sharif Saheb?'

He shook his head in a forthright admission of his literary limitations. Khalid Sharif was no longer embarrassed by his ignorance of Urdu literature. 'But I am reading Mir and Ghalib.'

Nazli smiled gravely and stroked his hand. She whispered hoarsely,

The memory of youthful days in old age
Is like the memory of a vanished dream.

Consistent with a youthful arrogance that spurned anything even minutely seared by mortality, Khalid Sharif's contempt for the old men sprang from the rumours and jokes about their waning sexuality. A disdainful aloofness characterised his conversations with them. That attitude changed markedly on the first night he was honoured with a place on the *takht* to reward his excellent progress. Khalid Sharif's knowledge of Islamic history and literature of India had improved significantly, and he began to speak Urdu without the obvious traces of Calcuttan colloquialisms.

'Learn from them, Sharif Saheb!' Tabassum Begum advised him. 'They are cultured men, even if they do not behave with the civility one expects from such people.'

On this occasion of thwarted intensions and unfulfilled desires, Khalid Sharif joined the two irascible old men as their uneasy truce began to sag under the weight of an argument about the relative merits of the two great rival cities, Delhi and Lucknow, and their contribution to Urdu poetry.

'The essence of great poetry is its language. Agreed?' Nur Mohammad, his face flushed and eyes glazed with the influence of wine, leaned forward belligerently in an effort to intimidate Rafi Murtaza into a tame acquiescence. 'The more refined the language, the more sublime the art. Hah *Bhai*?'

'The ultimate refinement of Urdu was, of course, achieved in Lucknow,' Rafi Murtaza responded cockily and called for more wine.

'*Bakwaas!*' Nur Mohammad slapped his thighs irritably. 'Rafi Murtaza, your observation is as weak as your erections! It is commonly known among scholars that the dialect, *Urdu-e-Mu'alla*, was specially developed for literary purposes under the guidance of Arzu in Delhi.'

'Who later migrated to Lucknow, worked and died there!' Rafi Murtaza was more interested in the wine than in Nur Mohammad's attempts to establish the cultural superiority of Delhi over Lucknow.

'*Ama yar!* All the great poets—Sauda, Mir and Dard—matured their art in Delhi!' Nur Mohammad's voice reached the high-pitched shriek of a whorling eagle sensing a vulnerable prey. He spilled more wine on his wet, stained *kurta*.

'And where did the poets go after Delhi was sacked in 1756? Where did the courtesans learn and improve their professional skills? Where did the *thumri* develop? *Bolyeh jeh?* Where? Hah? Where?' Rafi Murtaza waved a silver goblet in a wide arc. The linen *dastarkhwan* was plattered with drops of scarlet. In an act of mean-spirited triumph, he emptied the goblet over Nur Mohammad's head. 'Lucknow! That's where!'

Nur Mohammad screamed several obscenities and grabbed his walking stick. He swung wildly at Rafi Murtaza. Male servants appeared promptly to restrain the men. A wet towel was thrust into Rafi Murtaza's face and held there with some force. Without undue haste, he was led away, struggling and mouthing muffled abuses.

Nur Mohammad apprehended this to be a victory. In a moment of inebriated recklessness, he tore off his *kurta* and began a frenzied dance of triumph. Despite their training in handling such crises, the dancing girls panicked and ran off the floor as Nur Mohammad headed in their direction. The amused musicians, who had stopped to watch, were exhorted to play.

Led by my love for her, I decided to forgo
   the promised houri *in heaven.*
Mark the beginning of this happy-ending
   love affair.

Nur Mohammad wailed out of tune, blowing noisy kisses in the direction of the departing girls.

The restrained titter of merriment burst into a chorus of wild laughter.

Tabassum Begum was alarmed. That the dignity of an evening's gathering should be wrecked by an odiously vulgar display of drunkenness was a poor example for the novices, and bad publicity for *Khush Manzil*. It would tarnish the reputation of the house. She was angered by the exuberant enjoyment of Nur Mohammad's antics.

She stood up and clapped her hands. The chatter died down.

There was only one voice to be heard.

'*Na thein dein thah, na thein dein thah, na thein dein thah* . . .' Indifferent to the quietness around him, Nur Mohammad urged the *tabalchi* to continue playing.

'Mohammad Saheb!' Tabassum Begum's voice rolled over the uneasy silence like the boom of thunder splitting the night sky.

Unsteadily Nur Mohammad turned. For a moment his face reflected a stuporous bewilderment. Then, as he identified her voice in the swirling blur of images around him, his face cracked into a lecherous, open-mouthed smile. Waving the goblet over his head and thrusting his hips back and forth in a blatantly vulgar manner, Nur Mohammad lurched forward toward Tabassum Begum.

'Yes, my love-starved *koel*?' he slurred. 'Everything . . .' His eyelids twitched as he tried to wink at her. '*Everything* I possess is at your service.'

The ripple of suppressed giggles made Nur Mohammad feel popular with the men in the room. His bony frame was racked by a fiendish laughter.

Tabassum Begum inhaled deeply, her distress evident in the titanic heave of her bosom.

But when she spoke again, her tone was mellifluous and her voice without a shudder of anger. 'Mohammad Saheb!' Tabassum Begum looked at Rangeela standing near a side door. 'May I request a few minutes of silence for an important announcement?'

'We are to be lovers!' Nur Mohammad boasted.

Rangeela, accompanied by three servants, swiftly crossed the floor. They lifted Nur Mohammad and headed for the door.

'Unhand me, filthy defilers!' Nur Mohammad shouted, swinging his legs in protest. 'Only women may touch me! Save me, oh light of my heart . . . *Na thein dein thah, na thein dein thah, na thein dein . . .*'

A door slammed.

Tabassum Begum beamed with satisfaction. 'Esteemed guests, as you know . . .' She paused as a howl of pain, followed by the thud of a fall, interrupted her. 'As you all know,' she began again, 'the holy month of fasting begins next week. It is the established custom of this house that during Ramazan we cease all entertainment and *Khush Manzil* is closed to visitors. It is a time for fasting, prayers and charity work. Repairs and renovations are carried out.' Her voice assumed an uncompromising sternness. 'Under no circumstances are guests allowed access to this house during this period.' She looked around the room to ensure that her unwritten decree was understood by all those who were present. 'We shall, *inshallah*, meet again three days after *Eid-ul-Fitr* at a special celebratory dinner followed by a *mushaira* where poets, musicians and dancers from Delhi and Lucknow will honour us with their presence.' She named a few of the guest artists. 'An entertainment fit for royalty! Until then, *Khuda Hafiz!*'

Khalid Sharif's immediate and horrified response was to seek an assurance from Nazli that an exception could be made for him.

'There are no exceptions,' she said with a resigned firmness. 'Begum Saheba is our fate. It is pointless to defy her.'

Nazli's unruffled acceptance of their impending separation upset him even further. He had not ventured to contemplate the possibility that Nazli's view of their relationship could be, in any sense, incompatible with his.

'I shall ask Tabassum Begum,' Khalid Sharif resolved glibly. 'I must see you! Every day, if possible.'

He was still distraught, but hopeful, the next day when he sought the mistress of *Khush Manzil*.

Tabassum Begum welcomed him into the sitting room of her private chamber. She listened attentively, without interrupting. Khalid Sharif's impassioned plea for an exemption was met with a patient silence. Had he been alert and observant, instead of being wrapped up in his solitary obsession, he may have detected a flicker of compassionate understanding in her face. She was experienced and wise enough to know that youthful passions invariably managed to find reckless ways of circumventing rules, regardless of their stringency. Inwardly, Tabassum Begum allowed herself the rare indulgence of grieving for a young man who had ignored her advice and entangled himself in the sticky strands of a dangerous illusion. But her familiarity with men told her that any endeavour to make them relinquish their impossible and ephemeral dreams only strengthened their stubbornness.

'I cautioned you, didn't I, Sharif Saheb, not to be too intimate with us?' she said softly, with barely a hint of admonishment in her voice. 'We are like shadows that you can see but never catch and call your own. I cannot give you permission to come here. We need the time to ourselves to drop the masks, take off the make-up and survey our haggard lives. The music, the dancing and laughter . . . everything that we offer are passing acts to furnish your illusions. But the anguish and the tears, which you rarely see, are real. Once in a while they need to be fully released in thick streams instead of trickles. We are all bruised women here, and our weeping is an affirmation of our humanity. It gives us the will to live. We take a month off to repair our dignities and open the doors and windows to our locked dreams. Yes, we too have dreams, Sharif Saheb. They are common and boring—of husbands and children, houses and belongings.' There was a wistful sheen in her eyes as if she was viewing a distant world. 'We can only dream of all that is easily attainable for most women. You do not understand, Sharif Saheb?' She laughed bitterly. 'Men seldom do. They do not understand how mundane matters can become the focal point of our dreams.'

He looked at her without flinching, unable to speak of his own hurt and the wondrous uncertainties of the rides on those huge waves of feelings. The buffetings of love, passions and the associated pains. The falls and the desire to keep trying, even if Nazli's elusiveness continued to thwart and alarm him.

I do not know how to love. That was as much as she would say. He felt wretched and inadequate. But that wasn't enough to allow despair to overwhelm him. With time her affection would transform into . . . He couldn't give up. He had to be with her . . . *Every day, Begum Saheba! Can't you see that?*

He left quietly after being disarmed by Tabassum Begum's words. Khalid Sharif was sorely troubled by his incomplete understanding of life . . . love, desires, contentment . . . everything that mattered.

He kept away from Nazli, but every day of the holy month he delivered a basket of flowers and sweetmeats to *Khush Manzil* shortly before *Iftari*.

Firdaus questioned his nephew about the bills at the end of the month.

'That is an extraordinary amount of money you have spent in such a short time,' he commented dryly, without expecting a plausible explanation. 'There is a famine in Bengal, you know.'

Khalid Sharif looked thoughtful. 'There is a hefty price to be paid for such a high quality education,' he said laconically.

Khalid Sharif reacted slowly. The pounding on the window was alien to the sound pattern of his reveries about *Khush Manzil*. The wild shouting beyond the rattling window was fearfully close.

'Gentleness has disappeared from the world,' he murmured to himself. He was weary of the dark reality of India's changing political order. It was now like a human slaughterhouse—indifferent, mechanical and savage in the way it systematically sought the extinction of life.

Irritably he flung open the latticed, wooden shutters. The blinding light of the molten afternoon spilled into the room with a hurtful vitality, compelling him to throw a protective hand over his eyes. The moaning was not in his imagination. He stepped back into the shade of the room, feeling dizzy. Khalid Sharif rubbed his eyes with the knuckles of his hands. The fuzzy whiteness crystallised itself into a distinguishable shape.

A battered, bloody face confronted him. Red stained hands clutched the iron grills with a life-seeking desperation.

Khalid Sharif shook his head vigorously.

The apparition did not disappear.

The ghostly face of a white man destined to fade into India's past.

An *Angrez*, he concluded. One of those who had pillaged, exploited, hated and now divided a land caught in an uncontrollable turmoil.

A hand slipped between the grills and attempted to reach him in a silent plea for help.

Khalid Sharif stood unmoved. In his mind he became sanctimoniously unforgiving as he piled the sins of history on this unknown man. Somewhere inside him dark holes cracked open and primordial forces minced and swallowed compassion.

The vengeful noises were now below the window.

The darkness inside him was an irrepressible force, rushing and roaring, twisting judgement and banishing conscience.

The Englishman's hand inched a little further inside the room. The outstretched fingers wriggled like the legs of a scuttling spider and then stiffened into a despairing stillness.

The whisper was barely audible. 'Help. Please help.'

Khalid Sharif stepped back, retreating further into the shelter of his prejudices. He turned his back to the window and hurried to the door.

The piercing cries of triumphant hunters invaded the room.

Khalid Sharif hesitated, unable to resist a backward glance. He beheld the rawness of fear swimming in the orbs of grey. The mouth was open in a silent cry of disbelief against a fate that had singled him out to pay for the greed and foolishness of those who had rarely left the distant island.

The first stab of guilt spun him around. It was too late to convert regret into any kind of meaningful action.

The face slid down slowly. The hands clung desperately to the grills.

A scream of terror. Then he was gone.

Khalid Sharif ran to the window. He winced as he recognised the dull, thudding noises and the communal grunts of approval. The side lane was crammed with people intoxicated with violence. Men and young boys stood on the wall, their hands raised above their heads to herald a victory. They saluted Khalid Sharif and shouted their appreciation of his complicity in the savage destruction of life.

'We can hate just as fiercely!' someone yelled.

Those in the lane brandished *lathis*, butcher's knives, axes and roughly made spears.

Khalid Sharif grabbed the bars and strained to prise them apart. It was an abortive, exhaustive effort. He pressed his face against the rods for a better view of what was happening below. The hot iron burned his hands and singed parts of his face. His shout, imploring restraint, was lost in the din below.

The injured Englishman was nowhere to be seen.

After the crowd had dispersed and the lane was empty, Khalid Sharif became conscious of the pain in his face and hands. He had to apply considerable strength before he was able to uncoil his fingers from around the grills. His hands were puffed and the palms were streaked with red welts. His face was a gigantic throb, sweaty and swollen.

He stared at the window in wonderment as if it was a magical opening through which he had seen the enactment of an unhappy tale about the human condition. The rectangular blur appeared to be on fire. Twisting sheets of orange, diffused with an azure blue and a translucent white, fluttered in the light breeze that fanned the heat. Voices murmured the sadness of songs that belonged to another life. Tom-toms. Out of control. Pounding unambiguous messages of despair.

The Englishman's last look of condemnation.

Gradually they faded away. Like experiences . . . like life itself. He felt an affinity with the visible blankness of an inert sky. He was no more than a prisoner, convicted for his failures, destined to a harshly limited perception of the world through a jail window. Perhaps it was safer this way. People with his failings were an additional hazard to a dangerous world bereft of heroism.

Khalid Sharif sat down wearily on the chair behind the study table. A wall clock chimed the passage of another hour. Soon he would be summoned for afternoon tea. The rest of the house would stir after a disturbed sleep. They would discuss the noises and express their concerns.

Tea and biscuits. Card games. Ignorance about a life lost.

He would bear the secret.

The warm stickiness of his palms shuttered his face.

In the darkness the monsters appeared.

They were nearly home. Javed continued to harp on the dangers his father had invited with his unnecessary intervention.

'It wasn't any of your concern, Papa.' Javed was being patronisingly patient. 'They were kids. Probably carrying on an argument begun in school. You might have made it a lot worse.'

'It had to be done,' Khalid Sharif growled, indifferent to his son's nagging. 'I had to do something. I had to . . .'

Javed looked sharply at his father, unable to understand the fierce stubbornness with which the old man defended his act of rashness. Age had added disagreeable dimensions to his father's character. Javed felt the helplessness of distance. They were so far apart—they stood on opposite shores of the same river, with no means of crossing.

Javed wished he could talk openly to his father about the growing complications of middle-age, and seek some parental comfort. There was nothing very clear or certain about his life any more. The threat of transience hung over everything he contemplated. Too many prickly questions to stumble over. Doubts. Those faint whispers of mortality. Signs of decay. Hell! There was a fair bit to go yet. He was only in his forties. Little comfort there. The ageing process was relentless. It marched carelessly to time's tune, never pausing for a brief respite. He had to find a central purpose. New challenges. Stagnation induced despair. What else was there? More investments, another block of land, change of jobs, Theresa . . . A staleness shrouded the gamut of possibilities.

Even if I could talk to him, Papa wouldn't understand, Javed thought despondently. *He has led a dreary, conflict-free existence. Work, home, books, meals and conversation . . . financial security, an adaptable wife without professional ambitions or striving to be her husband's equal. His life has been without the extremes of emotions, dedicated to work and family. Quiet. Strong. His virtue has been his dependability. Is that what makes him boring? What can he look back on to give his life some distinctive character? Seventy-six years . . . that's . . . nine hundred and twelve months . . . more than twenty-seven thousand days. Of what? Does that haunt him? Is that why he has become so difficult? Does he look back and see his life as no more than a pile of cold ashes? Is he now rebelling against the flat greyness of his past? A belated, desperate flicker of a life without any high points of remembrance? He was a kind husband and a generous father . . . roles I find difficult to play. To be a good husband and father . . . whatever 'good' implies . . . Is that all one should seek?*

To Javed's surprise, Shanaz's car was in the driveway. She came out to greet them.

'I took off for a few hours,' she said, extending a supporting hand to her father-in-law. 'I am so glad you are all right, Papa!' Impulsively, she hugged him.

Khalid Sharif grunted non-committally. Secretly, he was touched that Shanaz was considerate enough to return home for him. He leaned on Javed and grasped Shanaz's hand as they walked to the front door.

'Zareen phoned from school. Mrs Barrett also rang to ask if she could come over later to see you,' Shanaz said brightly. 'Your little friend came around twice yesterday evening to ask about you.'

Alone in his room, Khalid Sharif read the card and admired the flowers from his grandchildren. He luxuriated in an aura of self-importance. The expressions of concern alleviated the chill of estrangement. The door had opened. He was no longer on the street, looking in on his son's family through a window.

'It could have been worse!'

Javed's booming voice carried through into Khalid Sharif's room.

'Much worse.'

After a brief chat and cups of tea with Khalid Sharif, both Javed and Shanaz left the house.

The old man hobbled to the phone in the kitchen, pausing frequently to rest his legs.

He had to tell Angela how it happened. He was apprehensive that she, too, would think his involvement in attempting to break up the quarrel was injudicious. The incident sounded quite ridiculous. A self-inflicted injury caused by a loss of balance as he sought to discover what was happening behind the bush. As he reached the boys, Khalid Sharif stumbled, lost his footing and crashed to the ground. The startled offenders panicked and fled.

Khalid Sharif brooded over the comments Javed had made in the car.

'No regrets!' he muttered absent-mindedly as he lifted the receiver. 'No regrets . . . Had to be done.'

It was only then that it occurred to him he had forgotten the phone number so assiduously memorised some weeks before.

ELEVEN

The bristles of the brush furrowed smoothly through the shampooed hair, layering the streaks of silver into an orderly prominence.

The effect was entirely undesirable. Parts of Javed's scalp became visible, like random clearings in a forest. He frowned and picked up the tweezers. The few unruly strands of white targeted themselves for removal.

Javed stopped in mid-sentence, leaning closer to the mirror.

Shanaz waited, smoothing over a quiver of irritation with the acquired patience of maturity. These egotistical rituals of her husband's were no longer amusing. Javed's obsession with the declining symptoms of middle age often manifested itself in comically futile endeavours to rid himself of the corrosive effects of mortality. The expensive pair of tweezers, the best that was available at the chemist, was the latest aid in a variety of trials intended to belie the unflattering reality of his increasingly haggard appearance.

Javed was still smarting over the comment he had overheard in the kitchen the previous day. There was no intentional malice in Asif's thoughtless reference to his father as *custard guts*, but its effect was to prompt Javed into a renewed determination to eat less, cut down on the beer and increase the number of sit-ups he endured every morning. He continually reminded himself that he was fit enough for vigorous games of squash, even if he was unable to control the sag and the increasing curvature of his belly.

The rebellious offenders extracted, Javed sat back on the stool and grunted with satisfaction.

It was a cue for Shanaz to pick up the conversation again. She looked at her watch. There was enough time before her presence in the kitchen would become necessary. The grabbing, elbowing and spillages invariably ignited the first of the morning's arguments. Ever since Shanaz had strictly allocated a maximum amount of time for the occupancy of the second bathroom for each of the children, the arena for the morning's hostility over individual rights had shifted to the kitchen.

'He hasn't quite reached the point where you can make decisions for him and expect an indifferent acceptance,' Shanaz observed guardedly, concerned about Javed's newly found fixation with his father's care.

'He is impossible,' Javed muttered, turning his head sideways to examine his face with gently probing fingers. The smoothness of the relatively unwrinkled skin was consoling. The jowls sagged like empty leather pouches, and there was that little extra flesh on the cheeks, but . . . all things considered . . . not bad . . . not bad at all. 'I don't know what he wants. I doubt if he is clear about it in his own mind.'

'He has already said he wants to go back,' Shanaz reminded her husband sharply, as she fumbled to tie a knot in the silk scarf around her neck. 'He is certainly not confused about that.' She was weary of Javed's tendency to plunge into impetuous commitments and then lament the burden of their consequences.

Javed turned to look at his wife as though she was being as unreasonable as his father. 'Yes, but he refuses to live in Calcutta with any of his daughters! He doesn't even want to be there on his own. He has this crazy idea of living in that dilapidated, old house in the village. For God's sake! How impractical can he be? Can you imagine living with Munir *Chacha*? Papa doesn't even think there is anything abnormal about his cousin!'

'Has it ever occurred to you that it may not always be necessary to view life as a practical proposition, especially at his age?' Shanaz retorted coldly, resentful of Javed's assumption that he had the prerogative to make all the vital familial decisions. His change of mind in asking Khalid Sharif to apply for permanent residence was a capricious gesture, articulated without seeking her opinion.

'I had to,' Javed explained later. 'It hit me the day I brought him back from hospital. He looked frail and vulnerable, struggling . . . really struggling with life. I cannot abandon him. I knew you wouldn't mind.'

Shanaz did mind, having experienced her father-in-law's disapproval—his fastidiousness with the food, the whining about his washed clothes being piled on the bed, unironed, his resentment and increasingly bitter complaints about the Polish cleaning lady who rolled through the house like an unstoppable tank, driving him to various corners, and, above all, his silent deprecation of their fractured family life. Conversely, he was also kind, gentle, generous and, at times, humorous in his conversations. Shanaz liked his strong spirit of independence that irked Javed. She had made a special effort to condition herself to his presence for a few months; but beyond the duration of his visit . . . that was a prospect to be actively discouraged. The extra work that would entail if he migrated and moved in with them! How would they manage when his health deteriorated? Javed's initial enthusiasm about looking after his father would wilt and disappear behind the excuse *I have too much to do* . . . and his long working days would stretch into the evenings. His promises to help with the housework were destined to shrivel into a verbal trickle of concern and sympathy for her.

No, she couldn't possibly manage her father-in-law as well

as her family and professional life. It sounded selfish. It *was* selfish. But that was the regrettable reality of modern living— a high standard of sanitised comfort, gadgets and possessions, earned with very hard work and stress, for oneself.

Javed was too preoccupied with the indignation, prompted by Khalid Sharif's curt rejection of his generous offer, to feel the sting of Shanaz's baited comment.

'That house in Modhunagar!' He shook his head disparagingly. 'You should see it! A real museum piece. It has no electricity or running water. No proper bathroom. There isn't a single, basic facility one has the right to expect,' Javed droned on in a low monotone. 'There isn't a hospital within a reasonable distance, and not a doctor or a dentist in case of an emergency. Plenty of quacks! Cunning peasants pedalling their amulets, charms, smelly herbal medicine and packaged prayers.' He threw up his hands in exasperation. 'And then there is Munir *Chacha*! Imagine spending the rest of your life in the company of a lunatic who tries to screw every female in sight and thinks that there are supernatural creatures in the forest. It's no way . . . no bloody way to live!'

Javed worked himself up to a state of extreme agitation as he recalled the previous evening's conversation with his father. He had taken Khalid Sharif out for dinner to one of those indistinctive Indian restaurants which offered a cuisine not quite compatible with the grandeur of its name. SHAHENSHAH was wedged between a men's clothing shop, enjoying a moderate success with its closing down sale, and a second-hand bookshop whose elderly proprietor was prone to be genuinely surprised when anyone actually bought a book from him.

On the outside the restaurant was like an ageing, gaudily made-up whore, desperate to attract attention with a splash of white and pink neon lights on the wide, full length window. An enlarged copy of the menu was stuck with blu-tack and displayed on the glass pane under one of the neon lights. On offer was a variety of meat and fish dishes, mostly cooked in a tandoor by a chef reputedly from a deluxe hotel in New Delhi. Neither the name of the chef nor that of the hotel was mentioned in the handwritten blurb on the A3 papers.

Except for a middle-aged couple, munching *pappadams* and sipping white wine, the restaurant was deserted when the Sharifs walked in. Inside it was dim and dreary. A dusty wooden statue of Ganesh, partly sheltered by the limp leaves of a rubber plant in an earthenware pot, greeted them near the entrance. The walls, covered with dark blue paper imprinted with black paisleys, added to the murkiness of the room. The wallpaper had peeled off in several spots, and behind the cheaply framed batik prints depicting Hindu deities in various phases of conflict with the forces of evil, there was probably more evidence of neglect and decay. The harsh effect of the spartan wooden chairs was partly offset by the spotless, white tablecloths which hung over the sides of the rectangular tables like loose-fitting clothes intended to hide unattractive body shapes. The restaurant was capable of accommodating perhaps forty or fifty people, although its maximum capacity had rarely been tested in the seven years of its unspectacular existence.

A man in dark trousers, white shirt and a black bow tie glided in like a doleful apparition from the depths of a forbidden territory. The frown on his sebaceous face cracked into a welcoming smile as he recognised Javed.

'Sharma!' Javed greeted him with a perfunctory handshake. 'It's been ages! How are you? This is my father.'

'*Namaste*, Sharif *jeh*! Welcome to my humble restaurant.' Sharma bowed obsequiously and led them to a table from where the wine glasses were whisked to another table by an alert waiter. 'Would you like a drink first? Orange juice? Mineral water? Coca-cola?'

'Plain water will do,' Khalid Sharif grunted, looking around him, unimpressed by the lighting that created sinister looking shadows around the tables.

'Mineral water please, Sharma,' Javed requested.

Even with the aid of his special glasses, Khalid Sharif couldn't read the menu. 'It's too dark in here!' He glared across the table at his son, suspecting an ulterior motive for this unexpected outing.

'I suggest we try the vegetable *samosas* and *pakoras* first,' Javed suggested, ignoring his father's hostility. 'Then we can have the tandoori platter with *naan*, rice and *raitah*. Maybe some *alluh bhaji*?' He looked expectantly at Khalid Sharif for approval.

'*Samosas? Pakoras?*' Khalid Sharif snorted in disbelief. 'Are we here for afternoon tea or dinner?'

The young waiter arrived with the drinks and a small bread basket with four *pappadams*.

'What's this?' Khalid Sharif asked suspiciously, leaning forward and peering into the basket.

'*Pappadams*, sir,' the waiter replied with a crisp efficiency, his voice reflecting the cool indifference with which he had learned to deal with those diners who hid their fear of spicy food behind aggressive questions and unflattering remarks.

'Why have you brought us *pappars*?' The old man turned to the waiter, eyeing him over the rim of his glasses which had slipped halfway down his nose.

'It's all right,' Javed intervened, waving the young man away. 'My father is not used to entrees in Indian food.'

The waiter nodded disinterestedly, turned and sauntered off toward the kitchen.

'Papa, this is the way Indian food is served in restaurants here,' Javed explained stiffly, his thoughts on the cordial phone conversation with the helpful man in the Immigration Department.

The feeble light from the lamp illuminated the lower portion of Khalid Sharif's face. His eyes and nose were veiled by a shadow that slashed diagonally across him, giving the impression that a mask was in place to hide his facial identity.

They ate their way through the *samosas* and *pakoras*, talking freely about Calcutta and Javed's memories of the city.

'Life is very hard there,' Javed concluded definitively.

The waiter placed fresh plates in front of them.

Javed sneaked a look at his watch.

The tandoori platter, with a variety of meat coated with spices, yoghurt and food colour, arrived with soft-peaked *naans*, glistening with melted *ghee*, saffron rice and a generous serving of curried potatoes.

Javed spooned meat and potatoes on his father's plate before helping himself. 'Papa,' he began cautiously, 'Shanaz and I have talked about your future. It is our considered opinion that you should transfer all your assets and come and live with us in Melbourne.'

Khalid Sharif tore a piece of bread, wrapped it around several pieces of diced potatoes and tasted it. He munched slowly. 'Good . . . a little more salt and chilli maybe . . . but very good. Just the right quantity of turmeric.'

'Papa, it is essential that we reach some agreement about your future!' Javed persisted, determined not to be sidetracked, confused and ultimately overcome by his father's diversionary ploys.

Khalid Sharif stabbed a cube of meat with his fork. He examined the succulent piece of chicken burnt at the edges. 'No saffron!' he exclaimed. 'They have used food colour!'

'Genuine saffron is impossibly expensive.' Impatience crept into Javed's voice. 'I know an Indian businessman who intends to go back. He is definitely interested in the Camac Street flat. He is willing to pay here in Australian dollars.'

'Both the flat and the house have been sold,' Khalid Sharif said quietly. 'The house in the village is being renovated and modernised. Electricity, running water, a bathroom inside the house. The sorts of things civilisation has inflicted on us. I will live there.'

The ensuing silence was not so much a reflection of Javed's shock, as further evidence of an insurmountable barrier between them.

Javed reacted with a childish petulance. He pushed his plate toward the middle of the table and gulped down the remainder of the mineral water.

'Your offer is kind and generous, but it would be a mistake for me to come and live here.' Khalid Sharif shook his head firmly. 'I don't wish to create any more regrets and burden myself with their consequences.' He leaned back in his chair, his face completely hidden in the shadows.

Javed wondered what his father meant. What regrets? Was it remotely possible that there were hidden dimensions unrevealed to his children? Aberrations in behaviour that they knew nothing about? Unlikely. Until recently he had been too predictably honest to bear secrets . . . a boring, uncomplicated man. But perhaps . . .

We are all really strangers to each other . . . even in the closest of relationships. How much do children know about their parents? Wives about their husbands? Their past . . . their thoughts . . . desires.

'What is it that you find objectionable about Melbourne? We have everything here. A standard of living that one could only dream of in Calcutta. It's a haven for elderly people—excellent hospitals, the best doctors, ambulance service, good food . . .' Javed choked in disbelief at his father's myopic rejection of an opportunity unavailable to most Indians.

'But elderly people do die here at some point in their lives, I take it?' Khalid Sharif inquired mildly. 'There is a finishing line for all of us?'

'Think of all that is to be enjoyed here! The shopping, the theatre, restaurants, sports!' Javed spluttered, too bewildered by his father's unyielding stance to be affected by the obvious sarcasm.

Khalid Sharif reached across the table to pat his son's hand that gripped an empty tumbler.

That's how old age appears to be sometimes. Transparent and empty. Drained of life's vitality . . . but we cling to the husk with an instinctive tenacity . . .

How was he to explain, that as much as he marvelled at the orderliness of the city, its easy-paced beat, its affluence and all the tangible benefits that wealth bestowed on it, he could never merge with it and become a part of its identity? He enjoyed the tram rides, loved to wander the streets, stopping to look at the displays, drift through the elegant shops, mindlessly sweeping his eyes over the well-stocked shelves, saying *No, thank you* . . . to the polite offers of assistance, pausing for a drink and a bite to eat without the itchy sensations of sweaty discomfort that was a familiar experience in the muggy heat of Calcutta.

Melbourne had added richly to his experiences. As a young man, Khalid Sharif had closely followed the events of the war, especially in Europe, and read about Judaism with a growing fascination about its legacy to Islam. He accumulated a formidable repository of factual knowledge about the oldest of the desert religions without ever meeting a Jew in his life . . . until a warm, March morning in Acland Street.

He had stopped in front of a cake shop, uncertain whether to indulge himself and risk increasing the pain that rarely left him. His eyes feasted on the cakes arranged in a seductive symmetry of colours and piled high in a familiar display of careless abundance that he identified with Australia.

'Good, huh?'

Khalid Sharif turned guiltily.

A crinkled, bearded face grinned at him. 'You speak English?'

'Yes.'

A hand was thrust forward. 'My name is Jacob.'

'Khalid.'

'You have been walking in front of the cake shops for some time. Can't make up your mind, huh?'

Khalid Sharif laughed uncomfortably. 'I have to think of consequences. Unfortunately, I am not yet past that state.'

The Jew looked at him thoughtfully. 'With us old people such delicacies are just like the difficulties beautiful women can create for young men.' He winked wickedly. 'Lovely to look at, delicious to have. But then, later, there is pain. No? Come in and take the risk of younger days.' He threw back his head and roared with a zestful laughter, as if some memory from a dim past had suddenly flooded his consciousness, reminding him of the careless vagaries of another era.

Khalid Sharif allowed himself to be guided inside the shop. He sat at one of the small round tables as Jacob excused himself and disappeared through the door behind the counter. He reappeared shortly and sat opposite Khalid Sharif.

'Coffee and black forest cake. Okay with you?'

Khalid Sharif nodded meekly. He would have preferred weak tea without the cake.

'What religion?' Jacob asked abruptly, staring at the Indian with an undisguised curiosity. 'Hinduism?'

Khalid Sharif stared back, their eyes meeting in a muted conflict of identities. 'I am a Muslim. You are . . . Jewish?'

Jacob frowned. Then, with a magnanimous smile, he shrugged his shoulders. 'What the hell!' he exclaimed. 'This is Australia! We bury such differences under our pleasures. Here no one cares much about anything except the sun, beer and the silly game with that funny shaped ball. We are too young to take history seriously. That is good in some ways.'

They lingered in the shop over more coffee and a pot of tea, relishing their new experience.

'I have never spoken to a Muslim before,' Jacob confessed. 'In all these years. Fancy that!'

Their conversation meandered lazily through the features of their lives until it reached the inevitable stage of evaluating what lay ahead.

'Will we live into the next century, do you think?' Jacob asked, as though his newly found companion was blessed with the gift of prophecy.

Khalid Sharif shook his head in an emphatic denial. 'I hope I don't.'

'We won't,' Jacob said cheerfully. 'You are like me. Tired of it all.'

'I wonder how people will look back at the twentieth century,' Khalid Sharif wondered aloud. 'Ultimately their views of the past will be shaped by the prejudices and preferences of historians. The monumental events of this century will be refurbished and repainted in fresh colours.'

'Some things must never be changed!' Jacob asserted sternly.

'Like what? Nothing escapes the human imagination. It is the source of all lies and everything that is great, foul, noble and evil.'

'My friend, the stench of Nazism must be allowed to linger, in case memory collapses and we forget what happens when the human soul goes mad and turns on its own kind. We owe the future a constant reminder of how much damage we can inflict on ourselves.'

'Were you . . .' Khalid Sharif stopped. He did not wish to offend.

Jacob understood and nodded slightly. 'My parents, two brothers, a sister, uncles . . .' He brooded with a glazed look of disbelief in his eyes.

'It isn't possible to live as long as we have without the pain of loss,' Khalid Sharif consoled him. 'Some of my memories don't hurt as much any more. That is why I sometimes wonder if all that I remember actually happened.'

'You have known much pain?'

'Of a different kind.' Khalid Sharif did not elaborate. The details were irrelevant to the essence of the experience.

They looked at each other and refrained from speaking. They knew that words could never convey the rawness of the hurtful moments cauterised in their minds. There were no adequate descriptions of the serrated edges of pain, and their reverberating echoes, which penetrated the layers of time, reaching them like freshly charged currents of sadness. Their memories were private and sacrosanct, not to be opened and dug up like graves, to search for secrets buried with the dirt-covered bones.

'Don't you wish to live beyond this century? Aren't you curious?' Jacob asked, relieved that they had tacitly agreed to leave the past undisturbed.

'No,' Khalid Sharif replied vigorously. 'Definitely not. I have no desire to be any more alienated from life than I am now. My curiosity is directed at what happened, not at what may be.'

To be alive at the birth of the twenty-first century would be a harsh punishment. It would entail stepping out of time, as he knew it, into a dimension requiring adaptations beyond his capacity. The prospect of such a dreadful eventuality, remote as it was, had nagged Khalid Sharif before.

What was life without the faculties to enjoy its gifts? Without the stimuli of books, music, friends and conversations? Without the possibilities of open spaces? The polarised tugs of coherent recollections? Without noises, movements, landscapes and dreams? It was an inordinately cruel fate to reduce life's joys to a few spoonfuls of painfully swallowed food, all smashed up into a pukey pulp. Vacant eyes and uncontrollable dribbles of saliva. A spartan bed, a wardrobe maybe, tables cluttered with trays of bottles, packets and half-empty tumblers of water. His greatest ally, an arsenal of drugs to keep him barely functional in the empty silence of an unfamiliar room. The sleeping and the waking, no more than the alternating phases of a life bereft of all meaning, responding to a beat that does not know when or how to stop. A shrivelled soul curled inwards, waiting . . . waiting . . . waiting. A state, Nietzsche described, where *oh everything human is strange*. A ragged puppet, attached to worn out strings, whose feeble movements relied entirely on the whims of others.

The distinct possibility of being unable to look after himself frightened Khalid Sharif. The indignity of confinement in a room stinking of shit and stale urine, being barely tolerated as an otiose entity, with only a feeble heartbeat to distinguish him from a well-preserved corpse, had hammered his pride into a resolution not to become a burden on his children. It wasn't as if he was uncertain of their love for him or their lack of responsibility; it was more the realisation of a relentless imposition which converted filial love into a tedious, resentful chore and, finally, wore itself down to a state of fatigued negligence.

Quite suddenly it occurred to Khalid Sharif that he didn't remember where he had kept the slip of paper with Jacob's address and phone number. He plunged his hands into his trouser and jacket pockets and groped around frantically. He took out everything. Loose change, small containers of pills, keys, handkerchief, wallet, a notebook, a biro.

Oblivious of his father's flustered condition, Javed continued to be garrulous about the necessity of being looked after in one's old age. He had worked out the remainder of his father's life with meticulous care. A couple or at the most three years with his son and Khalid Sharif would not be opposed to a bright, airy room with a view in one of the old people's homes. He had inspected a couple of the new ones which had been recently built and was impressed with the facilities they offered. Telephones, colour television and alarm switches in every room. A doctor and nurses in attendance. Two small shops where the whimsical fancies of old age could be satisfied. Khalid Sharif would be happy with the surroundings. There were walking tracks and a lovely garden. Communal activities—dances, card games, movies, bingo, parties. All that could be offered to insulate people from loneliness.

'Papa, you must think it over!' Javed insisted. 'There is absolutely no need to jump into a decision.'

'I have precious little time to think anything over!' Khalid Sharif frowned, puzzling over the lost bit of paper. Try as he did, he couldn't recall Jacob's surname. Ca . . . Ce . . . Ko . . . It had been written in capital letters on top of the address. The suburb . . . It had a very English sound to it. The word *cathedral* occurred to him several times. He was unable to make the connection.

Javed's voice intruded again.

'What you are planning is downright irresponsible!'

'Irresponsible to whom?' Khalid Sharif snapped.

'To everyone! To your children! Have you paused to think how worried we will be? What happens if you suddenly fall ill? There isn't a hospital or a doctor anywhere near the village. We cannot . . .'

'Now my responsibility is to myself and . . .' The old man interrupted and then stopped. 'You wouldn't understand. You belong to a generation that chooses its relationships with great care. Money. Prestige. Good looks. There are clear motives and tangible gains. Loyalty, I am certain, figures somewhere, even if it lags behind the rest of the reasons.'

'That is not true,' Javed protested weakly, wondering whether there was a deliberate ambiguity in his father's words. 'What you propose to do needs a reckless courage!'

'Courage?' Khalid Sharif stifled a bitter laughter. He honed in on the solitary word whose implications had been the centre of an intense and unsparing scrutiny at various times in his life. 'Courage is a virtue that belongs to others. Had I been blessed with even a small amount, it may have changed the entire course of my life.' He slumped back in his chair as if the accumulated disappointments of a lifetime were pressing against him.

'Am I to believe that you have regrets about the way things turned out? About your business and family? You have enjoyed an easy, wonderful life!' That Khalid Sharif could have experienced anything but a state of contentment with his family and professional life had a numbing effect of a heavyweight punch. It was an unexpected and unpleasant revelation for Javed.

'Is a life without regrets possible?'

'I don't have any!' Javed boasted readily. 'Nothing of any significance to cause me bitterness.'

'Then you are a very privileged man. It is a rare person who can look back without being haunted by the shadows of questionable decisions.' Khalid Sharif looked critically at his son. 'Perhaps some people don't need to turn inwards. Perhaps they know that there is little to be sorted out or agonised over. It is possible for life to be like an unlit room, lined with dusty bookshelves, but without books.'

Years of procrastination, cowardice and self-justification had effectively contained Khalid Sharif's curiosity and periodic yearnings to return to *Khush Manzil* for a discreet look from the outside. The desire arose from a cherished, but fallacious, assumption that the world he had known as a young man had been untouched by time, that only he had been blighted by change and grown older.

After Jahan Ara's death, it had become customary for Khalid Sharif to visit the graveyard in Gobra every fortnight. On the way back from work on alternate Fridays, the chauffeur had his instructions to take a detour and park the car in a lane, a short distance from the graveyard. Khalid Sharif stopped at a shop to buy incense sticks and candles before making his way to Jahan Ara's grave.

The time he spent there was not an indulgence in mourning or nostalgic self-pity. As he stuck the lit candles and incense sticks in the mound of earth, fringed by a low rectangular wall of plastered brick, Khalid Sharif felt calm and removed from the noise, the pollution and the hideous poverty of the city.

Usually the graveyard was empty. At that time of the day, it was too late for most visitors who were kept away by superstitious fears of the imminent darkness that enveloped Calcutta with a suddenness common to a tropical city. It was past the caretaker's working hours. The melancholy solitude of dusk had a restorative effect on his mind and emotions, and often made him reflect on the intricate mechanism of existence. He grappled with the conflicting voices that debated whether it was an inherent weakness that had prevented him from asserting a greater influence on his destiny.

Was he no more than a willing accomplice, seduced by his privileged circumstances, intended to function in accordance with the whimsical dictates of Fate? Was he like an exotic insect, pinned to a board, fluttering its wings and moving its legs in futile gestures of being alive? He resented the notion of being a helpless entity in a universe abandoned by God. He lived in a city that encapsulated such despair. There it was—Calcutta, the maligned city, all around the crumbling walls of the graveyard. It was like a dying beggar lacerated with sores and ravaged by diseases, prolonging life, beginning to think that even Death had bypassed it as a proposition too formidable for the dark pit of infinity. There were no resolutions to Khalid Sharif's knotty perceptions of life and the living, only angry impressions about the finiteness of everything created and then destroyed, as if there was a vindictive governing law that no one had managed to circumvent.

Initially it was a lingering guilt that made him a regular

visitor to the graveyard. *A man can easily love more than once!* the men in his family boasted, without exploring and fully understanding the nature of the emotion. Although he remained sceptical about the validity of such a generalisation, it made Khalid Sharif wonder whether he was freakishly stunted in the way his feelings had dried up, leaving him with a detached neutrality toward his wife.

He rarely felt any physical attraction for her. There were infrequent and joyless sexual encounters in the nocturnal confinement of their silent bedroom where they managed to procreate four children.

Brought up to believe that such acts of impropriety were necessary for propagation, Jahan Ara's sexual hang-ups received further confirmation as a result of her husband's more than obvious disinterest. Her confused passions retreated discreetly to the deep chambers of her psyche to languish and wither in exile.

The routine of his fortnightly visits to Gobra snapped suddenly on Khalid Sharif's last working day. Several months before he left for Australia, Khalid Sharif sold his business to a Marwari who insisted on concluding the deal with a celebratory lunch. Later, feeling bloated, sad and tired, the old man lurched into the back seat of the car, parked near the restaurant. He asked to be dropped off in Ripon Street. It was an impulsive decision. Irritably, he repeated the instruction to a bewildered chauffeur who kept looking in the rear view mirror to assure himself that the old man was not ill.

'Here!' Khalid Sharif leaned forward and tapped the front window with his walking stick. 'Stop! Go home. I shall take a taxi or a rickshaw later.'

Standing on a broken footpath, the old man waved to the reluctant chauffeur. He watched the car crawl behind a pushcart and several rickshaws until it disappeared around a bend.

He entered the lane and walked briskly for a few minutes, the worn bottom of the walking stick thudding on the bitumen surface as if he was announcing his arrival to a past that had given up on him. The muggy heat slowed him down and made him dizzy. His legs lacked strength and he panted heavily. Moving to one side, Khalid Sharif stopped and leaned on his walking stick. The world trembled. The houses moved and the sky shifted. His eyelids collapsed.

The darkness was a relief and, at the same time, a source of fear.

We are not now that strength . . .

The years retracted like a self-winding cord. There was Tabassum Begum admonishing him, telling him to leave.

You have no business here now, Sharif Saheb!

He's come to tell us why he broke his promises. Nazli spoke from behind her.

A stranger's concerned hand rested on his arm.

'I am all right,' he said gruffly, squinting to keep the prickly glare out of his eyes.

It was the wrong turning he was told. There was no mosque here. Further along Ripon Street there was another lane. The young man looked bemused.

There was no correspondence between what Khalid Sharif saw and all that he remembered. He couldn't tell whether his memory was lying or the world had changed capriciously beyond his recognition.

A pushcart clattered past him. Taxis honked, fume-belching Ambassadors and Fiats rumbled along the pot-holed street. Rickshaw pullers weaved through the chaotic traffic, sounding warnings with their little hand-held bells to pedestrians indifferent to the dangers of the onrushing vehicles. Time itself appeared to be surging past.

The *neem* tree had disappeared, replaced by an electricity pole. It was the same spot, Khalid Sharif convinced himself as he paused to examine the unfamiliar landmarks.

A hardware store stood where there should have been a tea stall.

He hesitated inside the entrance.

'Yes?' a man behind the counter asked impatiently.

'A mosque? Is there a mosque in the lane on the left?'

The man shook his head. There was a lane further up. About half a kilometre.

'Is there a tea stall at the corner of the turning?'

The shopkeeper shrugged his shoulders and turned his attention to a customer.

It was like taking a walk on the back of a giant snake. The lane wound and twisted its way without any visible sign of ending. Khalid Sharif frowned. It hadn't taken him this long to reach the mosque. There were double and triple-storeyed houses on either side. Crumbling, narrow old buildings with small windows.

It wasn't this far, Khalid Sharif thought wearily. He turned back despondently.

The sound of the *azaan* stopped him. It seemed to rise suddenly from the depth of the past to embrace him like an old friend. He stood quietly and listened to the muezzin's call. It wasn't, after all, the sound of a treacherous memory seducing him toward the disappointment of another illusion.

He looked up to see terraces crowded with drying clothes fluttering in a mild breeze. Khalid Sharif quickened his steps and walked past a group of rickshaw *wallahs*, squatting near their neatly lined vehicles, smoking and conversing animatedly. With a nervous anxiety he scanned the skyline, willing the muezzin not to stop.

He felt a surge of triumph, a quickening of his pulse as the dome of the mosque appeared against the haziness of the pale sky. It did not glitter as it once had, its shiny tiled surface reflecting the sunlight with a blinding sparkle. Years of grime and dust had turned it to a dull silver grey. The bronze crescent, which peaked the dome, was not visible. Broken and not replaced, Khalid Sharif concluded as he neared the front steps. Time had cheated him by removing an exact detail. One had to expect that in Calcutta. It was a living city of ruins—bruised, battered and overused.

Khalid Sharif paused in front of the steps where the bearded *mullah*, in a white skullcap, had been repulsed by the inquiry about the location of *Khush Manzil*. He smiled at the memory. The look of shock and disgust. Mumbled words of condemnation. The harsh judgement of a fundamentalist blinded by the vision of ethereal perfection.

Khalid Sharif's eyes swept across the wide, open doors, catching a glimpse of elderly men rolling out rugs and mats as they prepared to kneel and prostrate themselves in a ritual of unquestionable submission. The water trough was where he remembered it. It was now made of stainless steel with longer nozzled taps to facilitate *wazuh*.

The *azaan* blared over the loudspeaker again.

There was no urge to go inside. Words from Ghalib's *ghazal*, sung with an inebriated lustiness at a *mahfil*, were now injected with a sobering sadness.

> *Take delight in revelry, riotous passions*
>   *and luxurious living.*
> *Why dost thou die of thirst in the mirage*
>   *of religion?*

Revelry. Riotous passion. Fragments of a life beyond him. No shimmering mirages either. Shards of curiosity, rising from a death-bed, waiting to be quashed by an overwhelming disappointment.

He shuffled forward slowly, looking at the houses crowding the sides of the lane. Size, shapes, distinctive characteristics. Memory teased and then betrayed.

Somewhere here . . .

He went back a few steps. It had to be. *Somewhere here.*

Aadavarz hai . . . Welcome!

'*Shukuriya!*' He didn't intend to say the word quite as loudly.

A passing couple looked at him and then hastened their steps.

Shoddy, makeshift shops and more houses added to the confusion. Tailors and barbers. Garages and a laundry. A grocer's shop.

No trace of a bazaar.

The open space had disappeared, swallowed up by more houses. Labourers were crawling on bamboo scaffoldings, working on new buildings destined to climb high into the skyline.

The walls were scarred by furry growths of fungi. It had to be, he convinced himself. Dirty, broken windows. Some boarded up. A pile of rotting garbage near the steps. Flies and dogs in attendance. The unswept landing was covered with a layer of black scum.

'The *Flesh Trade Act* of 1958!' Ashraf had warned. 'It destroyed the courtesan culture. You won't find anything there.'

The front door had been replaced. Names and messages were carved on the wood. A few obscenities.

Anger, against the terrible work of time, surfaced with a bilious desire to smash through the barriers of the shrivelled present and reach back into a life he had briefly embraced.

'Is this . . . is this *Khush Manzil*?' he whispered to a man who came out with a sack of flour slung over his shoulder.

'Hah?'

'Is this *Khush Manzil*?'

'The shop is just inside.' The man grunted and went down the steps.

The unlocked door squeaked open to a dismal reality, far worse than Khalid Sharif could have envisaged.

What remained of the foyer was dimly lit with a single light globe that hung precariously from a cord attached to a charred ceiling. He looked up. Among the dark splotches there were no visible marks to indicate that a chandelier had once hung there like a cluster of brilliantly lit fruits.

Dust. Thick. Drifting. Rising and settling on the grimy cement floor.

The noise didn't belong here. The clatter of a primitive machine grinding wheat into flour. No wall or door in front of him.

There should have been a door.

A voice attracting angels.

It's at such gatherings
That lives are lost ...

A gaping hole. Unseen fists had obliterated what there was.

Jagged bricks. Peeling plaster. Dusty shelves crowded with sacks of rice, lentil, sugar, *besan* ... flour.

A young man in a black leather jacket, matching pants and boots. He was fiddling with the handles of a motor bike, disinterested in the affairs of the shop. Behind him a middle-aged man was stacking a shelf with bulging hessian sacks.

The ruins of the grand staircase on his left assured Khalid Sharif that he hadn't made an error. Cardboard boxes crowded the steps. The cracks on the wooden balustrade were stuffed with sticks and paper. And on the landing ... where she had often waited ... tea-chests and stacks of old newspapers.

The young man noticed Khalid Sharif. '*Kya mangtha hai*, man?' he asked sharply.

Anglo-Indian, Khalid Sharif deduced from the peculiar mixture of words articulated in a shrill voice.

'Is this *Khush Manzil*?'

'What?'

'*Khush Manzil*?'

'Hey Dad! The old fellow wants something.'

Khalid Sharif repeated the question to the father.

'*Khush Manzil*? I am afraid not! Never heard of it!' the man said cheerfully. 'My name is Gerald Carr. This is my son, Will.'

Khalid Sharif muttered his name as they shook hands. 'You live here?'

'In one of the flats upstairs.'

'How long have you been here?'

'All my life!' The Anglo-Indian grinned ruefully as if his acknowledgement exposed the limitations implicit in a lifetime spent in such grim surroundings. 'I was born here.'

Carr was about forty-five, Khalid Sharif estimated. Not old enough to know. 'And you have never heard this building being called *Khush Manzil*?'

'Never heard the name. *Khush . . . Khush . . .*' The word rolled out awkwardly. 'Doesn't it mean happy?'

'Yes.'

'Nice name! Hardly suits this place. Look, this house has seen quite a few alterations. There was a fire here, my father once told me. Nearly destroyed the whole building.'

'When?'

'Oh . . . before my old man moved in. Fifty years. Maybe more.'

With unsteady fingers Khalid Sharif pointed to the door to the left of the stairs. 'There was a hall there for . . .' He checked himself. The Anglo-Indian probably wouldn't know what a *mahfil* was. 'For entertainment.'

'That's the biggest flat in the building. The owner's son lives there,' Carr said gently. 'Could it be some other place? The houses here are very confusing.'

The memory of youthful days in old age
Is like the memory of a vanished dream . . .

Khalid Sharif remembered how the words had brushed against his invincible ego.

'And upstairs?'

'More flats.'

'The fire . . . How did it happen?'

Carr didn't know. The anguish on the old man's face

concerned him. 'Are you feeling okay? Here, why don't you sit down and have a drink of water, eh?'

Khalid Sharif murmured an assurance of his well-being. 'Do you know if anyone was killed or hurt in the fire?'

'I don't know. As I said, it happened before my family moved in.'

'May I stay a few more minutes?'

'As long as you like.' Carr returned to the shelves.

The old man was leaning on his walking stick, staring at the stairs as if they led to an imaginary world where he could be free from the encumbrance of age. He looked pathetic and useless standing there.

'There is nothing there for you, man!' Will called irritably. 'Go home! It's getting late. Do you know where you live?'

There was no response.

'Crazy old bugger!' the young man muttered under his breath, quickly banishing the intrusive stranger from his thoughts.

Silence. Thick. Choking.

The words had run out.

The silence of surrender. Or triumph.

'Well, if that is what you wish . . .'

Khalid Sharif nodded. 'That is how I want to live.'

Wearily Javed called for the bill.

TWELVE

'I doubt if I can beat that!' Khalid Sharif marvelled, injecting an awed admiration into his voice. 'The tree is too far for me to hit.'

Adam continued to lean over the treated-pine railing, staring glumly ahead. He remained unmoved with his triumph with the catapult. With the accuracy of a seasoned expert, he had knocked off a cluster of ripe plums from the tree.

Khalid Sharif made an elaborate show of aiming meticulously. From the distance the tree was a fuzzy, dark outline. He was anxious to ensure that even an accidental hit to match Adam's success was not a possibility. He aligned the catapult with what he guessed to be the lowest branch of the tree, and then imperceptibly lowered his shaking hands. The eyelid of the left eye closed.

'Why do you have to go?'

The pellet did not make it to the fence. There was a faint noise as it flew in a short arc and nose-dived into the earth, bouncing twice before it hit the fence and disintegrated.

'Missed!' Khalid Sharif announced dejectedly. 'You win!'

Adam kicked the surface of the deck with his right foot. 'Not fair!' he muttered fiercely, his chin resting on his forearm.

'We could go for an ice-cream before your mother comes

to pick you up,' Khalid Sharif suggested. 'I shall ask your grandmother if you like.'

It was an offer made with the sinking realisation that it might not be enough to placate the boy. Khalid Sharif felt inadequate and dishonest. A clumsy effort, he told himself, to circumvent the disarmingly direct question to which there was no simple explanation that would make sense to Adam.

The prospect of even a gentle stroll to the milk bar was not a pleasant proposition. Khalid Sharif's arms and legs were aching. His back felt tender and he had experienced several dizzy spells. The afternoon's furtive activity had exhausted him.

He had known that Angela would be away, shopping for groceries. Friday was her supermarket day, between two and about half-past three. Khalid Sharif found a plausible excuse for not accompanying her.

'I have to catch up with some correspondence,' he explained. 'Letters that should have been written several weeks ago.'

Angela conveyed her disappointment in an unmistakable frown. She had grown accustomed to their pots of tea and buns in the cafe after shopping. She had no right to impose her weekly schedule on him, she chided herself immediately and relented with a weak, twitchy smile.

'I shall come around to help you unload the groceries,' Khalid Sharif offered apologetically.

The bicycle was to be delivered at half-past two. At twenty to three, Khalid Sharif walked home and rang the shop.

The van was on its way, he was told. It had left the shop more than half an hour ago.

Khalid Sharif returned to the front of Angela's house to wait for the van. His breathing was laboured and he felt a tightness in his chest.

The van pulled up after another half an hour.

There was adequate space in the tool shed to store the bike.

As an afterthought Khalid Sharif decided to hide it behind the two old bookshelves cluttered with rusty, unused garden tools. The shelves were much heavier than they looked. He grunted and strained as he slid them away from the back wall to create enough room for the vehicle to be fitted in.

He kept checking the time. It was nearly twenty to four.

He closed his eyes. The world stopped wavering. Currents of pain were shooting up his arms.

She wouldn't stop for tea, Angela told him in a tone that made him remorseful about lying.

Any minute now . . .

The bolt in the door jammed. He panicked as he heard the car in the driveway. He pushed harder. It gave way with a sudden force and grazed the skin of his middle finger. Khalid Sharif wiped a smidgen of blood and dabbed the perspiration on his face with the sleeve of his shirt before he walked to the car.

'You are panting!'

Angela's concern made him concede that he was not feeling too well. 'I just feel a bit tired. Nothing too serious,' he said lightly.

'There is no need to do any more in the backyard,' she said firmly. 'No, I will take the bags in! Adam can give me a hand after putting away his school bag. Won't you, Adam?'

The boy grinned and dashed inside.

Angela came out from the kitchen with a tray laden with cups and saucers, a teapot, strainer, sugar pot, milk and thick slices of fruit cake.

'Adam, your mother's on the phone,' she said, laying down the tray on the outdoor table. 'She will be a little late in picking you up.'

'Don't care!' Adam said sullenly, banging the sliding door as he went inside.

Silently Angela poured the tea.

'The afternoons are no longer warm,' Khalid Sharif

observed, feeling the chill of a faint breeze which strummed the trees with a melancholic gentleness. He apprehended a slight resentment behind Angela's reticence. Her company was precious to him. He would miss their meandering, unhurried conversations that ignored the constraints of time.

'We don't experience such distinguishable autumns in Calcutta,' he reflected aloud. 'Here it has a very distinctive character. Everything is ripe and golden. Mature and settled. But . . .' He groped for the appropriate words to describe the contradiction he sensed in the ripeness of the season. 'There is something deeply sad about this sort of late afternoon, about its idyllic calmness, as if . . . as if it was quietly mourning its own transience. It is a season that hums the songs of mortality.'

She looked at him sharply. He looked haggard and dispirited, staring into the distance beyond the houses and the trees, as though he was mesmerised by the vista of another life he was forbidden to enter.

'Khalid . . .' She reached out to touch him and then quickly withdrew her hand before he turned to her. 'I . . . *we* . . .' she gestured toward the sliding door. 'We are disappointed that you are leaving.'

He smiled shyly and bit into the fruit cake. The haze began to thicken. *That hasn't changed . . . Regardless of my intentions, I remain a catalyst of other people's regrets. I am tired of expectations. There are those born to let others down . . . I have tried, God knows I have tried . . .*

'You may not think so,' she continued, 'but you have brought a stability to our lives.'

Khalid Sharif was flattered by her words. 'You have been very kind to me. Thank you for your generous friendship.'

'When you were in hospital, Javed gave me the impression that you would be coming back to live here permanently.'

'There is nothing permanent in my life now,' he said laconically, looking over the fence in the direction of his wilting tomato plants. 'Sometimes we make our lives unnecessarily difficult with words that ought to be discarded with age.'

'You know what I mean!' Angela snapped. Even in his most vulnerable moments he could be difficult.

His hands quivered as he accepted another cup of tea. 'It has never been my intention to become a burden on my children. I came to see my son and his family. A visit. Come to think of it, a prolonged goodbye. That was all it was ever meant to be.'

She noticed the tremor as he straightened up in his chair. 'Would you like one of Tom's old jumpers? A blanket?'

He shook his head.

'Would you like to go inside?'

'A little later perhaps. It's very peaceful out here. Winter must be cold.'

'It can be. The rain and the wind are quite depressing. This is my favourite time of the year.' Angela watched him closely. 'The only drawback is we shall lose daylight saving next Sunday.'

'Meaning?'

'The clocks will be put back an hour.'

'We get an extra hour added to our lives?' The idea amused him.

'In summer the clocks are put forward by an hour,' she said grittily.

'It hadn't occurred to me that time could be so manoeuvrable,' he chuckled. 'Backwards and forwards! Am I to believe that we are at liberty to move time at our whim? But why only an hour? Can't our illusions take any more than that? Why can't time be pushed back twenty years? Or forty? Fifty?'

Angela stopped paying attention to his steady flow of words. He was on his own again, garrulous and sliding into obscurity.

'You have had a terrific crop of tomatoes this year!' She broke into his reverie. 'There couldn't be many left.'

'What?'

'I said there couldn't be many tomatoes left in your garden.'

'There's lots left! Not ripe, but they are there!' he huffed. Even the remotest suggestion that the season might be near its end, that the plants did not have long to survive, drew a fiercely protective response from him. He had made up his mind not to touch the remaining fruits before he left.

'It's a pity that you are unable to stay for Adam's birthday,' Angela said quietly, unable to fully reconcile herself to Khalid Sharif's imminent departure. *A brief, terminal friendship. What was the point of it?* Angela felt a sad affection for this gentle, harmless man who did nothing to put her on the alert, unlike a couple of the frisky oldies at the RSL dances, with their wheezing breath and bony hands.

He is going home to . . . The errant thought flashed across her mind and unsettled her. *He knew! He hadn't told anyone . . .*

It was unavoidable, he had explained. His cousin in the village was ill . . .

Ashraf sounded rattled on the phone. His voice crackled with a helpless anger.

The renovations were done. The house looked entirely different. The white walls dispelled the gloom and made the rooms bright.

But Munir! Up to his old tricks again! Crying and complaining about severe headaches and shortage of money. But worse still, Khalid Sharif's cousin was in a Calcutta hospital with serious injuries.

Ashraf had lived in the house for a few days, waiting for some furniture to arrive from Calcutta. On his last night in Modhunagar, Ashraf was awakened after midnight by a group of distressed villagers clamouring for help under his window. There was an accident, they claimed. Munir was involved. Aided by the feeble light of several lanterns, Ashraf was led along a winding dirt track to a clump of *neem* trees on the edge of the village.

It was a cloudy night. The wind howled a warning of an approaching storm. Above the noise he heard pained groans from under the largest tree. Munir was lying on his back, stunned by several blows to his head, his face bleeding profusely. One arm was swollen and seemingly fractured. A party of farmers, returning from a wedding in a neighbouring village, had mistaken Munir for a supernatural creature, a wicked *djinn*, out to create mischief.

Khalid Sharif exploded in a torrent of angry words. How dare they hurt one of the Sharifs! He demanded to know whether the miscreants had been apprehended.

'The villagers cannot be entirely blamed,' Ashraf remarked cryptically.

'What was that?' Khalid Sharif shouted. There was a disturbing echo which made it difficult to hear what his friend was saying.

'The villagers are not to be entirely blamed. Munir was oddly dressed. Dinner jacket, bow tie, a black cape, top hat, gloves, carrying what he insisted was a wand. He must have bought the costume when he came to see me in Calcutta. Khalid? Khalid, are you there?'

'Yes,' Khalid Sharif whispered, the anger draining out of him.

'When the men came across him, Munir was running around the trees, waving the stick and speaking a language no one could understand. *"I am a magician! I control the tree spirits! I can make the world appear as it should be!"* he boasted when the peasants challenged him. He burst into a fiendish laughter and hurled abuses at anyone who came close.'

The men ran back to seek help. More villagers, armed with sturdy *lathis*, sought to determine the identity of the being under the trees. Most were secretly hopeful that whatever it was would have disappeared, as it was not in the nature of the spirits to make themselves visible in one place for a prolonged period of time. They were reassured by the presence of a *mullah* who could recite *surahs* destined to ward off all forms of evil and protect the villagers from harm.

The men approached the trees with trepidation. With a demeanour of supreme self-confidence, the *mullah* asserted his presence and insisted that his fellow mortals stay out of sight. The expulsion of nefarious spirits was a tricky business that needed the utmost concentration.

Holding a lantern in one hand and chanting words in Arabic, the *mullah* stepped boldly in front of the apparition from the dark world.

'In the name of Allah and His *Rasul*, I banish thee, evil spirit, from . . .'

A face materialised from the darkness. In the dim light of the lantern it appeared to be blacker than the night and more terrible than any imaginable visage of *Iblis*. A pink snake slithered out from the chasm of Hell and fluttered in front of the *mullah*'s face. Later the dazed man swore that he had seen the tip of a leaping flame emitting an infernal heat that had momentarily blinded him. The pernicious inhabitant of Darkness and Chaos was defiant and unaffected by the words intended to send the Evil One hurtling back to the fires of *Dozak*. The men heard a scream of terror. The *mullah* was in serious trouble. His cries for help and mercy activated the villagers into reckless action. Thirty armed men raised their sticks and charged blindly with cries of *Allah O Akbar*!

'They couldn't have recognised Munir in the light of the lanterns!' Ashraf insisted. 'Even I had difficulty when I arrived. Your cousin had blackened his face with shoe polish!'

Munir was taken to hospital in Calcutta and admitted to a private room. He was concussed. Fractured ribs and arms. Bruises all over his legs. Broken jaw. Recovery had been slowed down by his refusal to cooperate with the hospital staff. He refused the liquid diet and resisted medicine. Only after being told that Khalid Sharif would be displeased with his behaviour did he relent.

The case was reported to the local police who referred it to Calcutta, pleading a lack of experience in such matters.

Two Hindu detectives were sent to Modhunagar with the tedious task of interviewing the villagers and conducting a thorough investigation. Patiently, they listened to the varying accounts of the incident. The glaring contradictions in the epical narratives, stretched and spiced by fecund imaginations, made it impossible to piece together any sustainable evidence that could have led the detectives to the culprits actually responsible for the assault. The men from Calcutta's Intelligence Bureau were further hampered by the problems inherent in dealing with a predominantly Muslim community. They were under strict instructions not to provoke or intimidate people. Their manner of conducting the investigation was to be without overt signs of bias or religious prejudices, they were sternly told. The West Bengal Government had no intention of allowing a communal crisis to develop so close to the state elections.

After the first day the detectives gave up and relaxed. They fed on excellent fish curry and rice, yoghurt and sweetmeats, all provided by the friendly villagers who quickly sensed that the investigation was unlikely to lead to specific charges being laid against any inhabitant of Modhunagar. Hindu–Muslim harmony took a mega leap in this inconspicuous part of West Bengal, and it was the unanimous opinion of the villagers that the detectives were thorough gentlemen, a rare breed of Hindus to be welcomed to the village whenever they needed a break from their work.

The detectives returned to Calcutta with bulging folders and fond memories of their sojourn in the country. In due course they wrote their reports, after meticulously working out their claimable expenses.

As a result of conflicting evidence, the reports ended inconclusively. It was impossible to determine who had been involved in the unfortunate episode, the police regretfully informed Ashraf.

Case closed.

The news was receive in Modhunagar with exploding firecrackers and a *milad* to acknowledge the justice done to the men of the village. *Allah be praised!* Their innocence had been fully vindicated. It was an appropriate occasion for speeches, solemn procrastinations, special prayers and feasting.

After hearing the details of the unfortunate episode and examining the patient, the hospital doctors had recommended psychiatric help for Munir.

Ashraf sounded a note of warning. Khalid Sharif was to decide whether such a move was advisable, especially since the cost of his cousin's treatment was likely to be prohibitive.

'He is impossible!' Ashraf complained bitterly. 'His behaviour in hospital has been disgraceful! On the pretext of being in severe pain, he calls the nurses to his bedside at night and then insists on showing them a world of exotic pleasures with his magical wand.'

Khalid Sharif groaned with embarrassment.

'The nurses have taken it up with their union, and a formal complaint has been made to the hospital authorities. I expect a letter any day.'

'Is there any chance that he will be charged for his antics in the village?' Khalid Sharif was anxious to know.

'I doubt it. The police don't wish to involve themselves any further in the silly affair. Khalid, you must understand that I cannot devote all my time to looking after Munir. I am retiring next month, and I have to wind up everything before I finish. Besides, I am too old to be confronted with this sort of awkward and undignified situation.'

Khalid Sharif expressed his gratitude and assured his friend that Munir was not Ashraf's responsibility.

'He asks for you,' Ashraf said pointedly. 'Whenever he is asked to do something, his reply is, "Only if Khalid wants me to." When are you coming back? I have to tell him something to calm him down.'

'Soon. Very soon. Tell him that.'

He couldn't reveal the details of Munir's troubles and his own inextricable involvement in it. Even if he talked about it, Angela would be shocked into believing that the poor man ought to be in an asylum, and that it was too dangerous for Khalid Sharif to be near him.

He has no one. There are massive debts I owe him. I have profited from his selflessness. He was there when I needed him, willing to sacrifice himself to protect me . . . Like that time when we stripped the guava tree of all its fruits. He took the blame and the caning silently, without flinching . . . All those other times when I lied and left him with the consequences . . . He saved me from serious injury . . . Tried to share his world with me . . . The stories and the entertainment he provided when the children were young . . . Now I want to let go and take the risk of looking at life the way he does . . . Let loose all that has been kept imprisoned in the mind for the fear of being denigrated. Of course they will say I am crazy. Javed already thinks I am senile. What does it matter? Perhaps madness is a kind of imaginative fever . . . All that has been can be recreated with conviction . . . Now only the past remains . . . What is the harm if I wish to live among its ruins? . . . How bitter this incomplete remembrance . . . The bits now shrunken and stored in the dank cells of memory. Is that all life is? Flashes of recollections about times not to be repeated, experiences never to be redeemed? As I wait in the gathering mist of this purple dusk, I sense the flow of death gurgling as it empties life into the darkness . . . So I, too, shall disappear . . . A dot . . . A bleep . . . Silenced forever . . . Of what use are sensible and correct decisions now?

Angela remained unconvinced. 'Is that the only reason?' she asked with an uncharacteristic boldness.

'No.' He resolved not to confuse her with the necessities that were taking him back.

The old house awaited him with a muted greeting, its rooms empty and its white-washed walls like blank sheets of paper on which he could scribble fragments of vaguely remembered songs. He had to free himself from the dictatorship of time. Eat and sleep when there was a need. Fish and read. Swap stories with the villagers. Supervise the renovation of the school. Talk to the children. Relive a young man's life under a night sky that blazed with the gasping passion of a dying universe. There was much that his imagination had to behold. He would learn to believe that the stars were not really planets but distant holes through which one could enter other worlds and see other skies and dream other dreams.

'Khalid?'

'Yes?' His eyes followed the gaunt shadows as they stretched slowly across the housetops, preparing to close the shutters on another day.

'This may sound like a silly question . . .' Angela hesitated. 'But do you ever reflect on the purpose of your life? I mean, at our age, can there be a purpose beyond eating and sleeping, babysitting grandchildren and waiting for the next appointment with the doctor?'

'We are still capable of loving,' he replied, without taking his eyes off the tiled roofs and the trees across the road. The sun continued to hover on them like an angry eye, glowering with a faded energy, defiant and unwilling to relinquish its hold on a weary world longing for renewal.

'Is that the only reason for living?'

'It's the only one that brings consolation and teaches patience. To realise that we are able to energise someone else's life is an incentive enough to continue.'

'Do you ever feel a chilling loneliness inside you? The feeling that somehow you have been betrayed and left behind by those you loved?' She thought of her father and Tom. And strangely enough, Indra. They had carved an emptiness in her.

Angela surprised him. Those were not the kind of questions he expected from her. At last she seemed to be convinced that Khalid Sharif could be trusted to enter the cobwebbed side of her life, that dark corner where she preferred to hurt by herself.

He thought carefully. His feet were numb, as though they were dipped in iced water. How did it feel to be betrayed?

Ask her. She must have waited with a hope that briefly sparked her life and then dwindled into a slow death. Had she heeded her own warning about not building a life on a swamp? How had Tabassum Begum reacted? Was there any kindness in her professionalism to allow the young courtesan some time to recover, or did Nazli have to present herself at the next gathering to smile, comfort and teach another young man? Had she been relegated to a haveli to spend the rest of her days occupied with cooking, sewing and sweeping floors because she could not be trusted to maintain an emotional distance from the men who passed through Khush Manzil? Had she survived the malice of the fire? Was she left to carry on a whispered dialogue with her retarded dreams in the dimness of an ill-lit room?

He could tell that Angela hoped for a reply.

I only know what it feels like to betray. The footfalls of a thousand unanswered questions have never ceased to pursue me. If only you knew . . .

'I occupy myself with trivia. It insulates me against loneliness. I could go mad feeling the detachment from everything around me.' He grimaced as he leaned forward to place the cup and the saucer on the tray. It was peculiar how his legs had stopped hurting.

Angela was struck by the familiarity of what he was saying. 'But your family? You must love your family!'

'That is instinctive. But love does not necessarily lead to an understanding of people. It is now a different world in which I am a stranger.'

She poured her sympathy into another cup of tea.

'The number of people I know have shrunk alarmingly,' he complained moodily. 'These days my outings in Calcutta have a great deal to do with funerals. It is very inconsiderate of my friends to expose me so regularly to mortality without offering explanations.'

Angela smiled. He rarely failed to use his dry, ironic sense of humour to cover his helplessness.

A car honked and screeched to a halt. An angry voice.

Khalid Sharif frowned. Such a disturbance was unusual here. It interrupted the smooth passage of the autumn afternoon.

The tea was bitter. She had forgotten to add hot water to the pot.

'Do you often have such heavy fog in autumn?'

A peculiar question, she thought. Perhaps it was the phrasing which made it odd. 'It is not uncommon at night.'

My life is on an empty floor. Without the dancing . . . the music. Only the sound of curtains flapping against the open window. But I am not alone! Not alone! The past did happen . . . Didn't it? And what is this life now but a restless wandering in the winter chill of memories? I live in the solitude of their corridors, spinning illusions to hide the failings . . . My days are spent in revelries, my sleeping hours interrupted when she wakes me and commands . . . 'Remember!'

'Forgive me for saying this . . .' Angela bit her lower lip and debated the wisdom of articulating a personal observation. She knew him well enough, she decided. He would not be offended. 'I sometimes feel that there is a deep sadness in you.'

What was he to say? *Yes*, and then remain silent. *No, you are quite wrong* . . . and leave a lie incomplete. He pretended not to have heard her. It was, after all, a statement and not a question.

The sadness was a permanent blot on his psyche. It couldn't be explained. He felt its weight and perceived its greyness inside himself. Regret remained like an invisible enemy that struck at unexpected moments. Nazli was not the only reason. When Jahan Ara was alive, Khalid Sharif wished that he could come upon some magic potion that could evoke a genuine love for his wife. His unflagging kindness, attentiveness and the respect he had for her were inadequate compensations for the absence of feeling. He had failed her as well.

The revelation, that she knew far more than she should have, had affected him deeply. He had been unable to comprehend how Jahan Ara had managed to camouflage her vexations and live out the charade of a domestic contentment with such consistency. Perhaps that was her revenge—the knowledge that she was the one fooling him all the time.

The sliding door opened noisily. Adam looked slightly more composed.

'Mum said I was to have tea here.'

'I think we can arrange that,' Angela said light-heartedly.

Adam looked unforgivingly at Khalid Sharif. 'I am not eating that yukky stuff you make when *he* is here!'

'You can have a pie or sausage rolls. We shall eat that stuff. It's quite nice, you know.'

'Can I watch TV?'

'May I, please . . .' Angela waited patiently.

'May I please watch TV?'

'You may, but only for an hour. Pie or sausage rolls?'

'Pie . . . thanks,' the boy mumbled and followed his grandmother to the kitchen.

The fog again. This time in thick layers. Endless. Rolling toward him. With it came the cold. Long icy fingers stroking away the sensations.

He slumped in the chair.

A bubble began to form around him.

Like a beginning . . . a caul . . . but no darkness.

Faces emerged. Voices more vibrant than he remembered them to be.

The *tablas* were tuned. The musicians looked relaxed, talking quietly among themselves.

Munni Bai sat on a rug in the centre of the room, looking regally aloof.

Snatches of a song that had brushed past him.

Make the best of your time, for life will
  not come back to you . . .

Dard's *ghazal* was one of her favourites. She sang it more poignantly than anything else in her vast repertoire.

If some of your life remains, youth will
  not come back to you . . .

The words had meant nothing. The mask of life held the promise of eternity.

Angela's voice. From somewhere. 'You don't mind Strauss?'

He wanted to say *No*.

Why was she moving away?

'I won't be long. I'm making a chicken curry.'

She hadn't mentioned anything about dinner. He'd stay if she asked him. Javed had expressed a mild disapproval about the hours Khalid Sharif spent at her house.

Papa, you must be careful. People talk.

So do we. We cover great distances. Enter wonderful worlds. Time and space outside your experience.

The letter! He would tear up the letter he had written to her. The details about Adam's present required no alteration. Angela would fume and huff about the expense, but without the presence of the culprit to castigate and lecture on wastefulness. But the harsh finality of the farewell . . . That he would rephrase . . . Make it ambiguous. She would still grieve in a quiet, undemonstrative manner. There was nothing that could be said to prevent the mourning. But then anguish was the monumental culmination of everything human . . . of love . . . friendship. An affirmation that all that is precious cannot last.

The silhouette of the tree was blurry.

How like a woman waiting to be betrayed.

Nothing moved.

Trees. Houses. Parts of the sky.

There was some life left yet in the fading day.

Suddenly the sun slid behind a fluff of cloud, splattering light as if it was the last squirt from an empty tube of paint.

He was now inside. The door closed on whatever there was.

Once he had convinced himself that the outside world did not matter. From the small window of Nazli's room, they could see the terraces of other houses.

All that is important is here. Within this space. Out there is an unnecessary part of life. An illusion. You don't believe me? Have a look.

He cajoled her to sit up.

What do you see outside?

The sky. Terraces. Kites. Two eagles circling over a house.

He raised the crystal goblet to her eyes. *Look through that. What do you see now?*

I can't. It's . . . It's . . .

A scarlet blur?

Yes! What's the meaning of this game?

It isn't a game. Just shows how easily you can dispense with the trivial. Make it fuzzy. I have a cousin who says that we should see life with our heart.

You are strange. You sometimes say things which don't make sense. You cannot pretend not to see life as it is.

It's not a pretence! Why cannot the imperfections and the unimportant be blotted out?

Because it's all one. You have to accept what there is . . . The truth!

We create lies . . . Why can't the truth be invented?

The sky . . . the trees and roofs swung around and tilted. Fragments of cups and saucers were strewn around him.

I can see what I want to . . . What are you doing here? I have no wish to be with people from that world . . . I've finished with it.

I am not from the outside! I am from within.

Now I can be where I want to be . . .

Of course you can!

How did you get here?

You forget! I am a magician. I can be anywhere I choose to be. It is in my power to make you live wherever you please. I can make life whatever you wish it to be.

Who are they?

You know them.

He could barely see. Angela? A hand on her mouth . . . the other hand holding a blanket. Shanaz? Her arm around Javed's trembling shoulders. Zareen . . . The boys. Adam. Two men . . . Close . . . Full moons on the edge of a dark sky.

'I don't think he can hear us!'

'He is still breathing!'

Of course I am! Perhaps I should . . .

Khalid! Please! You are in the realm of a new knowledge.

The colours were like the breath of life itself, swirling and twisting as they embraced him into their folds. No demons or humans to interrupt him.

Aren't you coming?

The perfect peace of a twinkling twilight.

An empty lane.

Idle men with dreamy eyes.

The bazaar?

It is evening Saheb. There is now another life to be lived.

A brilliant white light jagged across the darkness, illuminating the house.

The vacant foyer. That voice! Sound beyond the door.

Aayeh *Sharif Saheb*.

He looked up.

He didn't have to be tempted.

It seemed perfectly natural for him to drift up the stairs to the landing where she waited.